DAYBRIDGE NECROPOLIS
WHERE SHADOWS KEEP THEIR SECRETS

THE ETHAN REEVES WEREWOLF DETECTIVE SERIES
BOOK TWO

RAE STONEHOUSE

LIVE FOR EXCELLENCE PRODUCTIONS

PROLOGUE: ECHOES

PROLOGUE: Echoes

Prague, Czech Republic

December 21, 1994

3:17 AM

The candles didn't flicker when Abby died.

Lila remembered that detail later — how the flames stood perfectly motionless, as if time itself held its breath while her sister's life slipped away. The chalk circles etched meticulously across the stone floor glowed with an unnatural silver light, arcane symbols pulsing in rhythmic patterns like heartbeats independent of the ritual participants. Her sister's body lay at the center, pale and still, surrounded by ancient grimoires bound in materials Lila preferred not to identify, their yellowed pages containing desperate hopes transcribed by generations of seekers.

"Again," Viktor whispered, his hands slick with Abby's blood as he adjusted the ceremonial dagger at the ritual's focal point. His aristocratic features were taut with concentration, dark eyes reflecting the eerie silver glow from the activating sigils. "The resonance is building. I can feel the dimensional thinning. One more push and we'll breach the veil between--"

"She's gone." Lila's voice cracked, the cold certainty of death overwhelming the academic detachment she'd maintained throughout their preparations. The power hummed through her bones like electrical current, dark and seductive in its promise, but Abby's hand was cold and lifeless in hers. "We failed."

"No." Viktor's eyes blazed with that terrible certainty she'd once found mesmerizing — the unwavering conviction that had drawn her into esoteric studies at the University of Prague five years earlier. "We're close. I can feel it. The boundaries between life and death are thin here, especially tonight. The winter solstice creates a natural dimensional alignment. We just need--"

"Viktor." Her tears fell on the meticulously drawn chalk lines, breaking their perfect geometry as the droplets carried her grief into the ritual space. "Please."

He knelt beside her then, setting aside the ceremonial implements to gather her into his arms. His heartbeat was too fast against her cheek, fever hot with the energies they'd channeled. "We knew there would be sacrifices, my love. For power like this -- for the ability to reach beyond conventional boundaries--"

"Not her." Lila clutched Abby's lifeless hand, still warm but rapidly cooling as whatever essence had made her sister laugh, dream, and love departed for realms they'd foolishly thought they could access through academic study and ritualistic precision. "It was supposed to save her. That's why we started this research in the first place."

The candles remained unnaturally still, their flames like painted images rather than living fire. In their unnatural light, shadows moved wrong -- stretching and contracting against the ancient stone walls of Viktor's family estate, reaching with hungry, elongated fingers toward the failed ritual's remnants. Toward Abby's cooling body.

"We can try again." Viktor's voice held that edge of obsession she'd been too desperately in love to fear until this moment. His fingers trembled as they brushed hair from her tear-stained face. "There are other ways. Darker paths we haven't explored. The Moravian grimoire mentions techniques that could--"

"No." Lila pulled away, the silver rings on her fingers -- family heirlooms inscribed with protective sigils passed through generations of her Romanian ancestors -- burning unnaturally cold against her skin. "This ends here."

His laugh held no humor, a brittle sound that echoed strangely in the ritual chamber. "Ends? My love, this is only the beginning. What we've learned, what we've opened -- the resonances are established now. They won't simply dissipate because we walk away."

The shadows lengthened further, stretching across the floor like grasping hands. The candlelight dimmed incrementally, as if something unseen were feeding on its illumination. And in that moment, as her sister's soul slipped finally, irrevocably into darkness beyond their reach, Lila Darkmagic made a choice that would define the remainder of her existence.

She placed her silver-ringed hand on the primary containment sigil, channeling her grief, rage, and newfound determination into its structure. The symbol flared brilliantly, then inverted its energy pattern -- converting from summoning to banishing, from invitation to severance.

"What are you doing?" Viktor's voice rose in alarm as the ritual energies they'd so carefully cultivated began to dissipate. "You can't just--"

"Watch me," she whispered, her voice finding new strength in opposition to the man she'd once believed would help her save her sister from terminal illness. "Some doors should remain closed, Viktor. Some knowledge isn't meant for human minds to comprehend or control."

As the protective circles collapsed inward, Viktor lunged for the central grimoire -- the ancient text that had led them down this dangerous path with its promises of transcending death itself. His fingers closed around its leather binding just as Lila completed the containment inversion.

The resulting energetic backlash threw them both against opposite walls of the chamber. When Lila regained consciousness minutes later, Viktor was gone -- along with the grimoire and several key ritual components. Only Abby's body remained, peaceful now that the unnatural energies had dissipated, looking almost as if she might be sleeping.

But the shadows still moved wrong in the corners of the chamber, suggesting that while their ritual had failed in its intended purpose, it had succeeded in opening something that would not be easily closed again.

The price of that night would echo through decades, following Lila across continents and through years of atonement and preparation for what she knew would eventually come.

Present Day

Daybridge City

October 31

2:13 AM

The body on Medical Examiner Choy's table had no marks. No wounds. No trauma that modern science could identify as a cause of death.

But its shadows were wrong.

Detective Alice Chen watched them twist at the corner of her vision, moving against the harsh fluorescent lights in patterns that defied conventional physics. Since the events at Daybridge Bridge six months ago, her perception had become increasingly sensitive to anomalies that existed at the boundaries of conventional reality. Beside her, Detective Ethan Reeves -- or the manifestation of him that could temporarily separate from his primary consciousness distributed throughout the bridge -- swore softly.

"Third one this month," he said, his voice carrying those subtle harmonics that reminded Alice of his transformed nature. "Same pattern of energetic depletion. It's like something extracted their life force without damaging the physical form."

"No pattern," Chen snapped on latex gloves with practiced efficiency, her tactical mind refusing to jump to supernatural conclusions despite her recent experiences. "Just emptiness. Like something reached inside and..."

"Took what it needed?"

They turned simultaneously toward the voice. A woman stood in the morgue doorway, silver rings glinting on every finger as she adjusted leather gloves designed to make the metallic bands visible while maintaining sterile protocol. Her dark hair was shot through with striking white streaks that appeared natural rather than cosmetic, framing a face marked by intelligence and experiences beyond conventional understanding. Her eyes -- sharp, assessing, and haunted -- had seen too much to maintain the comfortable illusions that most people wrapped around themselves like protective blankets.

"Lila Darkmagic." Reeves straightened, recognition in his slightly lumi-nous eyes. Through his connection to the nexus entity beneath Daybridge Bridge, he could perceive aspects of this woman's nature that transcended conventional observation. "The consultant from--"

"Prague." She moved to the autopsy table with fluid confidence, her own shadow falling wrong against the morgue's tile floor -- stretching and contracting independently of the overhead lighting. "It's happening again."

"What is?" Alice's question carried professional skepticism despite her recent exposure to forces beyond conventional understanding.

Lila traced symbols in the air above the body -- gestures precise and practiced, clearly meaningful though not immediately recognizable to either detective. Silver light flickered between her rings, responding to these movements in ways that suggested technological enhancement rather than mystical significance, though the distinction seemed increasingly arbitrary with each passing moment.

"Someone's trying to break the equations," she said softly, her accent reflecting Eastern European origins beneath years of international travel. "Someone who never learned that some doors should stay closed. Someone who refuses to accept that some debts can't be paid, regardless of what resources or sacrifices you're willing to commit."

"You know who's doing this," Chen said. Not a question but recognition of certainty in the consultant's demeanor.

"Yes." Lila's smile held grief and steel in equal measure, the expression of someone who had made peace with terrible knowledge while remaining determined to prevent its consequences. "He was my partner once. My love. My brilliant, ambitious Viktor. Until I chose differently."

She touched one of her silver rings to the corpse's forehead; the metal briefly flared with that same strange light. Where the ring made contact, the victim's skin revealed patterns invisible to conventional examination -- symbols etched at a cellular level in configurations that suggested deliberate composition rather than random effect.

"The Department brought me in as a consultant because I've seen this before," Lila continued, her voice taking on the clinical precision of a specialist reporting findings. "These deaths appear natural to conventional medicine -- heart failure, stroke, sudden neurological collapse. But they're actually systematic extractions of specific life-energy patterns. Harvesting, if you will."

Outside the morgue windows, storm clouds gathered with unnatural speed, lightning flickering in patterns that seemed almost deliberate. In the harsh fluorescent light, shadows continued to dance like memory given substance, reaching toward the corpse with hungry anticipation.

"Harvesting for what purpose?" Ethan asked, the harmonics in his voice intensifying as his connection to the nexus entity provided context beyond what Lila had explicitly stated.

"To pay a debt," she replied, her eyes meeting his with recognition of his transformed nature. "Or rather, to attempt the impossible -- to break a contract with forces that don't recognize conventional notions of negotiation or mercy."

Alice studied the consultant's face, her detective's instincts cataloging micro-expressions and vocal patterns that suggested personal involvement beyond professional consultation. "This isn't just another case for you."

"No." Lila straightened, adjusting her silver rings with practiced precision. "This is my responsibility. Twenty-eight years ago, I helped open a door that should have remained closed. I've spent my life since then developing methods to contain what escaped. But Viktor... Viktor never accepted our failure. He's been searching for alternative approaches ever since."

"And now he's found one," Ethan observed, his perception extending beyond the morgue's physical boundaries to sense disturbances in the energetic patterns flowing throughout Daybridge. "Here, in our city."

"Yes." Lila's expression hardened with resolve. "Daybridge has always been a nexus point for certain energetic configurations. The bridge itself serves as a conduit between dimensional frameworks in ways that most cities lack. After what happened six months ago, when the dimensional boundaries were significantly altered throughout the city, the resonance patterns have become even more accessible to those with the knowledge to detect and manipulate them."

And somewhere in the city, ancient powers stirred, hungry for what was promised long ago in a stone chamber in Prague. Forces that recognized no authority except the binding agreements established through ritual and sacrifice, patterns of energy and intent that had waited patiently for decades while pieces moved into position for resolution of debts long deferred.

The echoes of Prague were growing louder, resonating through Daybridge's transformed reality with increasing urgency as Halloween approached -- the night when boundaries between worlds traditionally thinned, when what had been contained might fully manifest if the proper conditions were established.

As Lila Darkmagic completed her examination of the body, her silver rings gleaming under the morgue lights, Ethan and Alice exchanged glances that conveyed shared understanding. Their investigation had just expanded beyond conventional homicide into realms they had experienced six months earlier beneath Daybridge Bridge -- dimensional forces beyond human comprehension, ancient patterns of energy and awareness that existed alongside conventional reality like parallel tracks occasionally converging with catastrophic results.

The cosmic chess game that had seemingly concluded with the redirection of the Obsidian Protocol was revealing itself as merely the opening gambit in a more complex configuration. And as Halloween approached, the players were moving into position for the next phase of a conflict that transcended individual lives or conventional understanding of reality itself.

~

COPYRIGHT

First Edition

Published by Live For Excellence Productions

ISBN:

Ebook: 978-1-998591-82-4

Paperback: 978-1-998591-83-1

Audiobook: 978-1-998591-84-8

CHAPTER ONE
GRAVE CONSEQUENCES

THE ACRID STENCH of decay hung heavy in the night air as Detective Ethan Reeves surveyed the desecrated graveyard. Shattered tombstones and gaping holes where coffins once lay greeted him like a macabre gallery of vandalism taken to disturbing extremes. The waning crescent moon cast a sickly glow over the scene, deepening the shadows that seemed to writhe with a life of their own—a phenomenon Ethan no longer dismissed as mere tricks of light since his transformation six months ago.

His heightened senses picked up nuances imperceptible to ordinary humans: the subtle shift in air currents that carried particles of disturbed soil, the whisper of movement from nocturnal creatures disturbed by an unnatural presence, and something else—a discordant note in the symphony of ordinary night sounds that made his skin prickle with instinctive warning.

"This is the third one this week," his partner, Alice Chen, murmured beside him. Her almond-shaped eyes narrowed as she took in the eerie sight, flashlight beam sweeping methodically across the violated earth. The beam illuminated fragments of splintered wood and tattered shrouds scattered among upturned soil and trampled flowers left by mourners. "What kind of sick freak gets their kicks robbing graves?"

The beam lingered on a particularly violent excavation where the coffin had been not merely opened but shattered, as if something had exploded outward from within. Alice's expression remained professionally neutral, but Ethan detected the subtle acceleration in her heartbeat, the microscopic dilation of her pupils that signaled controlled anxiety beneath her composed exterior.

Ethan crouched down, his keen senses picking up on the faint, cloying scent of something far more sinister than mere graveyard soil. It was the unmistakable reek of dark magic, like ozone and burnt offerings mingled with the coppery tang of freshly spilled blood. The smell activated ancient memories within him—not his own, but those accessed through his connection to the nexus entity beneath Daybridge Bridge, memories of rituals performed generations ago when the boundaries between worlds were manipulated by those seeking power beyond human limitations.

"Not just any freak," he growled, his voice taking on a rough edge as his inner wolf stirred in response to the dark energy permeating the air. The wolf aspect of his nature had become more integrated since the events at the bridge, no longer a separate entity fighting for control but a complementary awareness that enhanced his perceptions when threats manifested. "This is the work of a necromancer."

Alice's breath hitched, her hand instinctively reaching for the gun at her hip—a reflexive action born from years of police work rather than any expectation that conventional weapons would prove effective against supernatural threats. "A necromancer? In Daybridge? I thought they were just a myth."

She maintained remarkable composure despite the implications. Since witnessing Ethan's transformation and the cosmic confrontation beneath the bridge, Alice had adapted to their new reality with characteristic resilience, but even she had limits to what she could accept without question.

Ethan shook his head grimly, rising from his crouched position with fluid grace that betrayed his nonhuman aspects. "In a city like this, myths have a way of coming to life." His gaze swept the desecrated cemetery, penetrating shadows that would have been impenetrable to ordinary human vision. "Especially since the events at the bridge. The dimensional boundaries are thinner now, more permeable. Things that couldn't manifest before can find their way through more easily."

The silver pendant at Alice's throat—Father Muligan's parting gift inscribed with protective symbols—caught the moonlight as she surveyed the destruction. "Like the shadow anomalies we've been tracking downtown?"

"Similar principle, different manifestation," Ethan confirmed. "The shadow anomalies are echoes, impressions left by the thinning boundaries. This—" he gestured to the violated graves, "—is deliberate. Purposeful. Someone with knowledge and power is manipulating the weakened boundaries for specific ends."

As they picked their way through the desecrated graves, the detectives searched for any clues that might lead them to the perpetrator. Ethan's heightened senses were on full alert, his nostrils flaring as he caught the scent of something out of place among the earthy smells of the graveyard—a chemical tang that didn't belong, synthetic and sharp amid the organic decay.

"Over here," he called out, kneeling beside a mound of freshly turned earth. Embedded in the loose soil was a small, intricately carved object —a sigil, pulsing with an eerie crimson light that ebbed and flowed like a heartbeat. Ethan felt a shudder of revulsion ripple through him as he realized the carving was made from human bone, yellowed with age but meticulously crafted into patterns that seemed to shift subtly when viewed from different angles.

Alice joined him, her face paling as she caught sight of the macabre talisman. "Is that what I think it is?"

Ethan nodded grimly. "A necromancer's calling card. They use sigils like this to control the dead, to bend them to their will." He carefully extracted the sigil from the dirt, feeling the oily taint of dark magic clinging to its surface like a film. Through his connection to the nexus entity, he perceived how the object served as a focal point for energies that shouldn't exist in conventional reality—a conduit between worlds that allowed manipulation of life forces beyond their natural parameters.

"But why here?" Alice asked, scanning the surrounding graves with renewed attention. "This cemetery isn't particularly old or significant. There are historical burial grounds downtown that would have older remains, potentially more powerful for whatever ritual they're attempting."

Ethan turned the sigil over in his gloved hand, feeling its wrongness even through the protective barrier. "It's not about age or historical significance," he explained, drawing on knowledge that came partly from his own research and partly through his connection to the composite consciousness beneath the bridge. "It's about specific energetic patterns. This cemetery sits at a convergence point of what occultists call ley lines—natural channels of energy that flow throughout the earth. Combined with the thinning dimensional boundaries since the events at the bridge..."

"It creates ideal conditions for necromantic rituals," Alice finished, her analytical mind making connections despite her limited experience with the supernatural. "So, they're not just randomly robbing graves. They're targeting specific burial sites for specific purposes."

As he pocketed the grisly find in an evidence bag, a sudden sound caught his attention—the rasp of footsteps on gravel, like the shuffling gait of something not quite alive. Ethan's head snapped up, his eyes widening as he saw a figure lurching toward them through the darkness.

It was a corpse, its flesh grey and rotting, its eyes glowing with an unholy yellow light that illuminated the cavernous hollows of its face. The creature's movements were jerky and unnatural, like a marionette being puppeteered by an unseen hand. Ethan's nostrils flared as the stench of decay and dark magic rolled off the abomination in nause-ating waves—putrefaction accelerated and perverted by energies that violated natural order.

"Alice, get down!" he shouted, his voice echoing through the empty graveyard. In a blur of motion, he shifted into his werewolf form—not the painful transformation of bones and muscles that had once charac-terized his monthly ordeals, but a fluid integration of his lycanthropic nature with his human consciousness. His form expanded, muscles rippling beneath skin that sprouted silver-grey fur, his face elongating into a muzzle filled with gleaming fangs as his senses sharpened beyond human limitations.

With a roar that shook the earth, Ethan launched himself at the undead creature, his powerful jaws clamping down on the corpse's throat. The taste of rotting flesh and dark magic filled his mouth, making him gag even as his teeth tore through desiccated muscle and bone. The crea-ture fought back with unnatural strength, its bony fingers scrabbling at Ethan's face and chest as it tried to break free from his grip.

Behind him, Alice had taken cover behind a marble mausoleum, her service weapon drawn though she held her fire, waiting for a clear shot that wouldn't risk hitting her transformed partner. Her training had never covered combat protocols for werewolf-versus-zombie encoun-ters, but her adaptability had served her well in the months since discovering her partner's dual nature.

The undead creature's strength was formidable—far beyond what its desiccated muscles should have been capable of—but the werewolf's raw power was too much for the animated corpse. With a sickening crunch, Ethan's jaws crushed its skull like an overripe melon, dark ichor spraying across his muzzle as the unholy light in its eye sockets flickered and died.

As the creature crumpled to the ground, Ethan shifted back to his human form with practiced ease, his chest heaving with exertion. The integration of his lycanthropic nature since the events at the bridge had given him unprecedented control over his transformations, allowing him to shift at will without the pain or loss of self-awareness that had once accompanied the change.

Alice was at his side in an instant, her eyes wide with a mixture of awe and concern as she took in the sight of Ethan's blood-spattered face and torn clothing. "Are you alright?" she asked, her voice betraying only the slightest tremor as she holstered her weapon.

Ethan nodded, wiping his mouth with the back of his hand, grimacing at the foul taste that lingered. "I'm fine. But this is just the beginning." He gestured toward the fallen corpse, which was already beginning to decompose at an accelerated rate now that the animating energies had dissipated. "Whoever's behind this, they're not going to stop until they have what they want."

Alice's jaw tightened, her gaze hardening with determination. "Then we'll just have to stop them first. We'll find this necromancer, Ethan. We'll put an end to their sick little game."

Ethan met her gaze, his own eyes still glowing faintly with residual energy from his transformation. "Damn right we will. And when we do, they'll wish they'd never set foot in Daybridge."

He crouched beside the rapidly decomposing corpse, examining what remained before it disintegrated completely. "We need to document this before it's gone. The rate of decay suggests the animation was temporary—a sentry rather than a permanent resurrection. Whoever raised it only needed it to function long enough to alert them to intruders."

Alice was already photographing the remains with methodical efficiency, her professional training asserting itself despite the supernatural nature of their investigation. "So, the necromancer knows we're here now. That we're on their trail."

"Yes," Ethan confirmed grimly. "And they'll be preparing for us. We need to move quickly."

As they turned to leave the desecrated graveyard, the first rays of dawn began to peek over the horizon, casting a pale, watery light over the city. The skyline of Daybridge was visible in the distance—a jagged silhouette of skyscrapers and historical buildings intersected by the distinctive arch of Daybridge Bridge, its structure seeming to shimmer slightly in the early morning light as reality rippled around it in ways only Ethan could perceive.

Even as the sun rose, the shadows seemed to deepen, their inky tendrils ensnaring the unsuspecting city like parasitic vines seeking purchase on a healthy host. Ethan and Alice knew that their battle had only begun—that the darkness lurking at the heart of Daybridge would not be vanquished so easily.

But they were ready to face whatever horrors the necromancer had in store. They were the city's guardians, the thin blue line standing between the innocent and the monstrous. And they would not rest until the streets of Daybridge were safe once more.

The drive back to the precinct was a somber one, the weight of their grim discovery hanging heavy in the air. Ethan gripped the steering wheel of his battered old muscle car—a '69 Mustang that had seen better days but purred like a contented cat when he opened the throttle —his knuckles turning white as he navigated the rain-slicked streets. The city was beginning to stir, the first bleary-eyed commuters making their way to work as the neon signs of all-night diners and seedy bars flickered and buzzed in the grey light of dawn.

Alice sat silently in the passenger seat; her gaze fixed on the evidence bag containing the sigil they had found in the graveyard. The bone talisman continued to pulse with an eerie red light, visible even through the protective plastic. Ethan could almost hear the gears turning in her head as she tried to make sense of the macabre artifact.

"I've never seen anything like this before," she murmured, tracing the outline of the bag with a fingertip, careful not to touch the sigil directly despite the barrier. "The symbols, the craftsmanship... it's almost beautiful, in a twisted sort of way."

Ethan grunted, his jaw clenching as he remembered the foul energy that had pulsed from the sigil like a sickness. "There's nothing beautiful about dark magic, Alice. It's a corruption, a blight on everything it touches." The words came from somewhere deep within him—not just personal opinion but knowledge accessed through his connection to the nexus entity, memories of countless confrontations between natural order and those who sought to pervert it for personal gain.

Alice glanced up at him, her dark eyes searching his face. "You sound like you've had experience with this sort of thing before."

Ethan hesitated, his grip tightening on the steering wheel as he navigated around a delivery truck double-parked on Main Street. Despite everything they'd been through together—the cosmic confrontation beneath the bridge, his transformation and partial integration with the nexus entity—there were still aspects of his past he hadn't shared with Alice. Experiences from before they became partners, from the dark years following his initial infection with lycanthropy when he'd wandered the edges of society, learning to control his condition through painful trial and error.

"I have," he said at last, his voice low and rough with memories he preferred not to revisit. "More than I'd like to admit. The supernatural world, the things that lurk in the shadows... they've been a part of my life for a long time."

Alice was silent for a moment, digesting his words as rain began to patter against the windshield again—a persistent drizzle that matched the somber mood in the car. When she spoke again, her voice was soft but firm, carrying the steadfast loyalty that had defined their partnership through increasingly extraordinary circumstances.

"I know there's more to you than meets the eye, Ethan. I've always known. But whatever you're going through, whatever demons you're fighting... you don't have to do it alone."

Ethan felt a sudden lump in his throat, a swell of emotion that threatened to overwhelm his carefully maintained composure. In all his years as a detective, as a werewolf navigating a world that would fear him if they knew his true nature, he had never had someone who understood him, who accepted him for all that he was. But Alice, with her fierce loyalty and unwavering courage, had become more than just his partner—she had become his anchor, his guiding light in the darkness that constantly threatened to consume him.

"Thank you," he said at last, his voice hoarse with emotion he rarely allowed himself to express. "I... I don't know what I'd do without you, Alice."

She reached out and squeezed his hand where it rested on the gearshift, her touch warm and reassuring through the tactile connection. "You'll never have to find out. We're in this together, Ethan. No matter what happens, no matter what we're up against... I've got your back."

The simple statement carried weight beyond its words—a promise between partners that had evolved into something deeper since the events at the bridge. Not just professional colleagues facing danger together, but individuals whose lives had become intertwined through experiences that transcended conventional understanding.

Ethan felt a surge of warmth flood through him, a feeling of belonging he had never known before. For the first time in his life, he didn't feel like a monster, like an outsider looking in on a world that would never truly accept him. With Alice by his side, he felt like he could take on anything—even a necromancer hell-bent on plunging the city into darkness.

As they pulled into the precinct parking lot—a cracked concrete expanse littered with patrol cars and the personal vehicles of officers working the night shift—Ethan took a deep breath, steeling himself for the day ahead. He knew that they were in for a long and difficult investigation, that the road ahead would be fraught with danger and uncertainty. But with Alice by his side, he felt a newfound sense of purpose, a determination to see this case through to the end no matter what the cost.

They made their way into the bullpen, the usual bustle of activity and chatter washing over them like a familiar tide. The fluorescent lights hummed overhead, casting a harsh glow over tired faces and cluttered desks. The familiar scents of stale coffee, printer ink, and the lingering odor of fast food consumed during hurried lunch breaks created an olfactory landscape that Ethan had learned to associate with the routine of police work.

But as they approached their desks, Ethan noticed a strange hush falling over the room, a palpable sense of unease that set his nerves on edge. Conversations died mid-sentence, heads turned in their direction, and expressions shifted from professional neutrality to something more complex—a mixture of relief at their arrival and dread at what had necessitated it.

"What's going on?" he asked, his brow furrowing as he took in the worried expressions on his colleagues' faces.

One of the other detectives, a grizzled veteran named Simmons with a perpetual five o'clock shadow and eyes that had seen too much in thirty years on the force, stepped forward. His face was grim, the lines around his mouth deeper than usual as he clutched a case folder with white-knuckled intensity.

"There's been another one," he said, his voice low and urgent. "Another body found in an alleyway downtown. But this one... it's different."

Ethan and Alice exchanged glances, their hearts sinking as they realized the implications of Simmons' words. "Different how?" Alice asked, her voice tight with tension.

Simmons shook his head, his eyes haunted by whatever he had witnessed. "You'll have to see for yourself. But I'm warning you now... it's not pretty."

He handed the folder to Ethan, who flipped it open to reveal crime scene photographs that made even his hardened stomach churn with revulsion. The images showed a body—or what remained of one—displayed in a manner that went beyond murder into the realm of ritualistic desecration.

Ethan felt a chill run down his spine, a sense of foreboding he couldn't shake. Whatever they were about to walk into, he had a feeling that it would be worse than anything they had ever faced before—even considering the cosmic horror they had confronted beneath the bridge six months ago.

As they grabbed their gear and headed for the door, Ethan caught a glimpse of his reflection in the window—a man haunted by secrets, a werewolf torn between two worlds, now partially integrated with a dimensional nexus entity that existed beyond conventional human understanding. The complexity of his existence would have been over-whelming if not for the steadying presence beside him.

He met Alice's steady gaze in the reflection, drawing strength from her unwavering support. Together, they would face whatever horrors the necromancer had in store. Together, they would stop the darkness from consuming their city.

The crime scene was a nightmare made flesh, a twisted mockery of life that made even Ethan's hardened stomach churn with revulsion. The body lay sprawled in the center of the alleyway; its limbs splayed at unnatural angles like a discarded marionette. But the face—or rather, what was left of it—made Ethan's blood run cold.

The flesh had been stripped away with surgical precision, leaving only a grinning skull that leered up at them with empty eye sockets that seemed to follow their movements with malevolent awareness. The bones were cracked and splintered in specific patterns, not random damage but deliberate alterations that formed a grotesque parody of human features. But even more disturbing were the symbols carved into the bones themselves—intricate, arcane sigils that pulsed with the same sickly red light as the talisman they had found in the graveyard.

The alley itself had been transformed into a ritual space. Symbols drawn in what appeared to be a mixture of blood and ash formed concentric circles around the body, their patterns corresponding to the sigils carved into the victim's exposed bones. Candle stubs placed at precise intervals had burned down to nothing; their wax pooled in patterns that seemed too deliberate to be coincidental.

"My God," Alice whispered, her face pale and stricken as she took in the grotesque tableau. Her hand hovered near her service weapon, though what protection conventional firearms might offer against whatever had done this remained questionable. "What could do something like this?"

Ethan shook his head, his jaw clenched so tightly that he could feel his teeth grinding together. The wolf within him stirred restlessly, responding to the malevolent energies that permeated the scene like a miasma. Through his connection to the nexus entity, he could perceive how reality itself seemed thinner here, the boundaries between dimensions stretched to near-transparency by whatever ritual had been performed.

"This is no ordinary murder," he said, his voice low and grim as he crouched beside the body, careful not to disturb the ritual markings surrounding it. "This is a message, a warning. The necromancer is growing bolder, more powerful. And they're not going to stop until they get what they want."

As they began to process the scene, gathering what little evidence they could find amidst the grisly remains, Ethan's mind raced with possibilities. The forensics team worked methodically around them, photographing, measuring, and collecting samples with the detached professionalism of those who had seen too much to be easily shocked. But even these hardened crime scene technicians moved with unusual caution, as if subconsciously sensing that they were dealing with something beyond conventional violence.

"The victim appears to be male, approximately thirty to forty years old based on bone structure," the medical examiner reported, her voice clinically precise despite the horror before her. "Cause of death... well, that's more complicated. The flesh removal appears to have been done post-mortem, but I can't determine what killed him until we get him back to the lab."

Ethan nodded, his enhanced senses picking up details the ME couldn't possibly detect through conventional examination. "The body's been completely drained of life energy," he said quietly to Alice, keeping his voice low to avoid being overheard by the other personnel. "Not just blood or physical fluids, but the essential force that animates living beings. It's been extracted and channeled into whatever ritual was performed here."

Alice's expression remained professionally neutral, but her eyes reflected understanding of the implications. "Like batteries for a magical device?"

"Exactly," Ethan confirmed, grimly impressed by her quick grasp of supernatural mechanics despite her limited exposure. "Human life force is potent fuel for certain types of magic—especially necromancy. The more violent or traumatic the death, the more power it generates."

They spent hours at the crime scene, combing through every inch of the alleyway for any clues that might lead them to their quarry. The symbols, the ritual configuration, the specific mutilations inflicted on the victim—all of it spoke to a practitioner with extensive knowledge and alarming precision. This wasn't random experimentation or amateur dabbling in the dark arts. This was the work of someone who knew exactly what they were doing and had specific, calculated goals.

But as the sun began to set, and the shadows lengthened, Ethan knew that they were running out of time. The necromancer was out there somewhere, growing stronger with every passing moment. And if they didn't stop them soon, the streets of Daybridge would run red with blood.

As they made their way back to the precinct, Ethan's mind churned with dark thoughts. He couldn't shake the feeling that they were missing something, some important piece of the puzzle that would make everything fall into place. The sigils on the bones, the way they had pulsed with that eerie red light... there was something familiar about them, something that tugged at the edges of his consciousness like a half-remembered dream.

It wasn't until they were back at their desks, pouring over the evidence they had collected, that the answer finally came to him. The sigils on the bones, the specific configuration of the ritual space, the extraction of life energy rather than simple physical mutilation—he had seen something like it before, in a case he had worked years ago, before Alice had become his partner.

"Alice," he said, his voice low and urgent as he pulled a file from his desk drawer—a cold case that had never been officially solved. "I think I know what we're dealing with here. But if I'm right... we're going to need some help."

He spread the file contents across his desk—photographs of a similar ritual configuration found in an abandoned warehouse three years earlier, victim posed in the same marionette-like position though the mutilations had been less extreme. The case had been classified as a ritualistic homicide, possibly connected to cult activity, but had gone cold when no further victims had appeared and conventional investigation methods had yielded no viable suspects.

Alice studied the photographs with narrowed eyes, her analytical mind immediately connecting patterns between the old case and their current investigation. "The same perpetrator?"

"Not exactly," Ethan said, his expression troubled as he extracted a particular photograph showing a partial footprint preserved in ritual ash—a distinctive boot print with occult symbols embedded in the sole. "But I think they're connected. The methodology is too similar to be coincidental. And if I'm right about the magical signature..."

Alice looked up at him, her dark eyes searching his face. "What kind of help?"

Ethan hesitated, his mind racing as he weighed his options. He knew that what he was about to suggest went against every protocol, every rule he had sworn to uphold as a detective. But he also knew that they were running out of time, that the necromancer's power was growing with every passing moment.

"We need to talk to Lila Darkmagic," he said at last, his voice heavy with resignation. "She's the only one who might know how to stop this."

Alice's eyes widened, her mouth falling open in shock. "Lila Dark-magic? The consultant who just arrived from Prague? The one who set up that containment ritual in the morgue this morning?"

Ethan nodded, relieved that Alice's reaction wasn't as negative as he'd feared. "She has specialized knowledge in this field—experience with necromantic rituals and their countermeasures. If anyone can help us figure out what we're up against, it's her."

Alice was silent for a moment, her gaze searching Ethan's face as if trying to read his thoughts. At last, she nodded, her jaw set with deter-mination. "Alright," she said, her voice low and steady. "Let's do it. But if this goes sideways, Reeves... it's on you."

Ethan nodded, his heart heavy with the weight of responsibility. He knew that he was taking a risk, that bringing Lila more deeply into the investi-gation could have unforeseen consequences. The woman carried her own dark history—he could sense it in the way reality seemed to ripple around her, in the silver rings she wore on every finger, in the haunted look that sometimes crossed her face when she thought no one was watching.

But he also knew that they had no other choice. The necromancer was out there, growing stronger with every passing moment. And if they didn't stop them soon, the streets of Daybridge would run red with blood.

As they made their way out of the precinct and into the night, Ethan could feel the weight of the city pressing down on him like a physical force. The shadows seemed to writhe and twist with a malevolent intelligence, as if sensing the darkness gathering on the horizon. But as he glanced over at Alice, her face set with grim determination, he felt a flicker of hope kindle in his chest.

Together, they would find this necromancer, this manipulator of death and dimensional energies. Together, they would stop the darkness from consuming their city.

And if that meant enlisting the help of someone like Lila Darkmagic—a woman who clearly carried her own burdens of past mistakes and arcane knowledge—then so be it. When monsters lurked in every shadow and dark magic thrummed beneath the surface of reality, sometimes the only way to fight fire was with fire.

And Ethan Reeves, the werewolf detective of Daybridge, partially integrated with a dimensional nexus entity and partnered with the most steadfast human he'd ever known, was ready to burn.

～

CHAPTER TWO

SHADOWS OF THE PAST

THE MUSTY SCENT of old paper and stale coffee hung heavy in the air as Detective Ethan Reeves rifled through the dusty file boxes that lined the shelves of the precinct's evidence room. The fluorescent lights overhead flickered and buzzed, casting an eerie greenish glow over the cramped, cluttered space where decades of Daybridge's darkest moments lay cataloged and forgotten.

The room itself felt like a time capsule—windowless cinder block walls lined with metal shelves sagging under the weight of cardboard boxes and manila folders, each containing fragments of lives shattered by violence and tragedy. The air conditioning struggled valiantly against the persistent warmth generated by outdated electrical systems, creating pockets of cold and heat that Ethan's heightened senses detected as he moved through the narrow aisles.

Ethan's brow furrowed as he scanned the faded labels on the boxes, his keen eyes searching for the one case that had been haunting his thoughts ever since they had discovered the grisly remains in the alleyway. It was a case from his early days as a detective, before his partnership with Alice, before his partial integration with the nexus entity beneath Daybridge Bridge—a case that he could never solve and one that he could never forget.

"Should be in section C-7," muttered Sergeant Morales, the aging evidence clerk whose perpetually ink-stained fingers and encyclopedic memory had made him an institution in the department. "Cold cases from '18 through '20, organized by primary investigator. Might want to check the lower shelves too—some of those boxes got shifted around during the basement flooding last spring."

Ethan nodded his thanks, appreciating Morales' discretion. The sergeant hadn't asked why a homicide detective was suddenly interested in a five-year-old cold case, hadn't commented on the unusual authorization Ethan had secured from Captain Donovan to access sealed evidence. In a department where gossip spread faster than gunfire, Morales' silence was worth its weight in gold.

At last, he found what he was looking for—a battered old box tucked away in a corner, its label faded and peeling with age and neglect. The case number was barely legible, but Ethan would have recognized it blind: DPD-HC-19-0437, the alphanumeric code that had haunted his dreams for years.

With a grunt of effort, Ethan hauled the box down from the shelf and carried it over to a nearby table, his heart pounding with a mixture of anticipation and dread. Dust motes danced in the sickly fluorescent light as he set the box down, the cardboard creaking in protest as if reluctant to reveal its secrets after so many years of silence.

As he lifted the lid and began to sort through the contents, a wave of memories washed over him—memories of a time when he had been younger and more naïve, still new to the world of supernatural crime and only beginning to understand the implications of his own lycanthropic condition. His transformation had been relatively recent then, the wolf still an unpredictable force he struggled to control rather than the integrated aspect of his nature it had become.

The case had been a brutal one, a string of murders that had terrorized the city and left the police department scrambling for answers during a particularly harsh winter. The victims—seven in total—had been found in various states of dismemberment, their bodies displayed in ways that had seemed random to most investigators but had spoken of deliberate ritual to Ethan's increasingly supernatural senses.

The first evidence bag contained photographs, their colors slightly faded but the horror they captured undiminished by time. The initial victim, Marcus Delaney, 34, was found in the basement of an abandoned apartment building in the North End. The official cause of death had been exsanguination, but the medical examiner had noted anomalies in the tissue damage that didn't match any known weapon or animal attack.

But there had been something different about these murders, something that had set them apart from the usual run-of-the-mill crimes that Ethan had been used to dealing with. The victims had all been found with strange symbols carved into their flesh—not randomly placed but arranged in precise geometric patterns that Ethan now recognized as forming a complex sigil when mapped across all seven bodies. Their remains had been drained of blood and left to rot in the darkest corners of the city, often in locations with historical significance that had seemed irrelevant to the investigation at the time.

Ethan had been convinced that the murders were the work of a powerful vampire, a creature of the night that preyed on the innocent and left only death in its wake. His own recent transformation into a werewolf had opened his eyes to the supernatural world lurking beneath Daybridge's surface, and he had thrown himself into the investigation with a passion, determined to bring the killer to justice no matter the cost.

He recalled the skepticism of his colleagues, the raised eyebrows and concerned glances when he'd suggested connections between lunar cycles and the timing of the killings. His partner at the time, a veteran detective named Frank Mendoza, had humored him publicly while privately suggesting he seek counseling for stress-induced paranoia.

The second evidence bag contained soil samples taken from the third crime scene—the waterfront warehouse where Amy Carr had been found posed like a grotesque marionette, her limbs bound with copper wire that had left distinctive oxidation patterns on her skin. The lab results had been inconclusive, noting only "anomalous mineral content and organic compounds inconsistent with local soil composition."

Now, with his enhanced senses and connection to the nexus entity, Ethan could detect traces of the energy that had permeated those samples even after five years—a distinctive magical signature that resonated with the residue found at the recent grave desecrations. Not identical, but similar enough to suggest a connection or at least a shared methodology.

But as the weeks had turned into months and the body count had continued to rise, Ethan had found himself isolated within the department, his theories rejected, his insights dismissed as the ravings of a detective too close to the case. The evidence had been frustratingly sparse, the leads few and quickly evaporating like morning mist. And then, just when he had been on the verge of a breakthrough—tracking the geographic pattern of the killings to a potential convergence point beneath Old Town—the murders had suddenly stopped, as if the killer had simply vanished into thin air.

The third evidence bag contained the only physical evidence directly linked to the perpetrator—a fragment of black fabric found clutched in the hand of the final victim, Christine Weaver. The forensics report indicated unusual properties: "Material appears to be silk based but contains unidentified fibers resistant to standard testing protocols. Microscopic examination reveals patterns consistent with deliberate weaving rather than manufacturing defects."

Now, as Ethan stared down at the faded crime scene photos and yellowed witness statements that spilled from the box, he felt a sinking feeling in the pit of his stomach. The symbols on the victims' bodies, the way they had been drained of blood, the specific locations chosen for displaying the remains—it was all too similar to the recent spate of grave robberies and murders that had been plaguing the city.

With a heavy sigh, Ethan sank down into a chair and began to pore over the evidence, his mind racing as he tried to piece together the connections between the two cases. The metal chair creaked beneath his weight, its cold surface penetrating through the fabric of his slacks as he hunched over the scattered files.

He had always prided himself on his ability to see patterns, to find the hidden threads that tied seemingly disparate events together. But this time, the threads seemed to lead him down a dark and twisted path— one he wasn't sure he was ready to follow. If his suspicions were correct, if the recent killings were connected to the unsolved murders from five years ago, then the implications were staggering.

It would mean that the perpetrator had not simply disappeared but had been biding their time, gathering power, preparing for something more significant than a simple killing spree. And it would mean that Ethan's failure to solve the case the first time had allowed this darkness to fester and grow, to return stronger and more deadly than before.

As the hours ticked by and the precinct grew quiet around him, Ethan lost himself in the case files, his eyes straining to make out the faded handwriting and blurry photographs. The background noise of the station gradually diminished—the ringing phones giving way to the quiet hum of computers, the bustling detectives replaced by the skeleton crew of the night shift.

He could feel the weight of the past pressing down on him like a physical force, the guilt and regret he had buried deep within himself rising to the surface like a festering wound. Back then, he had been a different man—a newly turned werewolf struggling with his dual nature, a detective trying to prove himself while hiding a supernatural secret that would have seen him dismissed from the force or worse.

He had been so close, so very close to catching the killer all those years ago. But he had let his pride get the best of him, had allowed himself to be led astray by false leads and dead ends. His isolation within the department had made him reckless, pushing him to conduct unauthorized surveillance and follow leads without backup. And in the end, it had been the victims who had paid the price for his failure.

The fourth evidence bag contained the personal effects of Christine Weaver—a silver locket containing a photograph of her daughter, a set of keys to an apartment that had remained empty for months after her death, and a small notebook filled with increasingly paranoid entries about being watched, about shadows that moved independently of their sources, about whispers in the dark when no one was there.

Ethan's hand trembled slightly as he reached for the last folder in the box, his heart pounding with a sickening sense of foreboding. He already knew what he would find inside—the one piece of evidence he could never shake the one clue that had haunted his dreams for years.

With a deep breath, he opened the folder and stared down at the crime scene photo that lay within. It was a picture of Christine Weaver, the seventh and final victim, a young woman with pale skin and dark hair, her eyes wide and staring in death. But it was the symbol carved into her flesh that made Ethan's blood run cold—a twisting, serpentine design that wrapped around her torso like a constricting snake, its head positioned directly over her heart.

The same symbol he had seen etched into the bones of their most recent victim in the alleyway.

In that moment, Ethan knew that his past had finally caught up with him—that the killer he had failed to catch all those years ago had returned, more powerful and more deadly than ever before. And now, it was up to him to stop them before they could claim any more innocent lives.

But there was something else in the folder, something he had forgotten about or perhaps deliberately suppressed in the years since the case went cold. A small evidence bag containing a silver ring—not just any ring, but one bearing the distinctive design of intertwined serpents that matched the symbol carved into Christine Weaver's flesh. The evidence tag indicated it had been found at the scene of her murder, partially hidden beneath a radiator as if dropped during a struggle.

Ethan lifted the bag, studying the ring through the clear plastic. With his enhanced senses, he could detect faint traces of energy still clinging to the metal—a distinctive magical signature that resonated with something he had encountered recently.

The silver rings worn by Lila Darkmagic.

With a grim sense of purpose, Ethan gathered up the case files and strode out of the evidence room, his jaw set with determination. The connection he had suspected was now confirmed, though its implications remained unclear. Was Lila somehow involved in the original murders? Was she the perpetrator they had failed to catch, now returned to continue her work? Or was there some other connection, some shared history with the true killer that had brought her to Daybridge at precisely this moment?

He knew that he would need answers—and quickly—if he was to have any hope of stopping this new wave of killings. He needed help from someone who understood the dark forces that were gathering beneath the surface of the city, who could translate the arcane symbols and decipher their purpose before more innocent lives were lost.

And whether she was ally or enemy, Lila Darkmagic clearly held knowledge that was crucial to the investigation. Knowledge that might finally allow Ethan to close a case that had haunted him for five long years and prevent a darkness from consuming the city he had sworn to protect.

The precinct was nearly deserted as Ethan made his way through the bullpen, the night shift officers occupied with the usual parade of drunks and domestic disturbances that filled the quiet hours. No one questioned the evidence box tucked under his arm or the grim determination etched on his features as he headed for the exit.

Outside, the city glowed with artificial light that pushed back the darkness but never quite defeated it. Neon signs and streetlamps created pools of illumination in which people moved like fish in aquariums, unaware of the predators that lurked just beyond the light's reach. And somewhere in that urban wilderness, a killer was preparing their next move, drawing power from death and using it for purposes Ethan could only begin to imagine.

With his free hand, Ethan pulled out his phone and dialed Alice's number. His partner answered on the second ring, her voice alert despite the late hour.

"Chen."

"It's me," Ethan said, his voice tight with controlled urgency. "I found something in the old case files—a connection to our current situation. And possibly to Lila Darkmagic."

There was a brief pause before Alice responded, her tone shifting from professional to concerned. "Where are you?"

"Just leaving the precinct. We need to talk to Darkmagic—tonight, if possible."

"I'll meet you at her hotel in twenty minutes," Alice replied without hesitation, the sounds of movement suggesting she was already preparing to leave her apartment. "The Ridgewood on 7th. Room 318."

Ethan's brow furrowed in surprise. "How do you—"

"I asked the captain for her contact information after the morgue consultation this morning," Alice explained, a hint of defensiveness in her tone. "Thought it might be useful to have, given the circumstances."

A small smile tugged at the corner of Ethan's mouth despite the gravity of the situation. Alice's thoroughness and forward thinking had saved them countless hours over the years, her methodical approach complementing his more intuitive investigative style.

"Twenty minutes," he confirmed. "And Alice? Be careful. We don't know exactly what we're dealing with here."

"Never do," she replied with grim humor. "That's why we make such a good team."

As Ethan ended the call and made his way to his car, the weight of the evidence box seemed to increase with each step. Not just the physical burden of aged paper and preserved artifacts, but the weight of responsibility for lives lost and those that might yet be saved.

Whatever darkness had returned to Daybridge—whatever connection existed between the murders of five years ago and the recent desecrations—Ethan was determined to face it head-on. No more hesitation, no more isolation, no more failure to act when action was needed.

This time, he would stop the killer before the body count rose. This time, he had resources he lacked before—his integrated lycanthropic nature, his connection to the nexus entity, his partnership with Alice, and potentially the knowledge Lila Darkmagic possessed.

This time, the shadows of the past would not claim victory over the present. Not if Ethan Reeves had anything to say about it.

CHAPTER THREE

THE BLACK CAULDRON

THE BLACK CAULDRON was a seedy little occult shop tucked away in the heart of Daybridge's red-light district, its grimy windows and peeling paint a testament to the unsavory nature of its clientele. Wedged between a pawnshop with bars on its windows and an adult video store with permanently flickering neon, the establishment existed in a strange liminal space—visible to those who knew where to look but functionally invisible to the casual passerby or tourist. It occupied the ground floor of a pre-war building whose upper stories had been condemned after a fire in the 1970s, the brick facade blackened with decades of urban grime and supernatural residue.

Ethan had been there before, back when he had first delved into the supernatural underworld that lurked beneath the city's surface. In those early days after his transformation, desperate for answers about his condition, he had sought out anyone who might possess knowledge of the lycanthropic curse that had upended his life. The Black Cauldron had been one stop among many on a journey that had led him through Daybridge's hidden places—the spaces between normal reality where creatures of myth and nightmare conducted their business beyond the notice of ordinary humans.

The shop was owned by a woman named Madame Raven, a self-proclaimed psychic and medium who claimed to have a direct line to the spirit world. With her elaborate velvet gowns and theatrical mannerisms, she cultivated an image straight out of a Victorian séance parlor. Ethan had always been skeptical of her abilities, viewing them as part performance and part cold reading—the practiced techniques of someone who knew how to extract information from clients while appearing to divine it through supernatural means. But he couldn't deny that she seemed to have an uncanny knack for knowing things she shouldn't—things that could prove invaluable in his current investigation.

The streetlights cast elongated shadows as Ethan approached the shop, their amber glow reflecting off puddles from an earlier rain shower. The streets were relatively quiet for this part of town, the usual parade of night workers, club-goers, and denizens of Daybridge's underbelly temporarily subdued by the unseasonable chill that had descended on the city. A few enterprising dealers huddled in doorways, eyeing Ethan with professional wariness—his purposeful stride and the subtle bulge of his shoulder holster marking him as either law enforcement or serious competition. Neither was welcome in this neighborhood.

Through his connection to the nexus entity beneath Daybridge Bridge, Ethan sensed the subtle wrongness that permeated this part of the city —the way reality felt slightly thinner here, more malleable to those with the knowledge and power to manipulate it. The dimensional boundaries had always been weaker in the red-light district, even before the events at the bridge six months ago. Something about the convergence of desperation, vice, and human misery created conditions where other forces could gain purchase in the material world.

As he pushed open the door and stepped inside, the shop's interior hit him like a physical blow. The air was thick with the cloying scent of incense and the acrid tang of burnt sage, overlaying the more subtle aromas of rare herbs, musty paper, and the distinctive metallic odor of dried blood used in certain rituals. The walls were lined with shelves that groaned under the weight of dusty old books and arcane artifacts —crystal balls of varying sizes, animal bones arranged in complex patterns, jars containing substances Ethan preferred not to identify, and assorted talismans crafted from materials both mundane and exotic.

In the center of the room, a rickety old table was set up with a crystal ball and a worn deck of tarot cards, a single black candle flickering in the gloom. The flame burned with unusual steadiness, neither guttering in the draft from the door nor responding to Ethan's movement as he stepped further into the shop. Its light cast elongated shadows across the floor and walls, shadows that seemed to move independently of their sources in ways that would have disturbed Ethan before his own transformation had recalibrated his understanding of reality's boundaries.

The door closed behind him with a soft click, the bell that should have announced his entrance remaining ominously silent. The shop appeared empty at first glance, but Ethan's enhanced senses detected a presence in the back room—the subtle sound of breathing, the faint rustle of fabric, the distinctive scent of expensive perfume mingled with something more primal and unsettling.

"Detective Reeves," a voice purred from the shadows, sending a shiver down Ethan's spine. "I've been expecting you."

The voice was not Madame Raven's theatrical contralto but something altogether more refined and dangerous—a voice he hadn't heard in years but recognized instantly. A voice that belonged to someone who should not have been there, who had no business being in Daybridge after what had happened the last time their paths had crossed.

Ethan's hand instinctively went to the gun at his hip as he peered into the darkness, his eyes straining to make out the figure that lurked there. But as the candlelight flickered and danced, he glimpsed a face that he recognized—a face that he had hoped never to see again.

"Lila," he breathed, his voice hoarse with shock and disbelief. "What the hell are you doing here?"

The witch stepped out of the shadows, a wry smile playing across her full lips. She was as beautiful as Ethan remembered, her raven-black hair cascading down her back in glossy waves, her emerald eyes glinting with a mischievous light that had once captivated him before he understood the darkness that lay beneath her alluring exterior. She wore a tailored black suit that accentuated her slender figure, the jacket open to reveal a blood-red silk blouse. Silver rings glinted on every finger—protective talismans.

But there was something different about her now—a darkness that seemed to cling to her like a second skin, a sense of power that radiated from her like a physical force. Through his connection to the nexus entity, Ethan could perceive how reality bent slightly around her, how the shadows in her vicinity deepened and seemed to reach toward her as if drawn by some magnetic attraction.

"I could ask you the same question, Detective," she purred, her voice low and throaty as she moved with predatory grace around the table, trailing her fingers along its surface. "But I think we both know why you're here. You're looking for answers—answers that only I can provide."

Her scent triggered memories Ethan had long suppressed—intimate moments shared before he discovered her true nature, before he learned what she intended to unleash upon Daybridge. The mixture of expensive perfume, the natural musk of her skin, and the distinctive ozone tang of magical energy formed an olfactory signature as unique and recognizable as a fingerprint.

"Where's Madame Raven?" he demanded, his eyes scanning the shop for any sign of the proprietor. "What have you done with her?"

Lila laughed, the sound like crystal bells with an undertone of something darker. "Always so suspicious, Ethan. Madame Raven is perfectly fine—enjoying an all-expenses-paid vacation in the Bahamas, courtesy of my generous nature. She was quite happy to rent the shop to me for a few weeks. Apparently, business has been slow since that unfortunate incident with the hexed tarot deck."

She moved closer, her heels clicking softly on the wooden floor. "But you didn't come here for Madame Raven, did you? You came seeking information about the grave desecrations and the murder in the alley-way. About the symbols carved into human bone and the necromantic energies that have been detected at multiple locations throughout the city."

Ethan maintained his distance, acutely aware of the danger Lila repre-sented despite her outward charm. She had always possessed an almost supernatural ability to read his thoughts and emotions, to antic-ipate his moves before he made them. It had made her both an intoxi-cating lover and a formidable adversary.

"What do you know about the grave robberies?" he asked, his voice tight with barely suppressed anger. "And what do they have to do with the murders from five years ago?"

Lila's smile widened, her eyes glinting with a knowing light that suggested she had been waiting for precisely this question. "Ah, the murders," she murmured, her voice as soft as a lover's caress. "I was wondering when you'd make the connection. The symbols on the bodies, the way they were drained of blood... it's all part of a ritual, Detective. A ritual that's been centuries in the making."

She turned away, moving to a bookshelf where ancient tomes were arranged in a pattern that Ethan now recognized as deliberately designed to form a larger sigil—one that resonated with protective energies rather than the malevolent forces he had detected at the crime scenes. With graceful movements, she extracted a leather-bound volume whose cover bore no title, only an embossed symbol that matched the marking found on the most recent victim.

"The Grimoire of Eternal Shadows," she said, running her fingers along the book's spine with an almost reverent touch. "One of only three surviving copies. I've spent the last three years tracking it down after your... interruption... of my previous work."

Ethan's heart pounded as he listened to Lila's words, his mind racing as he tried to make sense of what she was telling him. He had always known that there was more to the murders than met the eye—that there was some deeper, darker purpose behind the killer's actions. But

he could never put his finger on what that purpose might be...
until now.

"The necromancer," he breathed, his eyes widening with sudden realization as pieces of the puzzle began to fall into place. "The one who's been robbing the graves and murdering innocent people. They're trying to complete the ritual, aren't they? The same ritual you were attempting three years ago."

Lila's expression shifted subtly, a flicker of something like respect crossing her features before returning to her usual enigmatic smile. "Not the same ritual, Detective. Something far more ancient and infinitely more dangerous." She opened the grimoire, revealing pages covered in text written in a language Ethan didn't recognize—spidery symbols that seemed to writhe on the page like living things. "What I attempted in Daybridge Park was a controlled summoning—a way to access power from another dimension while maintaining precise boundaries and limitations."

She turned the book so Ethan could see the illustrations—detailed drawings of ritual configurations that matched the patterns found at the crime scenes with disturbing accuracy. "What our necromancer is attempting is nothing less than a full breach of the dimensional barriers—a complete collapse of the metaphysical structures that separate our reality from others far less hospitable to human life."

Lila nodded, her expression grave as she closed the grimoire. "Yes," she said, her voice barely above a whisper. "And if they succeed, the consequences will be catastrophic. The ritual is designed to summon a being of immense power—a creature that feeds on death and decay, that thrives on the suffering of the living. If the necromancer completes the final sacrifice, this being will be unleashed upon the world... and nothing will be able to stop it."

The candle on the table flared briefly as she spoke these words, its flame doubling in height before settling back to its unnatural stillness. Through his connection to the nexus entity, Ethan sensed a ripple in the dimensional fabric of Daybridge—a subtle disturbance that suggested something was stirring in response to their conversation, as if the mere discussion of these forces was enough to attract their attention.

Ethan felt a chill run down his spine as he listened to Lila's words, his mind reeling with the implications of what she was saying. He had witnessed enough supernatural phenomena since his transformation to know that her warnings were not mere hyperbole. The threat she described could destroy Daybridge and potentially spread far beyond, consuming everything in its path like a cancer in the fabric of reality itself.

"How do we stop it?" he asked, his voice hoarse with the weight of responsibility. "How do we keep the necromancer from completing the ritual?"

Lila's eyes met his, her gaze filled with a grim determination that seemed at odds with the manipulative, self-serving witch he had known before. "We have to find them," she said, her voice low and urgent. "We have to stop them before they can make the final sacrifice. And to do that, we're going to need all the help we can get."

She placed the grimoire on the table and retrieved a rolled parchment from a drawer beneath the crystal ball. When she unfurled it, Ethan saw that it was a map of Daybridge, but not like any conventional map he had seen before. This one showed the city as a complex network of glowing lines and nodes—ley lines and power nexuses that formed a geometric pattern centered on Daybridge Bridge itself.

"The necromancer has been working methodically, establishing ritual sites at specific points in this network," Lila explained, indicating several locations marked with small red X's. "Each desecration, each murder, builds power toward the final ritual. Based on the pattern, I believe they will attempt the summoning here." Her finger came to rest on a spot that Ethan recognized with a sinking feeling in his stomach.

"The old cathedral in Blackwood Cemetery," he said softly. "Where the original founders of Daybridge are buried."

Lila nodded. "The oldest and most powerful nexus point in the city after the bridge itself. The perfect location for breaking through the dimensional barriers."

Ethan nodded, his jaw set with resolve. He knew that Lila was right—that they would need every resource at their disposal if they were to have any hope of stopping the necromancer and their dark plans. And he knew that meant putting aside his past differences with the witch, burying the hatchet and working together for the greater good, regardless of the personal complications their history created.

"Alright," he said, his voice filled with a newfound sense of purpose. "Let's do this. Let's find this bastard and put an end to their reign of terror once and for all."

As he turned to leave the shop, Ethan felt a hand on his arm—a touch that was both familiar and unsettling at the same time, sending a jolt of electricity through his body that was part memory and part warning. He looked down to see Lila staring up at him, her emerald eyes filled with an emotion that he couldn't quite name—something between concern and calculation, between genuine worry and strategic manipulation.

"Be careful, Ethan," she whispered, her voice soft and filled with an urgency that seemed genuine despite his lingering mistrust. "The path ahead is fraught with danger and deception. Trust no one... not even me."

The warning hung in the air between them, weighted with their complicated history and the knowledge that she had betrayed him once before, had used their intimate connection to further her own arcane agenda. Yet there was something in her eyes now that suggested a different motivation, a purpose beyond the selfish accumulation of power that had driven her previous actions.

And with those cryptic words, she stepped back into the shadows, the darkness seeming to embrace her like an old friend until she was no longer visible. The candle's flame guttered out, plunging the shop into momentary darkness before the mundane overhead lights flickered to life, transforming the mystical space back into what appeared to be a typical, if eccentric, retail establishment.

Ethan stood alone among the shelves of occult paraphernalia, the encounter leaving him with more questions than answers. He knew that he had just entered into a dangerous alliance, that trusting Lila even partially could prove to be a fatal mistake. But he also knew that her knowledge of the necromantic arts far exceeded his own, that her understanding of the ritual being enacted throughout Daybridge might be their only hope of stopping it before catastrophe struck.

As he stepped out into the neon-lit streets of the red-light district, Ethan felt a strange sense of calm wash over him despite the gravity of the situation. The familiar sights and sounds of urban nightlife—the distant thump of bass from underground clubs, the laughter of revelers moving between bars, the occasional siren wailing in the distance— grounded him in the reality he had sworn to protect.

He had faced down monsters before, had stared death in the face and lived to tell the tale. The confrontation beneath Daybridge Bridge had nearly cost him his humanity, but it had also granted him unprece- dented access to knowledge and power through his connection to the nexus entity. And he knew that he would draw upon every resource available to him—his lycanthropic abilities, his detective's training, his partnership with Alice, and now the dangerous alliance with Lila—to keep the darkness at bay.

For he was Detective Ethan Reeves, the werewolf cop of Daybridge, partially integrated with a cosmic entity beyond human comprehen- sion. And he would not rest until the streets of his city were safe once more, until the shadows that lurked in every corner were banished back to the hell whence they came.

No matter what it took, no matter what sacrifices he had to make... he would see this through to the bitter end. For the innocent, for the city he loved...

For his own immortal soul.

. . .

The candle flickered, casting eerie shadows across Nadia Marsh's study as she pored over the ancient tomes late into the night. Located in the converted attic of her Victorian home on the outskirts of Daybridge, the space was a scholar's sanctuary—walls lined with custom bookshelves, an antique mahogany desk positioned beneath a skylight that allowed her to work by moonlight when the mood struck, and carefully organized filing cabinets containing decades of research into the city's supernatural history.

The soft scratch of her quill was the only sound that broke the stillness as she meticulously recorded her findings in a leather-bound journal, its pages already filled with notes, diagrams, and observations from her ongoing investigation. As an investigative journalist, Nadia had dedicated her life to understanding the forces that shaped human belief in the supernatural.

But recent discoveries had transformed her academic interest into something far more urgent and personal.

Ever since uncovering the first hints of the Caligari Cataclysm during her investigations in Daybridge, Nadia had become obsessed with unraveling the truth behind this mysterious event that had nearly brought the world to ruin centuries ago. What had begun as research for her latest articles had evolved into a desperate race to understand a historical catastrophe that seemed increasingly relevant to current events in the city.

The pages spread before her contained fragments of accounts from multiple sources—church records describing a "great darkness" that descended upon the region in 1673, personal journals from witnesses who described impossible phenomena in the skies and waters surrounding what would later become Daybridge, and fragmentary references in occult texts to a "thinning of the veil" that allowed "entities of incomprehensible nature" to manifest briefly in the material world.

Her latest research pointed to a shadowy cult that may have played a key role, performing dark rituals that opened gateways to realms beyond understanding. The Brethren of Eternal Shadow, as they called themselves, had apparently existed across multiple countries and centuries, their membership including individuals of significant wealth and influence who shared a common belief that humanity's salvation lay in communion with extradimensional beings they referred to as "The Transcendent Ones."

The thought made Nadia's stomach churn, but she refused to shy away, driven by a hunger to understand no matter how disturbing the implications. Her academic colleagues had dismissed her theories as speculative at best and delusional at worst, but the patterns she had uncovered were too consistent, the connections too precise to be mere coincidence.

As she turned the brittle pages of a crumbling grimoire recovered from a sealed chamber beneath one of Daybridge's oldest churches, her eyes widened at the passage before her. Written in a spidery hand, the text described ritual preparations that bore striking similarities to the grave desecrations and murders recently reported in the local news—specific configurations of ritual sites, particular symbolic markings, and the extraction of life energy from sacrificial victims.

Hasty scribbles in the margins spoke of sacrifices, of lives snuffed out to fuel the cult's unholy rites. If true, it painted a picture more horrific than Nadia could have imagined—not isolated incidents of violence driven by individual madness, but a coordinated effort spanning centuries, each generation of cultists building upon the work of their predecessors toward some apocalyptic culmination.

Most disturbing were the diagrams showing how these ritual sites, when properly aligned and activated, would create a geometric pattern across the landscape—a pattern that, when overlaid on a modern map of Daybridge, corresponded precisely with locations where strange phenomena had been reported in recent weeks.

She felt the weight of her quest pressing down as she realized how much more there was to uncover about this catastrophe that had almost unmade the world once before and might be in the process of being recreated in the present day. The connections between past and present were becoming increasingly clear, suggesting that history was not simply repeating itself but continuing along a path laid down centuries ago.

Nadia's grip tightened on her quill, fresh determination coursing through her veins as she carefully transcribed the most relevant passages into her journal, adding her own observations and theoretical connections. The night was deepening outside her skylight, but she would not rest until she had gleaned every secret from the depths of history that might help prevent a modern recurrence of the Caligari Cataclysm.

Tomorrow, she would need to share her findings with someone who could act on this information—someone with both the authority and the specialized knowledge necessary to confront a threat of this magnitude. Her thoughts turned to Detective Ethan Reeves, whose name had appeared in connection with several unusual cases that aligned with her research. The rumors about him were fantastical, of course—whispers about supernatural abilities and confrontations with forces beyond human understanding—but after everything she had uncovered, Nadia was no longer so quick to dismiss even the most outlandish possibilities.

As she continued her work, the candle's flame suddenly jumped and swayed, though no draft had disturbed the still air of her study. The shadows in the corners of the room seemed to deepen momentarily, creating the unsettling impression that she was being observed by unseen eyes. A prickling sensation crept up her spine—the primitive warning system of human instinct responding to a threat not yet consciously perceived.

Nadia glanced toward her window, half expecting to see a face peering in from the darkness. But there was only the night sky, stars obscured by the light pollution of the city below. She returned to her work, but the feeling of being watched persisted, an unwelcome companion in her solitary research.

Unknown to Nadia, across the city in the depths of Blackwood Cemetery, ancient stones were beginning to resonate with energies awakened by her investigations. Knowledge was power, but it was also illumination—and in shining light into long-forgotten corners of history, she had inadvertently drawn the attention of forces that preferred to operate in darkness.

The game of cosmic chess was accelerating toward its endgame, with Daybridge as its board and its citizens as unwitting pieces. And as Nadia Marsh continued her desperate research, the necromancer moved another piece into position, one step closer to the cataclysmic ritual that would tear open the boundaries between worlds and usher in an age of darkness beyond imagining.

CHAPTER FOUR

BEFORE THE FALL

PRAGUE, 1994

CHARLES UNIVERSITY LIBRARY, Late Winter Evening

The reading room was officially closed, but shadows knew no hours.
Outside, snow fell in thick, lazy flakes across the ancient city. Inside the
library's Gothic architecture, time seemed suspended between
centuries—electric lights now illuminated spaces once lit by candles,
while weathered stone walls and vaulted ceilings had witnessed generations of scholars pursue knowledge without concern for
consequences.

Lila sat cross-legged on a reading table, surrounded by stacks of
ancient texts. Her dark hair was shorter then, wild with youth and
academic defiance, escaping from a messy ponytail as she bent over a
translation. Her fingers bore no protective rings—no silver bands
inscribed with the protective sigils that would later become her signature. Instead, ink stains marked her hands, the badge of a dedicated
researcher.

The library after hours was a sanctuary for privileged students granted
special access by impressed professors. Silence hung heavy, broken
only by the occasional turning of pages or scratch of pen on paper.

Most of the reading room lay in darkness, with only their corner illuminated by a desk lamp creating a small island of light.

"Found it!" Viktor emerged from between towering shelves, carrying a leather-bound volume with reverence. His footsteps echoed on the marble floor as he approached, excitement making him careless about noise. Candlelight caught his features—younger, softer, unmarked by what was to come. His face still carried the openness of a brilliant mind unfettered by disillusionment, his dark eyes still warm when they met hers.

At twenty-six, Viktor Kalishnikov was already making waves in Charles University's Department of Historical Anthropology, his controversial theories about prehistoric ritual practices earning him both admirers and detractors. His Russian heritage gave him exotic appeal among Czech students, while his family's wealth allowed him to pursue research avenues closed to those dependent on university funding.

"The Codex Mortis?" Lila made space among her papers, her voice betraying awe despite her scholarly skepticism. At twenty-three, she specialized in pre-Christian European magical practices, her facility with ancient languages making her an invaluable research partner. "I thought it was lost in the fire of 1789."

"Someone made a copy." He set the book down carefully, the leather binding creaking as it opened. The pages were yellowed with age, the handwritten text meticulously preserved. "And not just any copy. Look at these diagrams. The symmetry is... beautiful."

His voice contained the reverent wonder that had first drawn Lila to him—that capacity to see beauty in what others found disturbing. It was a quality they shared, this ability to look beyond conventional morality into deeper patterns underlying human experience.

Lila leaned closer, her shoulder brushing his as they bent over the ancient text. The contact sent a familiar warmth through her. The pages showed intricate patterns of interconnected circles and symbols, mathematical precision giving structure to what might otherwise appear as chaotic scribbles. These weren't random occult markings, but carefully calculated configurations designed to channel energies in specific ways.

"It's like music," she whispered, her finger hovering above the page. "You can almost hear it—the mathematical progression, the way each symbol builds on the last, creating harmonies and resonances."

"That's what drew me to this work. To you." Viktor's hand found hers, warm against her ink-stained fingers. "Most people see dark magic as crude and destructive. They don't understand the harmony in it. The perfect balance between life and death, creation and dissolution."

His voice took on the passionate quality that could captivate an entire lecture hall—the conviction of someone who saw connections others missed, patterns in what appeared to be chaos.

"Abby would love this." Lila traced a symbol in the air, visualizing how its curves would translate into energetic flows. Her voice caught as she mentioned her sister, emotion overwhelming her academic detachment. "She always said magic was just advanced mathematics that science hadn't caught up with yet."

The memory brought both warmth and pain—Abby's brilliant mind approaching problems from unexpected angles, seeing patterns where others saw only random events. At nineteen, her younger sister had already been outpacing her professors in theoretical physics before the diagnosis interrupted her academic rise.

Viktor squeezed her hand, understanding the complex emotions behind her words. "We'll cure her. The conventional treatments aren't working, but this..." He turned a page, revealing diagrams of energy manipulation that predated modern understanding of cellular biology by centuries. "This is real power. Power enough to rewrite the rules of death itself."

In the desk lamp's glow, his face showed the determination that had first drawn them together—the refusal to accept limitations when conventional wisdom failed to provide solutions.

"The professors say these rituals are forbidden for a reason," Lila said, her voice holding hesitation born not from personal fear but concern for the boundaries they approached. "That the price—"

"The professors are afraid," he interrupted, his voice hardening. "They hide behind traditions and academic caution while people suffer. While your sister suffers."

He turned to face her fully, taking both her hands in his. "We're different, Lila. We see beauty in the darkness. The potential where others see only danger."

The intensity in his gaze made her breath catch. This was the Viktor who had captivated her from their first meeting—passionate, brilliant, unfettered by conventions that restricted lesser minds.

She met his gaze directly, absorbing his certainty and allowing it to strengthen her resolve. In the candlelight, his eyes seemed to shine with inner fire.

"Together," he promised, his voice dropping to an intimate whisper, "we'll unlock secrets they never dreamed of. We'll save Abby. And then... then we'll change everything."

The promise contained multitudes—academic recognition, revolutionary understanding of forces dismissed by modern science, and most immediately, the desperate hope of saving her sister from terminal cancer. In that moment, any doubts Lila harbored seemed insignificant compared to the possibilities Viktor offered.

Lila kissed him among the forbidden books and guttering lamp, the ancient texts witnessing passions both intellectual and physical. Neither noticed how the shadows lengthened around them, reaching toward the opened Codex, or how the temperature dropped despite the building's heating system.

They were young. They were brilliant. They were in love.

And they were already falling—descending a path whose consequences would echo across decades and continents, eventually leading to Daybridge where the boundaries between worlds had grown perilously thin.

Present Day

Jake's Private Library

The hidden room behind Crossroads Books smelled of leather bindings and sage, with undertones of protective incense. Located through a concealed door in the back office, the space represented the true heart of Jake Steinman's life work—not the public face of legitimate bookselling but a private collection of texts too dangerous or valuable for public access.

Unlike the carefully curated classics in the public shop, this room contained works whose significance transcended monetary value. Floor-to-ceiling shelves held volumes in dozens of languages, many lacking conventional titles. Glass-fronted cases protected fragile manuscripts, their preservation systems maintaining precise temperature and humidity. The space felt like a sanctuary for knowledge the wider world had forgotten or deliberately suppressed.

Detective Ethan Reeves stood before a wall of photographs showing missing persons from the past five years. Red threads connected images, forming a complex web of relationships. His enhanced perception allowed him to detect patterns beyond the obvious—not just connections of age or occupation, but subtle linkages in energetic signatures lingering in the photographs.

"They all visited the shop first," Jake said, limping in with two mugs of coffee. A childhood polio survivor, he had never let physical limitations restrict his pursuit of knowledge. "Each one looking for specific books. Ancient texts. Grimoires."

At seventy-two, Jake's body might be compromised by age and illness, but his mind remained razor sharp. Behind wire-rimmed glasses, his eyes reflected decades of accumulated wisdom.

"Viktor's breadcrumbs," Reeves murmured, accepting a mug with thanks. The coffee was strong and black, brewed in the European style

Jake had never abandoned despite decades in America. "He's been recruiting."

"Or collecting." Jake settled into his worn leather chair with a slight wince betraying arthritic joints. "The young ones especially. Those with potential but no training. Raw talent, waiting to be shaped."

The word carried ominous implications. Ethan had seen enough of the supernatural world to understand that power often came at a terrible cost—particularly when wielded by those whose moral compasses had been compromised.

Reeves studied a photo of a teenage girl, her graduation portrait bright with promise. Melissa Baker, eighteen, reported missing three months ago after telling her parents she was meeting a professor who had offered a special research opportunity.

"Like Lila once was?"

"No." Jake's voice hardened. "Lila chose her path, however misguided that choice may have been. These ones..." He gestured at the wall of missing faces. "They never got the chance to choose."

The distinction was crucial—informed consent versus manipulation, partnership versus exploitation. Through his connection to the nexus entity, Ethan could perceive subtle energetic differences in the photographs supporting Jake's assertion. These weren't willing participants but resources being harvested, their potential tapped without regard for their autonomy.

"You've been tracking them all along," Ethan realized, admiration mixing with concern. "Before we even knew there was a pattern."

"I'm a librarian, Detective. We notice when certain books draw certain readers." Jake sipped his coffee, steam momentarily fogging his glasses. "And we notice when those readers disappear."

The bookseller's modest self-description belied his true role in Daybridge's hidden community of knowledge-keepers—those few who understood the city's unique position at the intersection of dimensional boundaries. While not possessing supernatural abilities himself, Jake had spent decades cataloging instances of dimensional bleed-through and those who exploited or contained such phenomena.

"Why didn't you come forward sooner?" Ethan asked, though he already suspected the answer.

"Would you have believed me? That a dark sorcerer was harvesting souls through rare book collections?" Jake smiled tiredly. "Besides, Lila asked me not to."

The admission hung between them, confirming a connection Ethan had suspected but couldn't verify. Lila Darkmagic's arrival in Daybridge had seemed too precisely timed to be coincidence.

"You knew her plan," Ethan said, a realization that shifted his understanding of the situation. The various players weren't moving independently but coordinating in ways he hadn't fully appreciated.

"I knew she carried guilt. Pain. The kind that makes people think they have to face everything alone." Jake stood carefully, using his cane for balance as he moved to the wall of photographs. "But guilt's a funny thing. It echoes. Creates patterns of its own."

He touched one of the red threads connecting a musician who had disappeared eight months ago to a nurse who vanished weeks later. "These disappearances aren't random. They're following the same sequence as the rituals in Prague. Viktor isn't just collecting power—he's recreating something specific. Something Lila would recognize."

The revelation aligned with what Ethan had sensed—that the energetic patterns of recent necromantic activities carried resonances of older workings. Not mere repetition but deliberate recreation, each step calibrated for maximum effect.

"Why?" Ethan asked, though he suspected the answer went beyond rational explanation into the territory of obsession and unresolved trauma.

"Because some echoes never fade." Jake suddenly looked every one of his seventy-two years, the weight of witnessing repeated cycles of darkness etched into his face. "And some patterns only make sense to those who drew them first."

The bookseller moved to another shelf, extracting a slim volume bound in faded red leather. "Lila came to me six months ago, shortly after the events at the bridge. She knew Viktor would be drawn to Daybridge once the dimensional boundaries were weakened. She's been preparing since then—gathering resources, establishing protective measures, trying to anticipate his next move."

He handed the book to Ethan—a journal filled with handwritten notes in a flowing script that matched the marginalia Ethan had seen at The Black Cauldron. "This is Lila's record of what happened in Prague. Not the official version, not the story she tells others, but her private account written in the aftermath."

Ethan accepted the journal carefully. "Why give this to me now?"

"Because time is running short," Jake said, moving to a window overlooking the street. "Viktor is accelerating his timeline. The final components are falling into place for whatever catastrophic working he's planning."

He turned back to Ethan, his expression grave. "And because Lila may not be telling you everything. Her guilt over what happened with her sister clouds her judgment where Viktor is concerned. Their history... it's complicated."

Ethan nodded, understanding the warning. Lila was an ally of convenience rather than absolute reliability, her motivations shaped by a past that continued to influence her decisions.

"There's something else you should know," Jake continued, lowering his voice. "The necromantic activities aren't just building toward a conventional summoning. The pattern suggests Viktor is attempting to recreate and complete the ritual that he and Lila began in Prague—the one that claimed her sister's life. But with modifications that make it far more dangerous."

"What kind of modifications?" Ethan asked, though the sinking feeling in his stomach suggested he already knew.

"He's incorporating elements from the Order of the Ebon Star's workings—specifically, their methods for manipulating dimensional boundaries. The gravestone desecrations, the symbols carved into bone... they're hybrid forms combining necromantic principles with the Order's approach to dimensional manipulation."

The implications were chilling. The Order's methods had nearly collapsed reality during the winter solstice confrontation beneath the bridge. Combined with necromantic energies that exploited death as a power source, the potential for catastrophic dimensional disruption was exponentially greater.

"How would he even have access to the Order's methodologies?" Ethan wondered. "Their practices were closely guarded, passed down through generations."

Jake's expression darkened further. "That's the most troubling part. Someone with intimate knowledge of both traditions has been helping him—providing texts, translating obscure passages, adapting the hybrid methodology to Daybridge's specific energetic landscape."

The unspoken implication hung between them: someone who had survived the winter solstice confrontation, a former Order member now serving a new master or pursuing their own agenda using Viktor as a tool.

"I need to talk to Lila again," Ethan said, tucking the journal into his jacket pocket. "Get some straight answers about what happened in Prague and what she thinks Viktor is planning now."

Jake nodded. "Be careful, Detective. Lila carries wounds that haven't healed despite the decades that have passed. Her desire to stop Viktor is genuine, but her judgment where he's concerned..." He paused. "Just remember that sometimes the most dangerous deceptions are the ones we tell ourselves."

As Ethan prepared to leave, his phone vibrated with a message from Alice: "Body found at Eastside Park. Matches pattern but with new elements. Captain wants us there ASAP."

"I have to go," he told Jake. "Another victim."

The bookseller nodded grimly. "It's escalating. Viktor is gathering the final components for whatever he has planned." He handed Ethan a small cloth bag. "Protective herbs and minerals. Won't stop major workings but might give you some warning before you walk into something you're not prepared for."

As Ethan turned to leave, Jake called after him one final time.

"Detective? When you finish reading that journal... you'll understand why Lila believes she's the only one who can stop Viktor. But remember—belief and truth aren't always the same thing."

With that cryptic warning echoing in his mind, Ethan left the hidden sanctuary for the harsh reality of another crime scene, another victim of a pattern whose full significance was only beginning to emerge from the shadows of the past.

The cosmic chess game continued, pieces moving across Daybridge with increasing urgency as players positioned themselves for a confrontation decades in the making. And somewhere in the city, Viktor Kalishnikov watched the pieces fall into place, each death bringing him one step closer to completing what had begun in a Prague library on a snowy winter night so many years ago.

~

CHAPTER FIVE
OLD WOUNDS
DAYBRIDGE POLICE STATION, 8:47 AM

DETECTIVE MARK SIMMONS stared at the crime scene photos spread across his desk, coffee growing cold beside his keyboard. The ceramic mug—a souvenir from his daughter's college graduation four years ago—bore a ring of brown stains marking the levels of countless refills. Third cup today, not that it helped with the exhaustion that had nothing to do with sleep and everything to do with the familiar dread creeping up his spine like an unwelcome visitor.

The surrounding bullpen pulsed with morning activity—phones ringing, officers filing reports, the steady background noise of a precinct coming fully awake. But Simmons barely registered the cacophony, his focus narrowed to the images before him, each one capturing a different angle of the desecrated Harrison family plot in Oakwood Cemetery.

The disturbed earth looked almost ordinary in the harsh flash photography, clinical and detached from the visceral wrongness he'd felt standing at the scene yesterday evening. But something about the precision of the excavation nagged at him like a splinter beneath skin —too methodical to be vandalism, too deliberate to be random. These weren't kids looking for thrills or typical grave robbers seeking jewelry or gold teeth. The cut through the soil was too clean, too... ritualistic.

Each grave had been opened with surgical precision; the earth removed in a specific pattern rather than simply piled aside. The coffins had been breached in exactly the same location—the head area shattered while the rest remained intact. And most disturbing, the skulls had been removed while the rest of the remains were left undisturbed, as if the perpetrators were harvesting specific components rather than desecrating out of malice or perversion.

"You're doing it again," Detective Maria Rivera said, leaning against his desk with a manila folder tucked under her arm. Her voice carried both professional concern and the familiar cadence of someone who had worked alongside him long enough to recognize his patterns. "That same look you had back in '98."

At forty-six, Rivera remained as sharp as when they'd first partnered fifteen years ago, though silver now threaded through her dark hair and reading glasses hung from a chain around her neck—a concession to age she'd fought until eyestrain headaches had forced the issue. Her tailored pantsuit and sensible shoes spoke of a detective who balanced professionalism with practical field work requirements.

Simmons didn't look up from the photos, his weathered hands rearranging them in chronological sequence. "This is different."

"Yeah? Because from where I'm standing, you've got that same obsessed expression you had with the Chapel Hill case. We both know how that ended."

The mention of Chapel Hill made Simmons' right hand drift unconsciously to his left shoulder, where the scar tissue still pulled tight in cold weather. The gesture was automatic, a physical manifestation of psychological wounds that had never fully healed. Twenty-five years on the force, and that case still haunted him. Three missing persons, a string of desecrated graves, and in the end... nothing. No arrests. No bodies. Just a detective with a career-altering injury and a file full of questions marked "unsolved."

The official report stated he'd been attacked by a suspect hiding in the cemetery—a convenient explanation for wounds that defied conventional description. Only Simmons knew the truth about what had emerged from the freshly opened grave that night, how it had moved with impossible speed, how its touch had burned through his jacket and shirt to the flesh beneath. How the darkness had seemed to deepen around it, becoming almost solid as it closed in.

"Look at this," Simmons said, pushing a photo toward Rivera. His finger tapped a specific detail—the soil pattern around the grave, the geometric precision of the excavation. "The soil pattern. The depth. The timing with the lunar cycle—"

"The what?" Rivera raised an eyebrow, professional skepticism overriding their years of trust and partnership. "Come on, Mark. Not everything is connected to your pet theories."

The department had a long memory for career missteps. After Chapel Hill, after his recovery and return from administrative leave, Simmons had developed what his colleagues considered eccentric investigative methods. He tracked lunar phases, researched historical burial practices, maintained detailed notes on soil composition at crime scenes. Most humored him, considering these peculiarities the harmless habits of an otherwise solid detective. A few, like Rivera, occasionally worried these fixations might lead him back to the breakdown he'd suffered after his injury.

Simmons opened his desk drawer, pulled out a worn leather notebook that had traveled with him through fifteen years and three partners. The binding was cracked, the cover softened by constant handling. The pages were yellow with age, filled with cramped handwriting and diagrams that made sense only to him—a personal codex of patterns and connections he'd observed but could never officially document in police reports.

He flipped to a page dated October 1998; the paper creased from frequent reference. The diagrams matched what they were seeing now —the precise measurements of grave excavations, the specific timing relative to lunar phases, the directional orientation of the disturbed sites.

"Same pattern. Same precision. Even the direction they dug..." He stopped, aware of how it sounded. How it had sounded back then, before everything went sideways and his career had nearly ended. How it had contributed to his divorce, to the estrangement from his son that had only recently begun to heal.

Rivera's expression softened, professional concern yielding to personal friendship. They'd been through too much together for her to dismiss him entirely, even when his theories ventured beyond conventional police work. "Chief's going to assign this to Narcotics. The preliminary report already suggests it might be connected to that designer drug case—'grave dust' or whatever they're calling it. Probably just some kids looking for old prescription burials or bones to grind for their latest high."

"No," Simmons said, more sharply than he intended. Several heads turned briefly in their direction before returning to their own work. He took a breath, steadied himself, modulating his voice to avoid drawing further attention. "I want this one, Maria. I need this one."

The emphasis wasn't lost on Rivera, who studied him with the penetrating gaze that had broken countless suspects in the interrogation room. "Because of Julia?"

The name hung in the air between them, heavy with implications and shared history. Julia Microft, nineteen years old, last seen near Chapel Hill Cemetery in October 1998. Her case file still occupied a box in the cold case storage room, one of the few Simmons periodically revisited despite official discouragement. The case that broke him, that drove him into the bottle for two years before Rivera had helped pull him back. The case he'd never solved.

"Because something's happening in this town," Simmons said quietly, leaning forward to ensure his words wouldn't carry beyond their immediate space. The bullpen's background noise provided cover, but old habits of discretion died hard. "Something like before. And this time, I'm going to stop it."

His gaze held steady, none of the feverish intensity that had characterized his obsession after Chapel Hill. This wasn't the desperate fixation of a detective losing perspective but the measured determination of a professional who recognized a pattern others missed. The distinction was subtle but crucial—the difference between obsession and legitimate concern.

Rivera studied him for a long moment, weighing his state of mind against her knowledge of his history. Their partnership had survived because she knew when to rein him in and when to trust his instincts, even when those instincts led places conventional police work rarely ventured.

"I'll talk to the Chief," she finally said, a concession that acknowledged both his experience and her reservations. "Make the case that this connects to your ongoing investigation into historical burial desecrations. But Mark?" She waited until he met her eyes, making sure her next words registered. "Don't let this become Chapel Hill again. You've got people watching your back this time. Use them."

The subtext was clear—don't go it alone, don't disappear down research rabbit holes without checking in, don't exclude the team from your process even when that process includes elements they might not understand or approve. Learn from past mistakes rather than repeating them.

After she left, heading toward the Chief's office with the determined stride that had earned her the nickname "The Missile" among junior officers, Simmons pulled out his phone. The device felt foreign in his hand—he'd never fully adapted to smartphone technology, preferring the reliability of landlines and face-to-face conversations. But some calls required privacy the precinct couldn't provide.

He pulled up a contact he hadn't called in years, finger hovering over the name: Jake Steinman. Maybe it was time to talk to that weird old bookstore owner who'd tried to warn him back in '98. The one he'd dismissed as a conspiracy theorist when the man had approached him with "relevant historical context" about the Chapel Hill case. The one who'd told him about things that hunted in graveyards and used human remains for purposes beyond conventional understanding.

At the time, Simmons had attributed Steinman's theories to the eccentric imagination of a man who spent too much time with obscure texts. After what happened in the cemetery that night, after what he'd seen and couldn't explain, he'd avoided the bookstore and its owner—not because he no longer believed but because he feared confirmation of what he suspected.

Now, with new grave desecrations following the same pattern and his cold case instincts screaming warnings, perhaps it was time to reconsider that conversation. To acknowledge that some mysteries extended beyond conventional criminal investigation into territories most officers preferred to ignore.

"Not this time," he muttered, reaching for his cold coffee and grimacing at the bitter taste. The familiar ritual grounded him in the ordinary world of the precinct even as his mind calculated lunar phases and grave orientations. "Not in my town. Not again."

He set the mug down with renewed purpose, gathering the crime scene photos into a precise stack that he slipped into a folder marked with the current case number. Whatever was happening in Daybridge —whatever connection existed between these new desecrations and what had occurred twenty-five years ago—he intended to face it with open eyes this time, regardless of where the investigation led.

As he rose from his desk, collection folder and notebook in hand, his gaze briefly met that of Detective Ethan Reeves across the bullpen. The younger detective nodded in acknowledgment, a subtle gesture between colleagues that nonetheless carried an undercurrent Simmons couldn't quite identify. Something in Reeves' expression suggested he understood more than he should about Simmons' current preoccupation—as if he too recognized patterns beyond conventional explanation.

That was a connection worth exploring, Simmons decided as he headed toward the evidence room to review the physical samples collected from the Harrison plot. Perhaps he wasn't the only detective in Daybridge who understood that some crimes extended beyond the boundaries of ordinary human malice into territories where ancient hungers and forgotten rituals still held sway.

And perhaps this time, with allies both within the department and beyond its institutional limitations, he might finally solve the mystery that had haunted him for twenty-five years—and prevent whatever dark culmination was approaching before more lives were lost to forces most people preferred to dismiss as superstition or madness.

Daybridge General Hospital

Autopsy Suite B

10:30 AM

"Time of death approximately between midnight and 2 AM," Dr. Eleanor Choy reported, her surgical mask muffling her precise diction as she continued the preliminary examination of their latest victim. "Male, Caucasian, early thirties. No immediate signs of trauma beyond the specific pattern of incisions noted here—" she indicated the geometric markings carved into the victim's chest, "—and here." Her gloved finger hovered over similar markings on the forehead.

Detective Alice Chen nodded, her own mask hiding her grimace at the distinctive pattern they'd now seen on multiple victims. "Same perpendicular placement as the others. And the same precision—these weren't made in a frenzy or with hesitation."

"Correct," Dr. Choy agreed, her professionalism keeping any personal reaction carefully contained. As Daybridge's Chief Medical Examiner for the past fifteen years, she had developed the detachment necessary for forensic work while maintaining the scientific curiosity that made her exceptional at her job. "Whoever did this understood human anatomy and worked with surgical precision. The depth is consistent throughout, suggesting familiarity with the procedure."

Beside Alice, Ethan Reeves studied the body with more than just visual examination. His enhanced senses detected what conventional investigation couldn't—the lingering traces of energetic manipulation, the distinctive signature of life force extracted rather than simply extinguished. Through his connection to the nexus entity, he perceived how the carved symbols functioned not as mere mutilation but as conduits, channeling the victim's essence for purposes beyond conventional understanding.

"Any preliminary thoughts on cause of death?" he asked, maintaining the professional facade necessary in the presence of the ME. While Dr. Choy had proven remarkably adaptable to Daybridge's increasingly unusual cases, there were aspects of Ethan's investigative methods that remained strictly need-to-know.

"Pending toxicology and further examination," Dr. Choy replied with characteristic caution, "but I'm observing the same cellular degradation pattern noted in our previous victims. As if—" she hesitated, scientific training temporarily at odds with what her eyes were telling her, "—as if something extracted essential components at a cellular level. The effect resembles extreme radiation exposure, but localized in patterns that don't correspond to any known radiation source."

The description aligned with what Ethan's enhanced perception had already detected—the systematic extraction of life force through the carved symbols, each marking corresponding to specific energy centers in the body. What Dr. Choy observed as cellular degradation was the physical manifestation of energetic harvesting—the necromancer's methodology for gathering power from living sacrifices.

"We found this clutched in his right hand," Alice said, indicating an evidence bag containing what appeared to be a small silver coin. "Any thoughts?"

Dr. Choy examined the bagged item without touching it, her experienced eyes noting details through the plastic. "Not immediately relevant to cause of death, but the positioning suggests he was holding it when he died—possibly given to him by the perpetrator or something he was carrying that became important in his final moments."

What neither Alice nor Dr. Choy could perceive, but Ethan immediately recognized, was the coin's true nature—not currency but a ritual token, its surface inscribed with symbols that matched those found in the Codex Mortis illustrations Lila had shown him at The Black Cauldron. A message, perhaps, or a component of the larger working being conducted across multiple sites throughout Daybridge.

"We'll need to expedite analysis on that," Ethan said, maintaining professional composure despite the surge of concern the token provoked. "And compare the symbol pattern with our previous victims. I suspect we'll find they form a sequence rather than mere repetition."

As Dr. Choy continued her examination, meticulously documenting each marking and tissue sample, Ethan's phone vibrated in his pocket. The screen showed a text from an unknown number:

"Harrison plot connection confirmed. Sequence accelerating. Meet at eastern entrance to Blackwood Cemetery, 3 PM. Come alone. — L,"

Lila Darkmagic's cryptic communication style hadn't improved since their encounter at The Black Cauldron, but the content confirmed what Jake Steinman had suggested—the pattern was accelerating toward some culmination, with the Harrison grave desecrations forming another component in Viktor's complex working.

Ethan glanced at Alice, weighing the decision to share Lila's message against the instruction to come alone. Their partnership had evolved beyond conventional professional boundaries into something approaching true trust—rare in his experience and not something he was willing to jeopardize without good reason. Yet Lila's warning to trust no one, combined with Jake's concerns about her own reliability, created a complicated calculation.

"I need to follow up on something," he said as they exited the autopsy suite, removing their protective gear in the anteroom. "A potential lead on the significance of the grave desecrations."

Alice's perceptive gaze suggested she recognized the partial truth in his statement. "Detective Simmons has been looking into those. Might be worth comparing notes—he's got some kind of historical perspective on cemetery violations going back decades."

The mention of Simmons was unexpected but potentially significant. Ethan had noticed the older detective's interest in the grave desecrations but hadn't connected it to historical cases. "Simmons worked similar cases before?"

"Chapel Hill, 1998," Alice confirmed, her efficient research skills evident in the immediate recall of details. "Three missing persons, multiple grave desecrations. Never solved. Simmons was injured during the investigation—took medical leave and nearly didn't come back to the force."

The timeline aligned with what Jake had shared about previous manifestations of necromantic activity in Daybridge—cycles of power-gathering that occurred approximately every 25 years, coinciding with specific astronomical alignments. If Simmons had encountered a previous iteration of what they were currently investigating, his insights could prove valuable.

"I'll talk to him," Ethan decided, mentally adjusting his schedule to accommodate both Lila's meeting and a conversation with Simmons. "See if there are patterns we should be aware of."

As they reached the hospital lobby, Alice paused, her expression shifting from professional detachment to personal concern. "Ethan, whatever you're not telling me about this case—whatever connection exists between these murders and whatever happened at the bridge six months ago—I need you to remember we're partners. That means we face things together, not split up when it gets complicated."

The statement cut closer to home than she could know, highlighting the tension between his instinct to protect her from supernatural dangers and his respect for her agency as a detective and partner. Alice

Chen had proven her resilience repeatedly, adapting to revelations about werewolves and dimensional entities with remarkable equilibrium. Excluding her from critical aspects of the investigation wasn't just professionally questionable but potentially deprived them of her considerable analytical skills.

"You're right," he acknowledged, coming to a decision. "There's a meeting at Blackwood Cemetery at three. A potential informant with specialized knowledge about these ritual killings."

"Lila Darkmagic?" Alice asked, her insight once again demonstrating why she'd risen so quickly through the detective ranks despite institutional resistance to her advancement.

Ethan nodded, impressed but not entirely surprised by her deduction. "She's requested I come alone, but given what we've seen so far, backup might be prudent."

"I'll maintain distance but stay within signal range," Alice suggested, the compromise acknowledging both the informant's request and the practical safety considerations. "Close enough to respond if needed, far enough that your contact doesn't feel cornered."

The solution exemplified their effective partnership—respecting boundaries while ensuring neither operated without support when facing potential threats. "Three o'clock," Ethan confirmed. "Eastern entrance."

As they parted ways—Alice returning to the precinct to coordinate with forensics while Ethan headed to his scheduled meeting with Jake Steinman to return the journal—both carried the weight of a case increasingly pointing toward catastrophic consequences beyond conventional criminal activity.

Somewhere in Daybridge, Viktor Kalishnikov continued his methodical harvesting of components for a ritual designed to breach dimensional boundaries permanently. Each grave desecration, each ritualistic murder, brought his working closer to completion—a sequence accelerating toward culmination as Halloween approached and the boundaries between worlds naturally thinned.

The cosmic chess game entered its middle phase, pieces positioned across Daybridge's transformed landscape with deadly purpose. And as Ethan navigated between potential allies with their own agendas and histories, the true nature of the threat—and his own role in either preventing or enabling catastrophe—remained obscured by shadows both literal and metaphorical.

Old wounds were reopening across Daybridge—not just Simmons' physical scars from Chapel Hill or Lila's emotional trauma from Prague, but the very fabric of reality itself, still healing from the confrontation at the bridge six months earlier. Whatever Viktor intended to summon through these bleeding boundaries would find entry far easier now than in previous cycles, with potentially devastating consequences for the city and beyond.

Time was running short, the pattern accelerating toward conclusion. And somewhere in the shadows, watching the investigators scramble to connect disparate pieces, Viktor smiled with the satisfaction of a strategist whose opponents still didn't understand the true nature of the game they were playing.

$$\sim$$

CHAPTER SIX
TEA LEAVES AND TRUTH
JAKE'S APARTMENT ABOVE
CROSSROADS BOOKS

MORNING After the Evidence Room Incident

The morning light filtered through crystal wind chimes suspended in the eastern window, casting rainbow fragments across Jake's kitchen table in an ever-shifting kaleidoscope of color. The apartment above Crossroads Books was a study in organized chaos—bookshelves over-flowing with volumes of varying ages and conditions, walls adorned with framed maps spanning centuries of Daybridge's evolution, and surfaces crowded with artifacts that blurred the line between academic curiosity and magical protection. The space reflected its owner's eclectic mind and his lifetime spent accumulating knowledge that conventional scholarship often rejected.

Lila sat motionless at the kitchen table, staring into her fourth cup of chamomile tea as if it might contain answers to questions she wasn't ready to ask. Her normally immaculate appearance showed signs of strain—dark hair pulled back in a hasty ponytail rather than her usual elegant styling, clothes rumpled from the night's events, and complexion pale beneath her olive skin tone. Her hands still trembled slightly when she lifted the cup, an involuntary reaction to the psychic toll of the previous night's confrontation.

"You haven't slept," Jake observed, settling into the chair across from her with his own steaming mug. The bookshop owner's movements had the deliberate care of someone accustomed to managing chronic pain, but his eyes were sharp behind wire-rimmed glasses that had been repaired multiple times with different colored wire at the hinges. At seventy-two, Jake Steinman carried his decades of occult knowledge in the lines of his face and the cautious wisdom in his gaze.

The apartment's kitchen maintained a pleasant warmth despite the autumn chill outside, the antique radiator supplemented by the heat from Jake's perpetually active oven. The scent of freshly baked bread mingled with the herbaceous aroma of the tea and the subtler notes of protective incense that burned in a small clay holder on the windowsill —Jake's habitual morning ritual for cleansing the space of any negative energies that might have accumulated overnight.

"Sleep isn't safe right now." Lila traced the rim of her cup with a finger adorned with one of her silver protective rings. The metal gleamed in the morning light; the intricate symbols etched into its surface briefly catching the rainbow refractions from the wind chimes. The rings were back on all her fingers after she had removed several during the evidence room incident, but they couldn't quite hide the lingering darkness beneath her nails—a side effect of the protective spell she had been forced to cast when the artifact in the evidence box had activated unexpectedly. "Not after... accessing those memories."

The evidence room incident had begun as a routine consultation. Captain Donovan had requested Lila's expertise in examining an artifact recovered from the most recent grave desecration—a small obsidian disk inscribed with symbols that matched those found carved into the victims' bodies. What should have been a simple identification had escalated when the disk had responded to her presence, activating latent energies that had lain dormant until exposed to someone with sufficient magical sensitivity to trigger them.

The resulting psychic backlash had temporarily overwhelmed the station's electrical systems and forced Lila to draw deeply on her own protective abilities to contain the released energy. In the process, she had inadvertently accessed memories stored within the artifact—impressions of its creation and previous uses that had left her shaken and confirmed her worst fears about Viktor's presence in Daybridge.

"Mm." Jake pushed a plate of toast toward her, the bread still warm from the oven and spread with local honey from the farmer's market he frequented each Sunday. When she didn't respond, he sighed, the sound carrying the weight of concern rather than impatience. "I remember when you first came to Daybridge. Five years ago. You walked into my shop, looked straight at the wards I'd hidden in the foundation, and said 'Your northwestern anchor is slipping.'"

The memory seemed to reach Lila in a way his direct concern couldn't, drawing her attention temporarily from whatever dark contemplation occupied her thoughts. A ghost of a smile touched her lips, softening the tension that had hardened her features. "Amateur work. The sigils were practically shouting to anyone with even basic sensitivity."

"You helped me fix them. Never asked for payment. Just borrowed books on local history and disappeared for weeks at a time." He paused, giving space for the recollection to bridge the gap between past and present circumstances. "I never asked why you chose my shop. Why here, in Daybridge of all places?"

The question hung between them, weighted with five years of unspoken history and the accelerating events of recent weeks. Jake had respected her privacy, recognizing in Lila someone carrying burdens that required careful handling rather than direct confrontation. Their relationship had evolved through shared knowledge and mutual respect rather than personal disclosure—until now, when circumstances forced greater transparency.

"You know why now." Her voice was barely a whisper, fingers tightening around the teacup as if seeking an anchor against memories threatening to overwhelm her composure. "After what happened at the station..."

"Because he's coming here. Has been, all along." Jake's tone remained gentle despite the gravity of his words, offering understanding without judgment. "And you've been preparing us. The wards around the city's major intersections. The protection charms you've discreetly placed in public buildings. The 'rare book consultations' that were really lessons in magical defense for those of us sensitive enough to understand what you were actually teaching."

The apartment's cozy kitchen suddenly seemed smaller, the weight of their conversation expanding to fill the available space. Outside, morning traffic increased on the street below, the rumble of delivery trucks and conversations of early shoppers creating a backdrop of normality that contrasted sharply with the subject of their discussion.

Lila closed her eyes, shoulders slumping with the release of a secret carried too long in isolation. "I should have told you. All of you. But I thought... I thought I could stop him before..."

"Before we became part of the story?" Jake supplied, his perception as always cutting through pretense to the heart of the matter.

"Before I dragged more people into our darkness." She looked up finally, eyes rimmed with exhaustion and something deeper—the bone-deep weariness of someone who had been running for so long they'd forgotten any other way to live. "I've spent so long running from what I was, what we did. Trying to be... better. Trying to help without revealing too much. Atoning without confessing. And now..."

"And now the past is here." Jake reached across the table, his weathered hand covering her ring-laden ones. The gesture bridged more than physical distance—it offered connection when her instinct was clearly to withdraw further into isolation. "But you're not facing it alone."

The morning light caught the crystals again, sending another wave of rainbow fragments dancing across the kitchen. The patterns briefly illuminated the protective symbols Jake had subtly incorporated into the apartment's decor over decades—carved into doorframes, painted into the designs on decorative plates, woven into the patterns of handmade rugs. His home was a fortress of accumulated knowledge and protective magic, though it presented as the modest dwelling of an eccentric bookshop owner to most visitors.

"That's what I'm afraid of." A tear slipped down her cheek, the first crack in the composed facade she typically maintained with such discipline. "Everyone who's ever helped me, everyone who's tried to..." Her voice caught, emotion overwhelming articulation. "They all..." She couldn't finish, the unspoken consequences of past alliances hanging in the air between them.

"Maybe that's why you need to stop trying to protect everyone." He squeezed her hands, his touch grounding and grandfatherly even though he wasn't much older than her—her apparent age a deception maintained through methods she had never fully explained. "Maybe it's time to let people choose to stand with you. Knowing the risks."

The wind chimes tinkled softly as a breeze found its way through the partially opened window, their crystalline notes adding an almost musical punctuation to Jake's suggestion. In the shop below, they could hear the first customers arriving—the bell above the door announcing their entry, the murmur of voices as Jake's assistant greeted them, the mundane world continuing despite the weight of ancient magics and older guilt pressing down on the apartment above.

"I don't know how to do that," Lila admitted, vulnerability replacing her usual self-possession. The confession seemed to physically diminish her, as if maintaining control had required constant energy she could no longer sustain. "I've been alone so long..."

"Well," Jake stood, joints creaking with the protest of age and early morning stiffness. He moved to the stove, where the kettle was just beginning to whistle—his timing as impeccable with tea as with his more esoteric practices. "You can start by actually eating something. Then maybe tell me the real story about Prague. All of it." He smiled, the expression warming his scholarly features with genuine affection. "I've got time. And more tea."

He refilled their cups with practiced movements, the ritual of tea-making offering a momentary return to normalcy amid extraordinary circumstances. The familiar actions created space for Lila to gather her thoughts, to consider what complete disclosure might mean after decades of careful omission and selective truth.

For the first time in days, Lila felt something loosen in her chest. Not hope, exactly—she had lived too long and seen too much to embrace hope without reservation. But maybe its shadow, a potential pathway through darkness that had seemed absolute just hours before.

She took a tentative bite of toast, the simple act of nourishment a concession to continuing existence rather than surrender to exhaustion. As she chewed, the decision crystallized—not suddenly but as the culmination of a process that had begun five years ago when she first entered Crossroads Books and recognized both the flawed protective wards and the genuine integrity of their creator.

"It was winter," she began slowly, her voice gaining strength as she committed to the path of disclosure. "The kind of cold that freezes memories into perfect clarity, preserving them like insects in amber. Prague in December feels ancient, as if the cold itself carries echoes from centuries past."

Jake settled back into his chair, his attention complete and judgment suspended—offering the rarest gift one person can give another: the space to speak their truth without interruption or immediate evaluation.

"Viktor and I were graduate students at Charles University—he in anthropology with a focus on prehistoric ritual practices, I in comparative linguistics specializing in dead languages. We met in the university library during extended hours, both of us seeking texts most students never bothered with." A hint of her former animation returned as she recalled that initial period, before everything darkened. "He was brilliant. Challenging. Saw connections between disparate fields that conventional academia kept separate."

She paused, sipping her tea as memories solidified into words. "My sister Abby was nineteen, a physics prodigy attending on scholarship. She'd been diagnosed with an aggressive form of leukemia that

autumn. Conventional treatments were failing, and the prognosis..."
Her voice faltered. "The doctors gave her months, not years."

The wind chimes moved again, their gentle music providing counterpoint to the gravity of her narrative. Below, the bookshop continued its
morning routine—customers browsing, the cash register chiming,
pages turning as lives continued unaware of the weight of history
being excavated above them.

"Viktor had theories about energy manipulation that went beyond
what modern science recognized—ideas drawn from ancient practices
across multiple cultures. He believed that certain ritual configurations
could access and redirect energetic patterns, including those governing
cellular deterioration and renewal." Her finger traced the rim of her
cup again, the silver ring catching light. "When he learned about Abby,
he suggested we explore alternative approaches—research pathways
that conventional medicine and academia dismissed."

Jake nodded, his expression neutral but attentive. As a collector of
esoteric knowledge, he understood the allure of forbidden wisdom,
especially when conventional approaches failed to provide answers to
life's most pressing questions.

"We began with theoretical research—historical accounts of healing
rituals, mathematical models of energy transference, linguistic analysis
of texts describing life-extension practices. It was academic at first, or
at least we told ourselves it was." Her gaze grew distant, seeing not the
kitchen but Prague's winter twenty-eight years earlier. "But as Abby
got worse, our research became more... practical. Experimental."

The apartment seemed to darken slightly, though the morning sun
continued to stream through the windows. Perhaps it was just a cloud
passing outside, or perhaps it was the weight of Lila's narrative
affecting the space itself—memories of dark practices casting shadows
across decades and continents.

"Viktor had access to his family's estate outside Prague—a property
with historical connections to certain medieval alchemical societies.
The estate contained a library of texts that had never been cataloged by

conventional academics, volumes passed down through generations of practitioners who understood that some knowledge exists in the spaces between recognized disciplines."

She paused again, gathering resolve for the most difficult part of her narrative. "On the winter solstice, when Abby's condition had deteriorated to the point where conventional medicine offered only palliative care, we attempted a working based on our research—a ritual designed to redirect the entropic energies consuming her body and replace them with regenerative forces drawn from... alternative sources."

The clinical description couldn't disguise the gravity of what she was describing—a magical working of significant power attempted by brilliant but inexperienced practitioners driven by desperation rather than wisdom.

"The ritual... failed." The simple statement carried the weight of catastrophe. "Not just failed—backfired in ways we couldn't have anticipated. Instead of healing Abby, it accelerated the entropic process, drawing her life force out through the very pathways we'd established to channel healing energy in."

Her hands trembled again, the memory physically manifesting in involuntary movement. "I tried to stop it, to reverse what we'd started, but Viktor..." She swallowed hard. "Viktor saw an opportunity in catastrophe. He believed we could redirect the process, use the energy being released not to heal but to transform—to elevate human consciousness beyond physical limitations."

Jake remained silent, allowing her to continue at her own pace, his expression reflecting compassion rather than judgment despite the increasingly disturbing nature of her confession.

"I chose differently." Lila's voice steadied, finding strength in the core decision that had defined her subsequent decades. "I sabotaged the ritual, disrupted the geometric configurations we'd established. But not before something... opened. A pathway, a connection to something that should never have been accessed. And in the chaos of that disruption, with energies discharging in unpredictable patterns, Abby died."

The kitchen fell silent except for the gentle music of the wind chimes. The shop below seemed momentarily hushed as well, though logically both knew the normal activities continued unabated.

"Viktor disappeared that night—taking certain texts and artifacts with him. I spent the next months learning everything I could about what we'd accidentally accessed, about the nature of the breach we'd created and its potential consequences." Her gaze met Jake's directly for the first time since beginning her narrative. "I've spent twenty-eight years trying to contain what we released, trying to prevent Viktor from completing what we began."

Understanding dawned in Jake's expression as connections formed between Lila's personal history and current events in Daybridge. "And now he's here, attempting to recreate the working—but with modifications based on what he learned from your initial failure."

Lila nodded, relieved at being truly understood without having to explicitly connect all the dots herself. "The grave desecrations, the ritualistic murders—they're components in a working designed to create a more stable breach, a permanent connection between our reality and... something else. Something that exists beyond conventional dimensional boundaries, that perceives human consciousness as both sustenance and medium for manifestation."

"And Daybridge offers ideal conditions for such a working," Jake concluded, his academic knowledge of the city's unique properties allowing him to grasp implications without extensive explanation. "Especially after the events at the bridge six months ago, with the dimensional boundaries already compromised."

"Yes." Lila finished her tea, the simple act of completing something providing momentary stability amid overwhelming circumstances. "Viktor's working is approaching culmination—each component carefully placed and activated according to a precise sequence. If he completes the final stages..."

She didn't need to finish the sentence. Jake's lifetime of studying occult phenomena gave him sufficient background to understand the catastrophic implications of a successfully completed working of the magnitude she described.

"So now you understand," Lila concluded, exhaustion returning as the catharsis of disclosure faded. "Why I came to Daybridge five years ago when I first detected Viktor's preliminary workings. Why I've been establishing protective measures throughout the city. And why I've been reluctant to fully disclose my history or intentions—even to allies like yourself."

Jake considered her words, his scholarly mind weighing implications and potential courses of action. When he spoke, his voice carried the measured certainty of someone who had spent decades cultivating wisdom rather than mere knowledge.

"What happened in Prague was tragic, but it doesn't define who you are now." He reached across the table again, his touch offering connection rather than absolution—he was too honest for easy forgiveness of actions whose full consequences remained unknown. "Your choices since then matter. Your efforts to contain what was released, to prevent worse catastrophes—these aren't nullified by past mistakes."

The simple acknowledgment of her efforts—neither dismissing her culpability nor allowing it to overshadow her subsequent attempts at atonement—seemed to reach Lila in ways that conventional comfort couldn't have. Her posture straightened slightly, some of her characteristic composure returning.

"There's something else you should know," she said, decision evident in her renewed focus. "Something I haven't told Detective Reeves or anyone else in Daybridge."

Jake waited, creating space for this final disclosure without prompting or pressure.

"The working Viktor is attempting isn't just about opening a breach between dimensions. It's specifically designed to resurrect Abby — or what he believes is Abby — from whatever exists on the other side of that breach." Her voice quieted but remained steady. "He never accepted her death as final. He believes that her consciousness survived, that it persists in some form accessible through the right configuration of energies and intentions."

The implications were staggering—not just a general breach between dimensions but a targeted attempt to retrieve a specific consciousness from whatever lay beyond conventional reality. Such precise manipulation of interdimensional forces exceeded even what Jake had imagined, suggesting a level of theoretical understanding and practical capability that made Viktor far more dangerous than a conventional practitioner of forbidden arts.

"And you?" Jake asked gently. "What do you believe happened to Abby?"

The question cut to the heart of motivations that had driven Lila for decades—the uncertainty that had prevented complete closure despite years of atonement and protective work.

"I don't know," she admitted, the simple confession clearly costing her more than the detailed narrative of past events. "That's the truth that haunts me. I don't know if something of her persisted beyond physical death. I don't know if Viktor's theories about consciousness transcending biological limitations have validity. I only know that whatever he's attempting to retrieve isn't just Abby — that the entity responding to his workings has intentions and capabilities far beyond what a human consciousness should possess."

The wind chimes moved again, their crystalline notes suddenly discordant despite no change in the gentle breeze animating them. Below, the shop's entry bell rang with unusual force, as if responding to energetic patterns generated by their conversation.

"So, the question becomes not just how to stop Viktor's working, but how to address whatever has been responding to his attempts at communication." Jake's academic training automatically reformulated the problem, breaking it into components that could be addressed systematically despite their esoteric nature.

"Yes." Lila nodded, her own analytical mind engaging with the reformulated challenge. "And to do that effectively, I need to stop working alone. I need to trust others with the full context of what we're facing—not just the immediate threats but the historical background and my own role in creating the situation."

"Starting with Detective Reeves," Jake suggested, naming the most obvious candidate for full disclosure given his unique capabilities and central role in Daybridge's supernatural community.

"Yes, though that conversation will be... complicated." Lila's expression suggested there were aspects of her history with Reeves that remained unshared even in this moment of unusual candor. "But also, Detective Chen, whose analytical capabilities exceed conventional parameters despite her lack of supernatural sensitivity. And possibly others whose specific knowledge or abilities might contribute to containing both Viktor and whatever he's attempting to contact."

The decision represented a fundamental shift in Lila's approach—from solitary guardian carrying the burden of past mistakes to potential coordinator of a more collaborative response. The transition wouldn't be easy, requiring vulnerability and trust that decades of isolation had atrophied. But as the morning light continued to fill Jake's kitchen with rainbow fragments from the crystal chimes, the possibility of shared responsibility offered a pathway that solitary atonement had failed to provide.

"Well," Jake said, rising to refresh their tea once more, "the first step in any significant undertaking is proper nourishment. Finish your toast, have another cup, and then we can begin crafting an approach that acknowledges both the urgency of our situation and the need for careful disclosure to potential allies."

The simple practicality of his suggestion—addressing immediate physical needs before tackling cosmic challenges—drew a genuine smile from Lila, brief but authentic.

"Thank you," she said, the words encompassing more than the tea and toast. "For listening. For not..."

"For not running screaming into the street shouting about dimensional breaches and necromantic rituals?" Jake finished with gentle humor.

"My dear, when you've spent six decades studying the places where conventional reality frays at the edges, very little remains truly shocking. Concerning, yes. Requiring immediate attention, certainly. But not beyond comprehension or response."

As they settled into planning mode—Jake retrieving notebooks and maps from his extensive collection, Lila drawing on both her historical knowledge of Viktor's methodologies and her more recent tracking of his activities in Daybridge—the apartment above Crossroads Books transformed from a place of confession to a command center for what might well be the most significant magical confrontation in Daybridge's history.

The tea leaves at the bottom of their cups settled into patterns too complex for conventional interpretation, but in their swirling configurations lay possibilities beyond the binary outcomes of catastrophe or salvation. As morning shifted toward afternoon, Lila Darkmagic found herself navigating unfamiliar territory—not just the collaborative planning session with Jake but the internal landscape of cautious hope that partnership had begun to nurture where isolation had previously fostered only grim determination.

The wind chimes continued their gentle music, rainbow fragments dancing across maps of Daybridge where red pins marked known locations of Viktor's working components. And somewhere in the city, Detective Ethan Reeves was preparing for a meeting that would irrevocably alter his understanding of both the current threat and the woman who had returned to Daybridge to confront it.

The cosmic chess game accelerated toward its middle game, pieces moving with increasing urgency as Halloween approached and the natural thinning of dimensional boundaries enhanced the potency of Viktor's necromantic workings. But for the first time in twenty-eight years, Lila was allowing others to see the board from her perspective—a vulnerability that carried risk but also the potential for strategies beyond what solitary vigilance could achieve.

~

CHAPTER SEVEN
PARTNERS
O'MALLEY'S BAR

2:17 AM

The neon beer signs cast alternating red and blue shadows across their corner booth, creating a visual rhythm that matched the subdued pulse of classic rock playing through the bar's aging speakers. The glow transformed ordinary surfaces into something almost otherworldly— appropriate, given the day's events that had stretched the boundaries of what either detective considered reality.

O'Malley's was a cop bar in the most traditional sense—wood-paneled walls adorned with badges and patches from departments across the country, a scarred bar top that had absorbed decades of stories too dark or strange for official reports, and an unspoken understanding that what was discussed here remained here. The establishment had served Daybridge's finest since the 1970s, maintaining its deliberately anachronistic atmosphere despite the gentrification that had transformed much of the surrounding neighborhood.

Alice Chen stared at her half-empty glass of bourbon, the amber liquid catching the neon glow as she slowly rotated the tumbler. Her normally impeccable appearance showed signs of strain—hair slightly disheveled from repeatedly running her fingers through it, the collar of her shirt unbuttoned, the faint shadow of exhaustion beneath her eyes. Across from her, Ethan Reeves methodically shredded a paper napkin into precise squares, the mindless activity channeling nervous energy while his enhanced senses remained alert to their surroundings.

The silence between them wasn't uncomfortable—they had worked together long enough to communicate without words when necessary —but it carried the weight of experiences that had fundamentally altered their understanding of the world and their place in it. Some partnerships fractured under such pressure; others emerged stronger, forged in fires most would never comprehend.

"Want to talk about it?" Ethan asked finally, breaking the silence with the gentle directness that characterized their professional relationship.

"About which part?" Alice's laugh held no humor, the sound sharp-edged with stress and lingering disbelief. "The necromancy? The soul-binding ritual we interrupted at Harrison's grave? Or how about the fact that I can still see those symbols floating when I close my eyes?"

She rubbed her temples as if trying to physically erase the afterimages that persisted hours after they'd witnessed Lila Darkmagic perform what she'd called a "containment working" on the obsidian disk recovered from the most recent crime scene. The disk had begun emanating energy that interfered with the station's electrical systems, necessitating immediate intervention before it could complete whatever activation sequence had been triggered by its removal from the ritual site.

"I was thinking more about what happened in the evidence room. When Lila..." He trailed off, searching for words adequate to describe what they had witnessed without sounding like he belonged in a psychiatric evaluation rather than a detective division.

"When she channeled enough dark magic to make the air taste like copper?" Alice took another sip of her bourbon, the alcohol providing momentary warmth that did little to dispel the chill that had settled into her bones since the incident. "Yeah. That's definitely making my highlight reel of 'things they didn't cover at the academy.'"

Her attempt at humor barely masked the underlying processing of trauma—the way the room's temperature had plummeted as Lila had begun speaking in languages neither detective recognized, how the lights had flickered and then shattered, how the shadows had seemed to gather around her like obedient pets as she manipulated energies beyond conventional understanding. Most disturbing had been the way the obsidian disk had responded—symbols appearing on its surface that matched those found carved into victims' bodies, pulsing with sickly red light before Lila's countermeasures had contained them.

The late-night crowd had thinned to a few regulars at the bar—a retired detective nursing his customary scotch, two patrol officers unwinding after a difficult shift, and the perpetually present Malone, whose actual rank and department remained the subject of ongoing speculation. None glanced at the two detectives huddled in their corner booth; O'Malley's was unofficial cop territory, where badges came to process the things they couldn't put in reports without risking psychiatric evaluation or administrative leave.

"You know," Ethan said carefully, his tone suggesting the significance of what he was about to share, "I never told you about Indianapolis."

Alice looked up, interest immediately piqued. In three years of partnership that had evolved into one of the most effective investigative teams in the department, Indianapolis remained the one case Ethan never discussed. She had respected his silence, understanding that some cases left scars too deep for casual conversation, but her detective's curiosity had filed away the omission as significant.

"My first homicide rotation," he continued, his fingers momentarily stilling their methodical destruction of the napkin. "Body in an abandoned church. Male victim, mid-thirties, no identification, no matches in the system. He had these... markings. Like brands, but they moved when you weren't looking directly at them." His hands resumed their shredding, the mechanical movement betraying tension his voice controlled. "My partner said it was gang related. Captain said to close it quick, write it up as drug violence and move on. But I knew... I'd seen those symbols before."

The admission hung between them, weighted with implications that extended beyond professional disclosure into personal history Alice had never been privy to, despite their close working relationship.

"Where?" she asked, her tone carefully neutral to encourage continued sharing rather than retreat.

"My grandmother's stories." Ethan's expression softened briefly with the memory. "She was from a small village in Romania. Came to America after World War II, brought nothing but her clothes and her stories. Used to tell me about... things. Powers in the old forests. Deals made at crossroads. Creatures that wore human faces but weren't human at all." He smiled tightly, the expression not reaching his eyes. "I always thought they were just stories. Something to scare a kid into behaving."

"Until Indianapolis," Alice supplied, connecting the narrative threads with the perceptiveness that made her an exceptional detective.

"Until I followed a lead to this bookshop in the Hungarian district. Found an old woman who took one look at my case photos and started crying. Speaking half in English, half in something older." His voice dropped, ensuring their conversation wouldn't carry to the few remaining patrons despite the unlikelihood of being overheard. "She said I had to burn the body. Salt the ashes. Or it would..." He stopped shredding napkins, his hands finally stilling as he met Alice's gaze directly. "Well. Let's just say she was right."

The implication hung unspoken but clear—whatever had happened in Indianapolis had provided Ethan's first direct encounter with forces beyond conventional explanation, long before his transformation into a werewolf or his partial integration with the nexus entity beneath Daybridge Bridge. It explained both his relative composure when confronted with supernatural phenomena and his occasional reluctance to dismiss explanations that extended beyond standard investigative parameters.

Alice was quiet for a moment, absorbing this new information about her partner and mentally recalibrating her understanding of his investigative approach. When she spoke, her voice carried the same measured trust his disclosure had demonstrated.

"Second year on the force," she said finally, reciprocating his confidence with her own. "Domestic disturbance call in Oakland Heights. Neighbor reported screaming, possible violence. My partner and I found a teenager in the bathroom, covered in blood. But it wasn't hers." The memory remained vivid despite the years that had passed, details preserved with the perfect clarity trauma sometimes etched into consciousness. "She kept saying her stepfather deserved it, that she'd 'wished him away.' There was no body. No evidence of violence beyond the blood. Just... empty clothes on the kitchen floor, still warm."

The account was clearly one she rarely shared, the experience filed among those that didn't fit neatly into conventional understandings of crime and justice—the category of "unexplainable" that most officers accumulated over years of service but discussed only with colleagues they implicitly trusted.

"What happened to her?" Ethan asked, professional concern momentarily overriding curiosity about the metaphysical implications of Alice's account.

"State psychiatric facility initially. I checked on her last year. She's doing better. Living independently, working as a graphic designer. Says she doesn't remember that night." Alice traced a finger through the condensation on her glass, drawing patterns that unconsciously mimicked the symbols they'd seen in the evidence room. "But sometimes I dream about it. The look in her eyes when we found her. Like she'd touched something vast and terrible and wonderful, and it had touched her back."

"Like Lila's eyes in the evidence room," Ethan observed, connecting past and present with uncomfortable precision.

"Yeah." She shivered despite the bar's warmth, goosebumps rising on her arms at the memory of how Lila's normally green eyes had shifted to silver during the containment ritual, how they had seemed to reflect light that had no source within the evidence room itself. "We're in deep on this one, aren't we?"

The question wasn't merely rhetorical but a genuine assessment of their current situation—professionals taking stock of circumstances that had progressed beyond standard operating procedures into territory where instinct and adaptability might prove more valuable than formal training.

"Past our depth and swimming further," Ethan confirmed with grim humor, signaling for another round with a raised finger toward the bartender. The gesture was acknowledged with a nod—O'Malley himself working tonight, his understanding of his clientele evident in his minimal intrusion on their private conversation. "Question is, do we keep going?"

The query represented more than professional consideration—it acknowledged that they had reached a juncture where continued involvement represented personal choice rather than merely fulfilling their official duties. They could, theoretically, step back—request reassignment, cite conflict of interest, allow specialized units to handle aspects that extended beyond conventional criminal investigation. The department had protocols for unusual situations, bureaucratic pathways that would allow them to distance themselves from phenomena that defied standard categorization.

Alice thought about the silver light in Lila's eyes during the containment ritual. The way shadows moved wrong around her now, extending and contracting independently of light sources. The feel of ancient power humming through the evidence room, vibrating at frequencies that seemed to resonate with something deep within human consciousness—something usually dormant but awakened by proximity to energies beyond conventional understanding.

But she also thought about Jake's missing customers, their photographs forming a grim mosaic in his hidden library—people who had sought knowledge and found something darker instead. About graves that wouldn't stay closed, their occupants disturbed for purposes that violated not just law but natural order. About a young woman in Prague who made a terrible choice for love of her sister and had spent decades attempting to contain the consequences of that decision.

"We took an oath," she said finally, decision crystallizing not despite the unusual circumstances but because of them. "To protect and serve. Nobody said what we were protecting people from had to be... normal."

The simplicity of her statement belied its significance—a recommitment to their professional responsibilities even as their understanding of what those responsibilities entailed expanded beyond conventional parameters. It acknowledged that protection might require methods not covered in police training manuals, that service might extend to confronting threats most citizens remained blissfully unaware existed.

"Partners?" Ethan held up his glass, the gesture transforming a casual toast into something more significant—a renewal of their professional bond in light of extraordinary circumstances, an acknowledgment that whatever lay ahead, they would face it together.

"Partners." They clinked glasses, the sound bright in the subdued atmosphere of the nearly empty bar. Alice's tension visibly eased as the decision was confirmed, her characteristic pragmatism reasserting itself. "But you're doing the paperwork on this one. I don't even know how to categorize 'consultant performed a necromantic ritual in the evidence room.'"

"Property damage due to unexpected equipment malfunction?" Ethan suggested, his deadpan delivery momentarily restoring normalcy to their extraordinary circumstances.

"Now you're thinking like a detective."

They shared a laugh that was only slightly hysterical, the release of tension momentarily transforming their corner of O'Malley's into an island of relative normalcy amid the expanding strangeness that had come to characterize their investigation. Outside, the storm clouds were gathering again, their unnatural patterns forming configurations that meteorologists struggled to explain with conventional atmospheric models. But in their corner booth, two detectives who had glimpsed the darkness chose to face it together, drawing strength from a partnership that transcended ordinary professional boundaries.

The symbolism wasn't lost on either of them—darkness gathering while they sought illumination through shared experience and mutual support. Their professional training emphasized objective analysis and methodical investigation, but both recognized that the current situation demanded additional resources—intuition, flexibility, and willingness to consider explanations that extended beyond conventional understanding.

As O'Malley approached with their fresh drinks, his weathered features betrayed no curiosity about their hushed conversation. His decades behind the bar had taught him when to engage and when to simply provide the space officers needed to process what they encountered in the line of duty. He set the glasses down with a nod and retreated, his discretion as much a service to Daybridge's finest as the alcohol he served.

"So," Alice said once they were alone again, her tone shifting from personal disclosure back to professional analysis, "what's our next move? Jake's research suggests Viktor's working is approaching culmination, and Lila's containment ritual in the evidence room confirmed the artifacts are connected to some larger pattern across the city."

Ethan nodded, mentally transitioning from the personal moment they'd shared back to the immediate challenges of their investigation. "We need to identify the final components of whatever ritual Viktor is constructing. Jake's analysis of the historical pattern suggests it requires seven primary nodes positioned at specific geometric intervals throughout the city, with Blackwood Cemetery as the focal point."

"And we've confirmed four sites so far," Alice continued, their investigative partnership functioning with practiced efficiency despite the unusual subject matter. "The Harrison plot, the alleyway behind Seventh Street, the abandoned church on Riverside, and the fountain in Memorial Park."

"Which leaves three unidentified locations," Ethan concluded. "And based on the accelerating timeline of incidents, Viktor is likely to activate them within the next seventy-two hours, culminating on Halloween night when the dimensional boundaries naturally thin."

The practical discussion of next steps provided familiar ground amid increasingly unfamiliar territory—the investigative process giving structure to circumstances that might otherwise seem overwhelming. Their years of partnership had developed routines and rhythms that remained effective even when applied to phenomena beyond conventional criminal activity.

"We should coordinate with Simmons," Alice suggested, referring to the detective whose historical knowledge of similar cases had proved unexpectedly valuable. "His insights on the Chapel Hill incident might help us anticipate Viktor's remaining target locations."

"Agreed. And we need another conversation with Lila—a comprehensive briefing rather than the piecemeal information she's been providing." Ethan's expression suggested complex feelings about their occult consultant, a mixture of professional respect and personal wariness that reflected their complicated history. "After what happened in the evidence room, I think she's ready to be more forthcoming. Jake seems to have that effect on people."

Their discussion continued, strategizing next steps with the methodical thoroughness that had made them effective investigators long before supernatural elements complicated their caseload. The familiar process provided an anchor amid increasingly strange circumstances—a reminder that while the nature of the threat might be unprecedented, the fundamental principles of investigation remained applicable.

As they prepared to leave—both recognizing the need for at least a few hours' rest before continuing their investigation—Alice paused, her expression sobering as she considered implications beyond their immediate tactical planning.

"Ethan," she said quietly, "what happens if we can't stop this? If Viktor completes his working and whatever's on the other side of that breach comes through?"

The question acknowledged the stakes more directly than their previous discussions had—moving beyond investigation of individual crimes to consideration of potentially catastrophic consequences for Daybridge and beyond. It was the kind of question that separated theoretical understanding from emotional comprehension, acknowledging that their current case might have implications far beyond conventional law enforcement parameters.

"Then we adapt," Ethan answered after a moment's consideration, his response reflecting both his personal history of transformation and his professional commitment to protecting Daybridge regardless of the form threats took. "We find new ways to serve and protect. We work with whatever allies we can gather—Lila, Jake, others who understand what we're facing—and we contain the damage as best we can."

The answer wasn't as reassuring as either might have hoped, but it carried the authenticity of honest assessment rather than false confidence. It acknowledged both the gravity of potential failure and the commitment to continue functioning as guardians regardless of circumstances—an approach that had served them well through previous crises.

"One step at a time," Alice agreed, finding comfort in the pragmatic approach that had characterized their partnership from its beginning. "First, we find those remaining sites. Then we disrupt whatever Viktor's planning. Then we can worry about interdimensional breach containment protocols."

"I'm pretty sure those aren't covered in the department handbook," Ethan observed dryly, his humor a welcome counterpoint to the gravity of their situation.

"We'll improvise," Alice responded with equal dryness. "It's practically our specialty at this point."

As they finally left O'Malley's, stepping into the unnaturally still night air, both felt the subtle shift in Daybridge's atmosphere—a tension building not just in weather patterns but in the fabric of reality itself. The streets seemed emptier than usual for a weeknight, as if the city's inhabitants unconsciously sensed approaching danger and sought the illusory safety of their homes. Shadows pooled more deeply in corners and alleyways, seeming almost viscous in their unnatural density.

And somewhere in the night, ancient powers took notice of two mortal detectives who had glimpsed beyond conventional reality yet chosen to stand their ground rather than retreat into comfortable denial. Such awareness carried both threat and opportunity—human consciousness providing both potential gateway and obstacle for entities that perceived reality through fundamentally different frameworks.

As Alice and Ethan parted ways—she to her apartment in the revitalized warehouse district, he to his isolated cabin on the city's wooded outskirts—neither was entirely alone. Their partnership had created something that transcended individual vulnerability, a connection that provided resilience against forces that might otherwise overwhelm isolated consciousness.

In the cosmic chess game accelerating toward its conclusion, they represented pieces whose significance remained to be determined— potential sacrifices or unexpected factors that might disrupt carefully calculated strategies. And as Halloween approached, bringing natural thinning of dimensional boundaries that would enhance Viktor's necromantic workings, the partnership forged in O'Malley's Bar would face its most significant test.

Not just as investigators sworn to protect and serve, but as human beings confronting forces that challenged fundamental understanding of reality itself—standing at the boundary between light and darkness, choosing to face the unknown together rather than retreat into comfortable ignorance separately.

The storm clouds gathered more densely overhead, unnatural patterns forming configurations that defied conventional meteorological explanation. And beneath them, Daybridge continued its uneasy sleep, most citizens unaware of the cosmic drama unfolding in their midst—or of the detectives who had chosen to place themselves between ordinary reality and the darkness gathering at its edges.

CHAPTER EIGHT
AMENDS
DAYBRIDGE CEMETERY

DAWN, Present Day

The morning mist clung to Lila's ankles as she walked the familiar path through Daybridge Cemetery, tendrils of white vapor curling around her like spectral fingers reaching up from the earth. The world existed in half-tones at this hour—the sun not yet risen, the moon having set, leaving only the liminal light that belonged wholly to neither day nor night. The cemetery's wrought-iron gates had opened silently at her approach, responding to the silver rings on her fingers and the purpose in her heart.

Daybridge Cemetery was one of the oldest in the city, established in the 1830s when the settlement was still little more than a trading post at the convergence of river and forest. Unlike the more elaborate Blackwood Cemetery with its ornate mausoleums and carefully tended grounds, this place maintained a quieter dignity—simple headstones and family plots telling the story of generations who had lived and died in relative obscurity. The oldest sections held graves whose inscriptions had been worn nearly smooth by time and weather, while the newer areas reflected modern memorialization practices with their polished granite and occasional digital tributes.

Lila moved through this chronicle of mortality with practiced steps, following a route she had walked countless times over three decades. Her boots left momentary impressions in the dew-covered grass, tracks that would vanish as the day progressed—temporary markers of a vigil that had become ritual. The weight of memory and responsibility pressed against her shoulders, a familiar burden that had shaped her posture over years of carrying it.

The eastern sky showed the first hints of approaching dawn, a faint lightening at the horizon that would soon transform into true sunrise. But for now, the cemetery remained in shadow, gravestones standing like sentinels in the half-light. The only sounds were Lila's measured footsteps and the occasional call of early birds beginning their day— nature's cycles continuing regardless of human drama or cosmic significance.

She stopped before a modest headstone in the cemetery's western section, an area devoted to those who had passed in the mid-1990s. Unlike many surrounding it, this grave bore no religious symbols, only a simple geometric pattern carved into the marble at its crown—an interlocking series of circles that resembled both atomic structure and cosmic configuration, science and mysticism intertwined in stone.

ABBY ALEXANDRA DARKMAGIC

1977 - 1994

"Beloved Sister, Brilliant Light"

The inscription remained as clear as when it had been carved, protected perhaps by the subtle preservation spells Lila had integrated into the stone itself—magic disguised as conventional treatments against weathering, invisible to any but those with eyes to see such things. Though Abby's actual remains lay in Prague, this memorial marker had provided Lila with something physical to visit during her years of wandering and eventual settlement in Daybridge.

She knelt before the headstone, brushing leaves from its face with gentle fingers. Her silver rings clinked against the marble, each one catching the predawn light with subtle gleams that seemed almost to respond to the carved geometric pattern. The sound echoed briefly before being absorbed by the surrounding mist, a momentary connection between the living and what lay beyond.

"I'm sorry I haven't visited lately." Her voice was soft in the predawn stillness, intimate as a confession. "Things are... complicated. Again. Like Prague." She smiled sadly, the expression visible only to the stone that bore her sister's name. "You'd hate that I'm still apologizing to you. You always said I took too much responsibility for everything."

The one-sided conversation carried none of the awkwardness that might have characterized similar graveside monologues from others. Lila spoke with the natural cadence of ongoing dialogue, as if continuing a conversation that had merely been paused rather than severed by death. Whether this represented healthy processing of grief or something more complex—influenced perhaps by her unique understanding of dimensional boundaries and consciousness—remained a private matter between sisters.

From her messenger bag, crafted of worn leather adorned with subtle protective sigils worked into its design, she drew out a small bundle of wildflowers—not the formal arrangements typical of cemetery visitations but meadow blooms gathered at dawn from specific locations around Daybridge. Each flower had been selected for both symbolic meaning and inherent energetic properties, a bouquet that represented both personal sentiment and magical purpose.

Alongside the flowers, she removed a piece of chalk—not ordinary classroom variety but a specialized composition containing minerals gathered from significant locations across multiple continents, bound together with substances better left unidentified. In appearance, it resembled nothing more unusual than artist's chalk, but its properties extended beyond mere pigmentation.

"Viktor's back. Or maybe he never left." She arranged the wildflowers at the base of the headstone with careful precision, each bloom positioned according to patterns only she fully understood. "The things we did, the power we touched... it echoes. Like ripples in a pond that never stop."

She began drawing protective symbols around the grave with practiced motions, the chalk leaving marks that appeared conventional to casual observation but contained geometries and intentions that operated on multiple levels simultaneously. These weren't the desperate, improvised protections of their youth but refined workings developed through decades of study and practice—elegant in their precision and economy of form.

"I thought I was saving you. We both did." The symbols took shape under her guidance, forming a circle that encompassed the grave and extended slightly beyond its physical boundaries. "But we were so young, so certain we knew better than everyone else. So convinced that the rules didn't apply to us because our cause was just, our need greater than conventional limitations."

The eastern sky continued its gradual transformation from darkness to light, the approaching dawn lending energy to Lila's workings as natural cycles aligned with her intentions. The chalk symbols began to glow faintly, responding to both the changing light and the power she channeled through her silver rings—protection and connection intertwined in a working that honored both emotional and metaphysical realities.

"I dream about that night sometimes. Not the ritual—before." Her voice caught slightly, emotion momentarily overwhelming the composed exterior she typically maintained. "When you told me to let you go. 'Death is just another kind of mathematics,' you said. 'The equation has to balance.'"

Tears fell on the marble, crystalline drops that traced paths through the morning dew already gathering on the stone's surface. Unlike conventional expressions of grief that might have diminished over three decades, Lila's emotion carried the immediate quality of wounds that had never fully healed—preserved perhaps by her unique awareness of what had truly been lost that night in Prague.

"But I wouldn't listen. Couldn't. And Viktor... he understood that desperation. That need to break all the rules for love." Her chalk continued its precise movements, each symbol building upon the last to create a comprehensive protection that operated on multiple dimensions simultaneously. "He gave that desperation form and direction, channeled it into workings that should never have been attempted. And I followed willingly, because the alternative was accepting a world without you in it."

She finished the circle of symbols, the completed working humming with subtle energy that resonated with the approaching dawn. Within its boundaries, the air felt cleaner somehow, as if the protective circle had established a space where natural order prevailed against forces that might otherwise disturb it. The working would maintain Abby's memorial against both conventional vandalism and the more esoteric disruptions that Viktor's activities might generate throughout Daybridge.

"I'm going to face him today. Finally." Lila's voice steadied, resolution replacing momentary vulnerability. "And I'm scared, Abby. Not of dying, but of becoming that person again. The one who would do anything, break anything, to save what she loved."

She pressed her hand to the cold stone, establishing a physical connection with the memorial that represented her most profound loss and greatest regret. Through that contact, memory flowed—not just of Abby's final days but of their shared childhood, of scientific debates that stretched late into the night, of a sister whose brilliance had illuminated those around her with both intellectual insight and emotional warmth.

"I need you to remind me, one last time, what you taught me about equations." The request wasn't mere sentiment but a genuine seeking of wisdom across the boundary between life and whatever lay beyond —a connection that transcended conventional understanding of death as absolute severance.

The rising sun broke through the mist, its first rays stretching across the cemetery in golden shafts that transformed the landscape from monotone to living color. For a moment, in the play of light through morning dew, Lila almost thought she saw her sister's smile—a trick of light and memory perhaps, or something more significant for someone whose understanding of reality's boundaries extended beyond conventional parameters.

"They have to balance," she whispered, finding an answer in memory if not in supernatural response. "Always."

The principle had been central to Abby's understanding of both physics and ethics—the fundamental truth that actions generated consequences, that energy could change form but never truly disappear, that attempts to circumvent natural laws created distortions that eventually demanded correction. It was the lesson Lila had refused to accept as a grieving sister, the wisdom she had spent three decades integrating into her understanding of both magical practice and personal responsibility.

She stood, brushing dirt from her knees with movements that served as a transition between memorial reverence and the practical demands of the day ahead. The protective circle would hold, maintaining Abby's rest regardless of what energies might soon be unleashed throughout Daybridge. This at least she could ensure—that whatever consequences arose from confronting Viktor, they would not disturb this place of remembrance and connection.

"I understand now, little sister. Thirty years too late, but I understand." The admission carried neither self-pity nor dramatic emphasis but simple acknowledgment of truth—recognition that wisdom often came through experience rather than intellect alone.

She touched the headstone one final time, completing the ritual of visitation that had sustained her through decades of atonement and preparation. Then she turned away, her path now leading not toward the cemetery gates but deeper into Daybridge's industrial district where an abandoned foundry awaited—a location Jake's research had identified as the most likely site for Viktor's next working.

The mist swallowed her figure as she walked, her silhouette gradually dissolving into the vaporous boundary between visibility and obscurity. With each step, her posture shifted subtly—grief and reflection giving way to purposeful determination, the set of her shoulders and the rhythm of her stride transforming from mourner to hunter, from penitent to guardian.

Behind her, the chalk symbols pulsed once with pure light as the sun's first direct rays touched them, then faded into apparent ordinariness—visible now only to those with eyes to see such things, their protective function continuing without visible manifestation. A sister's last gift of protection, perhaps, or the natural resolution of properly balanced magical equations.

The cemetery resumed its morning routine—groundskeepers arriving to begin their day, early visitors coming to pay respects before work, birds continuing their chorus from trees that had witnessed generations of human grief and remembrance. Nothing in its outward appearance suggested that anything unusual had occurred, that boundaries between dimensions had been momentarily thinned through one woman's practiced workings and sincere connection.

Yet something had changed—not just in the protective energies surrounding Abby's memorial but in Lila herself. The visit had provided not merely ritual closure but genuine resolution, transforming her approach to the confrontation ahead from desperate prevention to balanced correction. Viktor's workings represented fundamental disruption of natural order, equations forced out of balance through manipulations that violated both physical and metaphysical principles. Her task was not to defeat him through superior power but to restore equilibrium—to ensure that whatever energies he had set in motion found proper resolution rather than catastrophic release.

As she reached the cemetery's western boundary, passing through a small pedestrian gate rarely used by visitors, Lila paused briefly to orient herself toward the abandoned foundry that awaited her attention. The rising sun now illuminated Daybridge's industrial district in the distance, morning light catching on weathered brick and rusted metal—structures that had once represented the city's manufacturing pride now repurposed or abandoned as economic patterns shifted.

Among those buildings, the Harrington Foundry stood as a particular testament to faded glory—its massive chimney still dominating the skyline though no smoke had risen from it in decades. Established in 1892 to serve the regional railway expansion, the foundry had operated continuously until the 1980s, when changing economic conditions had rendered its operations unprofitable. Since then, it had passed through various owners with redevelopment plans that never materialized, eventually becoming one of Daybridge's many liminal spaces—neither fully abandoned nor actively utilized, caught between past function and future purpose.

This transitional quality made it ideal for Viktor's purposes—a location with rich historical resonances, positioned at a significant junction of the city's energetic pathways, and sufficiently isolated to allow complex workings without immediate discovery. Jake's research had identified it as the most likely site for the penultimate component of Viktor's pattern, based on both geometric alignment with previously activated locations and historical significance in Daybridge's industrial development.

Lila's path took her away from residential areas toward the industrial zone, her purposeful stride carrying her through neighborhoods transitioning from slumber to morning activity. Few noticed the dark-haired woman with silver rings, and those who did saw nothing unusual— just another early riser with somewhere to be, unremarkable in a city beginning its daily routines.

Yet as she walked, subtle changes occurred in her immediate environment—shadows lingered slightly longer than natural light would dictate, morning dew gathered more densely where her footsteps had been, birds altered their songs to minor keys when she passed beneath their perches. These were not conscious manipulations but unconscious influences—reality responding to the presence of someone whose connection to natural forces operated at levels beyond conventional awareness.

By the time she reached the chain-link fence surrounding the foundry complex, the sun had fully cleared the horizon, casting long shadows across rusted equipment and weed-choked yards. The official entrance remained secured with heavy chains and padlocks, but Lila moved confidently toward a section where the fence had been cut and crudely repaired multiple times—evidence of regular unauthorized access that suggested the location served purposes beyond mere abandoned property.

As she slipped through the gap, momentarily vulnerable while navigating the sharp edges of cut metal, Lila sensed rather than saw movement deeper within the complex—a shift in energetic patterns that indicated she was not the first visitor that morning. Whether Viktor himself or one of his followers preparing the site for his arrival remained to be determined, but the subtle wrongness in the foundry's atmosphere confirmed Jake's assessment of its significance.

The main building loomed before her—a massive brick structure with arched windows now mostly broken or boarded over, its original grandeur still visible beneath decades of neglect. The foundry floor had once housed massive furnaces and casting equipment, the production of railway components providing employment for hundreds of Daybridge residents across generations. Now it stood empty except for scattered remnants too large or worthless to salvage, its vast interior spaces perfect for activities requiring both privacy and specific geometric configurations.

Lila paused at the building's entrance, her hand hovering near the rusted door handle as she extended her awareness beyond physical senses. The protective rings on her fingers responded to energies already accumulated within—residual industrial energies from decades of metal transformation mingling with more recent and deliberate manipulations of dimensional boundaries. The combination created patterns that resonated with specific frequencies, preparations for a working whose design she recognized all too well.

"Oh, Viktor," she whispered, recognition bringing both confirmation and sorrow. "Still trying to bring her back. Still refusing to accept the equation's balance."

For a moment, standing at the threshold between preparation and confrontation, Lila felt the weight of three decades collapse into singular purpose. The morning's visit to Abby's memorial had provided more than comfort or closure—it had crystallized understanding that had been developing through years of study and atonement. Viktor's workings weren't merely dangerous manipulations of forbidden energies but fundamental disruptions of natural balance, attempts to force equations that demanded equilibrium into configurations that served individual desire regardless of cosmic consequence.

With clarity born of both magical knowledge and personal reconciliation, Lila grasped the door handle and stepped into the shadowed interior of Harrington Foundry. Whatever awaited within—whether Viktor himself or merely the next component of his grand working—she would face it not with the desperate power of her youth but with the balanced wisdom of someone who had finally accepted what her sister had tried to teach her on that winter night in Prague.

The equation had to balance. Always. And if Viktor wouldn't accept that fundamental truth, then Lila would ensure balance was restored—whatever personal cost that restoration might demand.

The heavy door closed behind her with a finality that seemed to mark a transition between worlds—the ordinary Daybridge continuing its morning routines outside, while within the foundry's cavernous interior, forces gathered that would determine whether those routines could continue undisturbed or would soon be irrevocably disrupted by energies beyond conventional comprehension.

And somewhere between those worlds, in a cemetery now fully illuminated by morning sunlight, protective symbols maintained their vigilance around Abby Darkmagic's memorial—a sister's gift ensuring that whatever cosmic balancing might soon occur, it would not disturb the peace that had been so dearly purchased three decades earlier.

The equation would balance. One way or another.

CHAPTER NINE
CHOICES
DAYBRIDGE PARK

2:14 PM

The park bench overlooked the river, where autumn leaves danced on the surface like dying flames against the dark water. Daybridge Park formed a green corridor through the city's urban landscape, providing residents with respite from concrete and commerce. On this October afternoon, the park was relatively quiet—most people were at work or school, leaving the paths to retirees, young parents with strollers, and the occasional jogger.

Alice found Lila exactly where the text said she'd be, though she hadn't expected the paper coffee cup in the witch's hands. The image seemed incongruously mundane—a woman who could manipulate dimensional energies holding a branded cup from the local coffee chain.

"Peppermint tea," Lila said without looking up as Alice approached. Steam rose from the cup, carrying the bright scent of mint into the crisp air. "Some habits of the living are hard to break."

The comment carried implications Alice wasn't entirely ready to explore—suggestions about Lila's nature that extended beyond human practitioner into something more complex. Since witnessing the

96

evidence room incident, Alice had been reassessing her understanding of their consultant.

Alice sat, leaving careful space between them. The bench creaked slightly beneath her weight. "That's why you asked me to come? To discuss beverage preferences?"

"No." Lila set the cup down on the bench between them. Her rings caught the afternoon light, but the silver seemed darker somehow, tarnished in ways that defied explanation. "I asked you to come because you're the only one who saw the evidence room footage. The only one who knows what I really am."

The security camera had captured the incident in its entirety—Lila's transformation as she contained the energies emanating from the obsidian disk, the shadows gathering around her, the silver light that had replaced her normal eye color as she spoke in languages that had never existed on Earth. Captain Donnovan had ordered the footage sealed, citing equipment malfunction, but not before Alice had viewed it multiple times.

"A practitioner of necromantic magic who's trying to stop her ex-partner from raising an army of the dead?" Alice kept her tone light, using humor to bridge the gap between ordinary human interaction and the extraordinary circumstances. "We've all got baggage."

That earned a small smile from Lila, a momentary softening of the intensity that had characterized her demeanor since their first meeting. "Detective Chen—"

"Alice," she corrected, making a deliberate choice to reduce formal distance between them.

"Alice." Lila watched a leaf spiral down from an overhanging maple. "What do you know about choice?"

The question seemed simultaneously philosophical and urgently practical—not academic pondering but genuine seeking of perspective.

"Professionally or philosophically?" Alice asked, giving herself time to consider the deeper implications.

"Both. Neither." Lila's fingers traced patterns in the air between them, leaving momentary shadows that lingered slightly longer than natural light conditions should allow. "When does a series of choices become who you are? And when does who you are determine the choices you'll make?"

The question revealed vulnerability beneath Lila's composed exterior —uncertainty not about her capabilities but about her identity, about the relationship between past actions and future possibilities.

Alice thought about case files, about perpetrators and victims, about the thin line between them that often blurred under careful examination. Her years as a detective had shown her the complexity of human choice— how circumstances, history, and momentary impulse combined to create actions that sometimes contradicted an individual's own self-concept.

"You're worried you'll make the same choice again. When you face him," Alice observed, connecting Lila's philosophical questioning to the immediate concern of confronting Viktor Kalishnikov.

"Wouldn't you be?" Lila turned, meeting Alice's gaze directly. Her eyes held that silver fire witnessed in the evidence room—not fully manifested but present beneath the surface. "You've seen what I can do. What I'm capable of. The power is... seductive. It whispers solutions. Simple ones. Dark ones."

The admission carried weight—acknowledgment of temptation that continued despite decades of restraint, of knowledge that could never be unlearned.

"But you haven't chosen those solutions. Not since Prague," Alice said, offering perspective Lila might have lost in her focus on potential failure.

"Haven't I?" Lila's response carried genuine uncertainty. Her fingers clenched, the silver rings catching light. "Every protection spell, every ward... they all draw on death magic to some degree. I tell myself it's different, that I'm using it for good, but..." She clenched her fists. "The darkness doesn't care about intentions. It just wants to be used."

A jogger passed their bench, entirely unaware of the cosmic implications being discussed mere feet away. A child laughed somewhere distant, the sound carrying across the park with innocent joy. The mundane world spun on, unaware of dimensional boundaries growing thinner.

"When I was a rookie," Alice said carefully, drawing on personal experience, "my training officer told me something I never forgot. He said 'The gun on your hip isn't good or evil. It's just potential. Every time you draw it, you're making a choice about who you are.'"

The analogy bridged their different worlds—connecting Lila's esoteric abilities to tools more familiar in Alice's professional context.

"And if you've made the wrong choice before?" Lila asked, the question carrying weight beyond philosophical consideration.

"Then you make a different one next time. That's what redemption is." Alice leaned forward. "It's not about erasing the past. It's about choosing differently in the present."

The simplicity of the statement belied its profound implications—acknowledging that while past actions couldn't be undone, they need not determine future choices.

Lila was quiet for a long moment, her gaze returning to the river. When she spoke again, her voice carried vulnerability rarely displayed in their previous interactions. "And if you're not strong enough to choose differently?"

"Then you let others help you choose." Alice reached over and gripped Lila's hand, feeling the cold metal of the rings against her palm. "You're not in Prague anymore. You're not alone."

The gesture represented more than momentary comfort—it was a deliberate choice to establish connection despite knowledge of potential danger.

"That's what I'm afraid of." Lila's voice cracked, emotion briefly overwhelming her composure. "Everyone who's ever helped me—"

"Has made their own choices," Alice's grip tightened, interrupting the spiral of guilt. "Just like I'm making mine now. Just like Ethan and Jake have made theirs."

The statement asserted agency not just for Lila but for all those who had chosen to stand with her despite potential consequences.

A cloud passed over the sun, casting a momentary shadow across the park bench. In the dimness, Lila's eyes seemed to hold both silver fire and human tears—contradictory elements coexisting.

"The foundry," she said softly, decision forming from their conversation. "Tonight. He'll have prepared. The power there... it will be overwhelming."

The disclosure confirmed what Ethan and Jake had suspected—that the abandoned Harrington Foundry would serve as the penultimate site in Viktor's working.

"Then we'll be overwhelmed together," Alice smiled, the expression conveying determination rather than naivety. "Unless you're planning to knock me out and go alone in some misguided attempt to protect me?"

The gentle challenge acknowledged tropes they both recognized from countless stories where powerful protectors made unilateral decisions "for the good" of those they sought to shield.

Lila laughed, though it was watery with barely contained emotion. "Would it work?"

"Not a chance. I've got your number now, Darkmagic." The use of her surname carried affectionate teasing, transforming what had begun as professional consultation into something approaching genuine partnership.

They sat in comfortable silence, watching leaves dance on the river's surface. The metaphor wasn't lost on either woman as they contemplated the collaboration necessary to confront whatever awaited at the foundry.

Finally, Lila spoke again, her voice steadier and carrying genuine emotion. "Thank you."

"For what?" Alice asked, though she suspected she knew the answer.

"For seeing the choices I could make, not just the ones I have made." The distinction captured the essence of their conversation—acknowledgment of potential futures rather than deterministic imprisonment in patterns established by past actions.

Alice stood, brushing off her slacks with practiced movement. "That's what partners do." She held out her hand, the gesture both practical assistance and symbolic invitation. "Ready to make some better ones?"

Lila took it, her silver rings warm now despite their earlier chill, and if Alice felt the hum of ancient power beneath those metal bands, she chose not to flinch.

As Lila rose from the bench, their silhouettes momentarily merged in the afternoon sunlight, casting a single shadow that seemed to shift and flow in ways that defied conventional physics.

Sometimes, redemption was as simple as that—one hand extended, another accepting; one choice connecting to another until new patterns emerged from what had seemed inevitable repetition.

CHAPTER TEN
FIRE AND SHADOW

THE ABANDONED Harrington Foundry loomed against the darkening sky like a hulking beast. Once the pride of Daybridge's manufacturing sector, the massive structure had stood vacant for decades. The three-story brick facade remained relatively intact, but the rear sections had partially collapsed, creating a labyrinth of debris and shadowed corners.

The air was thick with the acrid stench of chemicals and rotting garbage. Through his connection to the nexus entity beneath Daybridge Bridge, Ethan perceived additional layers beyond what human senses could detect. The foundry radiated wrongness—reality itself felt stretched thin around the building, dimensional boundaries warped by deliberate manipulation.

Beside him, Alice Chen scanned the area with keen eyes, her hand resting lightly on her gun. Despite lacking Ethan's supernatural senses, her trained observation skills noticed the recent tire tracks in the muddy approach, the absence of typical urban wildlife, and the unnatural stillness in the air.

They had received an anonymous tip that morning—coordinates and a cryptic warning about "the culmination drawing near." Combined with

Lila's information about Viktor's methodical activation of ritual sites throughout Daybridge, the foundry represented the penultimate location in what appeared to be an elaborate working designed to breach dimensional boundaries.

Ethan couldn't shake the feeling of unease that prickled along his neck. He had been a cop long enough to know when things didn't feel right —and everything about this place screamed danger on both conventional and supernatural levels.

The wolf aspect of his nature stirred restlessly, responding to invisible threats his human consciousness couldn't fully articulate. Since his partial integration with the nexus entity, this internal communication had become more nuanced—less the struggling of separate identities and more the harmonization of complementary awareness systems.

As they approached the foundry's massive doors, Ethan held up a hand, signaling for Alice to stop. He could hear something coming from inside—a low, rhythmic chanting that seemed to vibrate through the ground beneath their feet.

"We need to be careful," he whispered. "Whatever's going on in there, it's not good. The energetic signature matches what we encountered at the other sites, but significantly stronger."

Alice nodded grimly, drawing her service weapon. Together, they inched forward and carefully pushed open one of the heavy metal doors.

The sight that greeted them was like something from a nightmare.

The foundry's main floor had been transformed into an elaborate ritual chamber. The air was heavy with the scent of incense and decay. Flickering candlelight illuminated the space, hundreds of black candles arranged in precise geometric patterns across the floor, forming a massive sigil when viewed from above.

In the center of the room, a makeshift altar had been erected from repurposed industrial materials. Upon this altar lay what appeared to be human remains—not a complete body but components harvested from multiple sources, arranged in a pattern that suggested they would ultimately form a composite vessel.

But it was the figure standing behind the altar that sent a spike of terror racing through Ethan's veins.

He was tall and gaunt, his skin the color of parchment stretched over a frame that seemed too angular to be fully human. His eyes were sunken deep into their sockets, but within those hollows burned intelligence that radiated both brilliance and madness. His robes were elaborately embroidered with symbols that matched those carved into the victims' bodies they had discovered throughout Daybridge.

"Viktor Kalishnikov," Ethan breathed. "I thought you'd be older."

The necromancer's head snapped up at the sound of Ethan's voice, his movements possessing the unnatural quickness of predatory insects. His lips twisted into a grotesque parody of a smile, revealing teeth that appeared too numerous and sharp for an ordinary human mouth.

"Detective Reeves," he rasped, his voice like the scrape of a rusty blade against bone. "I'm afraid the years have been kinder to me than most. The benefits of specialized knowledge, you understand."

Ethan felt a surge of white-hot anger pulse through him at the casual way Viktor spoke, as if they were colleagues discussing academic research instead of adversaries confronting each other across a moral and metaphysical divide.

"What are you doing here, Viktor?" Ethan demanded, his voice shaking with barely contained rage.

Viktor spread his hands wide, the gesture theatrical in its expansiveness. "Why, I'm simply fulfilling a promise made long ago, Detective. A promise to bring back what was unjustly taken. To restore what was lost through interference and misunderstanding."

"The grave robberies," Alice murmured beside him. "The murders. The specific pattern of ritual sites activated throughout Daybridge. It was all you, wasn't it? Building toward whatever this is."

Viktor's smile widened. "Very good, Detective Chen. You always were the perceptive one. Seeing patterns where others notice only isolated incidents."

Ethan's fingers tightened around his gun. "But why? Why go to all this trouble? What could be worth dozens of lives and the risk of dimensional collapse?"

Viktor's eyes flashed with a complex mixture of emotions—madness certainly, but also grief, determination, and something that might almost be described as love, twisted by decades of obsession. "Reunion, Detective," he hissed. "The restoration of what was wrongfully separated. The recovery of brilliance extinguished before its time."

"You're trying to bring back Abby," Ethan said, connecting the pieces based on Lila's account. "But whatever you're reaching for isn't her anymore—not really. You have to know that."

Something shifted in Viktor's expression—a flicker of doubt quickly suppressed. "You understand nothing," he snarled. "She persists beyond conventional boundaries—her consciousness preserved through the very working that appeared to fail. I've communicated with her, Detective. Heard her voice through the thinning veil between dimensions."

"You're being used," Alice stated with direct clarity. "Whatever is communicating with you isn't Abby—it's something using her memory, her connection to you, to gain access to our reality. The pattern of your workings throughout Daybridge doesn't create a pathway for a single consciousness to return—it's establishing a permanent breach that would allow unrestricted access between dimensions."

Viktor's features contorted with rage. "You think I haven't considered that possibility? That I haven't tested and verified the authenticity of the consciousness responding to my workings? I who have spent decades studying the boundaries between dimensions, who have sacrificed everything in pursuit of this single goal?"

Dark energy began to gather around his hands like condensing shadow. The robed figures surrounding the altar began to move with greater purpose, their chanting increasing in both volume and complexity.

"Insane or not," Ethan snarled, his finger tightening on the trigger, "we won't let you tear open the boundaries between worlds and unleash whatever's waiting on the other side. It ends here, Viktor. Now."

With a roar that contained elements of both human resolve and lupine ferocity, Ethan charged forward, his gun blazing as he fired shot after shot at the necromancer.

Viktor responded with disturbing speed, his body twisting and contorting as he dodged the bullets with movements that defied ordinary human limitations. The necromantic energy surrounding his hands expanded outward, forming a shield-like barrier that absorbed the few projectiles that might otherwise have found their mark.

Alice was right behind Ethan, her own weapon spitting fire as she took aim at the robed figures that had begun to surge forward. Unlike Ethan's conventional ammunition, her backup weapon contained silver-loaded rounds—specially prepared by Lila with additional enchantments designed to disrupt necromantic energies. Lila had channeled some of her rings' ambient protective energy into Alice's silver rounds, providing a temporary counter-charge against necromantic constructs.

The air filled with the stench of blood and gunpowder, the sound of screams and chanting mingling in a cacophonous din. But even as they fought, Ethan could feel the tide turning against them. The robed figures seemed to shrug off even the most grievous wounds, while Viktor remained untouched—a blur of motion as he wove complex patterns in the air.

Ethan felt a searing pain rip through his shoulder as one of the necromancer's spells found its mark. He stumbled back, his vision momentarily blurring.

Beside him, Alice cried out as she too was struck, her body flung backward by the force of the blast. Ethan's heart seized as he saw her crumple to the ground, leaving him divided between continuing the assault and ensuring his partner's safety.

Drawing on his connection to the nexus entity, Ethan reached beyond his lycanthropic nature to access energies that offered power beyond what his werewolf form alone could provide.

His spine arched painfully as muscle and bone reshaped. Claws of obsidian unsheathed from his fingertips and fangs like ivory blades glinted in the gloom. Silvery fur rippled down his back and across his chest, his body swelling with supernatural strength.

His senses heightened to incredible levels—the stench of death and dark magic overwhelming, the frenzied chants drilling into his skull. But the enhanced perception also revealed patterns previously obscured—the specific configuration of Viktor's working, the way it drew power from the geometric arrangement of ritual sites throughout Daybridge.

With this expanded awareness came understanding—Viktor's working wasn't merely opening communication with whatever entity he believed was Abby's consciousness but establishing a permanent conduit between dimensions that would allow unrestricted transfer in both directions.

With a howl that echoed through the foundry, Ethan launched himself at Viktor in a whirlwind of flashing claws and snapping teeth. The staccato of gunshots and screams faded into the background as his world narrowed to the sole purpose of disrupting the necromancer's connection to the dimensional breach forming above the altar.

Sickly green light erupted from Viktor's hands like hellfire, slamming into Ethan's chest with enough force to shatter concrete. The impact sent him crashing into a stack of abandoned equipment. The smell of charred fur filled the air as necrotic energy attempted to consume living tissue, but the nexus power flowing through Ethan's transformed body provided unexpected resistance.

Recovering with supernatural quickness, Ethan sprang back to his feet. This time he charged with greater strategic awareness, using his enhanced speed to circle rather than approach directly—forcing Viktor to divide attention between maintaining the dimensional working and defending against physical attack.

The approach succeeded in disrupting the necromancer's concentration, but at significant cost as Viktor responded with a wall of purple-black flames that materialized in Ethan's path.

The necromantic fire seared his flesh like liquid nitrogen. He howled in agony as the unnatural flames danced across his skin, temporarily paralyzing nerve pathways while attempting to separate his consciousness from physical form.

Viktor's laughter rang out like graveyard bells. "Pathetic mongrel," the necromancer sneered, lightning arcing between his fingertips as he prepared to deliver a finishing strike. "I'll send you to beg table scraps from Cerberus in the Underworld itself."

His gloating speech cut off abruptly as Alice's silver dagger sprouted from his bony chest, black ichor bubbling from the wound. Her throw had been true despite the chaos of the melee, the weapon spinning end over end before embedding itself precisely where Viktor's heart would be if his body still functioned according to ordinary biological principles.

Viktor staggered to his knees, his magic momentarily disrupted. The purple-black flames imprisoning Ethan flickered and dissipated, freeing him from their paralyzing effect.

Ethan didn't hesitate. Free of the dark flames, he launched himself at Viktor's fallen form in a snarling blur of teeth and claws. The necromancer barely had time to react before Ethan's powerful jaws clamped down on his throat.

But as the werewolf's teeth sank deeper, Viktor's body suddenly dissolved into a swirling mass of inky shadows and acrid smoke. Ethan stumbled forward, his jaws snapping shut on empty air as the necromancer's form dissipated.

A chilling laugh echoed through the foundry, seeming to come from everywhere and nowhere. "Foolish creature," his voice taunted. "Did you really think it would be so easy to overcome decades of preparation? This is merely one component of a greater working—a single note in a symphony you cannot yet comprehend!"

With a final, mocking cackle, the shadows coalesced into a churning vortex before vanishing altogether. But the dimensional breach above the altar remained, though significantly reduced in size from what it had been approaching.

As Viktor's presence faded, the entire foundry seemed to shudder—physical reality adjusting to the sudden reduction in dimensional distortion. The swirling portal of necrotic energy above the altar began to shrink further, collapsing inward as the carefully established geometric pattern sustaining it was disrupted.

The remaining robed figures crumpled to the ground as the necromantic energy animating them dissipated, their bodies revealed as neither living cultists nor fully animated corpses but something between—ordinary humans partially transformed through exposure to death magic.

Ethan shifted back to his human form in gut-wrenching crunches and snaps. He limped slightly as he made his way to Alice, who had retrieved her silver dagger from where it had fallen when Viktor's physical form dissipated.

Without a word, he gathered her into a tight embrace, both too drained for verbal processing after their desperate fight. The connection between partners transcended words in that moment—shared survival creating bonds that didn't require articulation.

But even as they clung to each other, Ethan couldn't shake the feeling this was only the beginning. Viktor's final words echoed in his mind, a chilling promise of escalation rather than retreat. The necromancer had slipped through their grasp, and Ethan knew with sick certainty that it was only a matter of time before he resurfaced—likely at Blackwood Cemetery, the final point in the geometric pattern they had identified.

For now, though, they had won a temporary reprieve. This component of Viktor's grand working had been disrupted, the dimensional breach collapsing before it could achieve a stable connection between worlds. But as Ethan and Alice made their way out of the building, they couldn't escape the lingering sense of unease, the knowledge that their battle against the forces of darkness was far from over.

Viktor Kalishnikov would return, and when he did, they would need to be ready. The final confrontation would likely occur at Blackwood Cemetery on Halloween night, when natural thinning of dimensional boundaries would enhance Viktor's necromantic workings and provide optimal conditions for his ultimate goal.

The fate of Daybridge—and potentially reality itself—hung in the balance.

CHAPTER ELEVEN

THE TRUTH IN SHADOW

THE RAIN FELL in sheets over Daybridge, turning the city's streets into a labyrinth of glistening asphalt and neon reflections. Each droplet caught fragments of colorful light from storefronts and traffic signals, creating a shimmering mosaic that transformed the urban landscape. The downpour had begun shortly after their confrontation at the Harrington Foundry, as if the natural world itself responded to the dimensional disruption they had temporarily contained.

Detective Ethan Reeves sat hunched over his desk at the precinct, the fluorescent lights overhead casting harsh shadows across his face as he pored over the Viktor Kalishnikov case files. His coffee had gone cold hours ago, the mug pushed aside to make room for the sprawling array of photographs, reports, and evidence logs.

It had been three days since their confrontation with the necromancer —three days of endless paperwork and unanswered questions. The official report had carefully sanitized the supernatural elements, transforming a confrontation with necromantic forces into something that could be filed within conventional law enforcement parameters.

A sudden commotion from the front of the precinct jolted Ethan from his brooding thoughts. The bullpen's normal background noise shifted abruptly, silence spreading outward from the entrance. He looked up to see a figure striding through the space, her high heels clicking against the scuffed linoleum with precise timing.

She was dressed all in black, from her form-fitting leather jacket to her stiletto boots, her raven hair cascading down her back in glossy waves. But it was her eyes that caught Ethan's attention—twin pools of emerald green that seemed to glint with otherworldly light as they locked onto his across the bullpen.

"Hello, Ethan," Lila Darkmagic purred as she reached his desk, her full lips curving into a smile that was equal parts invitation and challenge. "Did you miss me?"

Ethan felt his heart skip a beat at the sound of her voice, a familiar mix of attraction and wariness rising inside him. He had first encountered Lila three years ago, when unusual energy signatures had been detected near Daybridge Bridge. Their initial professional collaboration had evolved into something more complex during the crisis that had led to his transformation.

When that crisis had been resolved, Lila had disappeared without explanation, leaving Ethan to navigate his newly transformed existence alone. Her unexpected return during the current investigation had reopened wounds he thought had healed.

"What are you doing here, Lila?" he asked, his voice rough with tension as he rose from his desk. "I thought we agreed you'd maintain a lower profile during this investigation."

Lila's smile widened, her eyes glinting with amusement as she studied him. "Oh, Ethan," she murmured, her voice like honey poured over gravel. "You should know by now that I adjust my approach based on evolving circumstances. Especially when there's trouble brewing in a city I've become rather fond of."

Ethan's brow furrowed at her words, a prickle of unease running down his spine. "What's changed? Have you identified Viktor's next move?"

Lila's expression sobered, her eyes darkening with gravity that transformed her from mysterious seductress to battle-hardened veteran. "More than identified," she said quietly. "I've confirmed his final target. The necromancer you confronted at the foundry—he's accelerating his timeline. The disruption you caused has forced him to compress his remaining preparations."

She glanced around the bullpen. "We need to talk privately. What I've discovered goes beyond what can be discussed in official settings—even with your department's unusual tolerance for unconventional methods."

"What do you know about Viktor's endgame?" he asked, gathering his jacket as he prepared to accompany her outside.

Lila hesitated, her eyes searching his face. "Viktor is attempting to complete what we began in Prague thirty years ago," she said at last, her voice barely audible. "But with modifications that make it infinitely more dangerous. His research into the Order of the Ebon Star's methodologies has allowed him to combine necromantic practices with dimensional manipulation techniques—creating a hybrid approach that could potentially tear permanent breaches between realities."

Ethan felt a wave of cold dread wash over him. The Order of the Ebon Star had nearly succeeded in collapsing reality during the winter solstice confrontation beneath Daybridge Bridge—the event that had triggered his partial integration with the nexus entity.

"Blackwood Cemetery," he stated rather than asked, connecting the geometric pattern they had mapped throughout Daybridge to its logical focal point.

Lila nodded. "Yes. The oldest burial ground in Daybridge, established on land that held spiritual significance to indigenous peoples long before European settlement. The cemetery occupies a natural power nexus—a location where dimensional boundaries have always been thinner than surrounding areas."

"When?" he asked, professional focus temporarily overriding emotional response.

"Halloween night," she replied. "When the dimensional boundaries naturally thin and cosmic alignments enhance necromantic workings. The window of optimal conditions begins at midnight and extends for approximately three hours—giving us a specific timeframe for intervention."

The timeline provided less than forty-eight hours for preparation—a dangerously narrow window given the scope of the threat they faced. Conventional law enforcement protocols would prove woefully inadequate against necromantic forces and dimensional manipulation.

"Alright," he said at last, decision crystallizing. "Let's continue this discussion somewhere more private. I need to bring Alice up to speed as well—her analytical approach has provided critical insights throughout this investigation."

Lila's lips curved into a smile that contained genuine appreciation rather than her usual calculated charm. "Detective Chen has indeed proven herself remarkably adaptable to circumstances beyond conventional parameters. Her perspective will be valuable in formulating our approach."

As they moved toward the precinct exit, Ethan felt the weight of responsibility settling more heavily across his shoulders. The confrontation ahead represented more than merely apprehending a criminal—it potentially involved protecting reality itself from fundamental disruption.

"There's something else you should know," Lila said as they stepped outside into the continuing downpour. "Viktor believes he's communicating with Abby—with her consciousness preserved beyond physical death. But whatever is responding to his workings isn't my sister—at least, not solely her. It's something that existed before her death, something that recognized opportunity in our failed ritual and has been guiding Viktor's research ever since."

The revelation added new dimensions to their understanding. Not merely a grieving researcher pursuing forbidden knowledge, but potentially a manipulated pawn serving entities with agendas beyond human comprehension.

"What kind of entity are we talking about?" Ethan asked as they hurried toward his unmarked department vehicle.

"Similar but distinct from what the Order sought," Lila replied, her expression grave. "The Order sought contact with entities that existed entirely beyond our dimensional framework. What's manipulating Viktor appears to be something that once had physical form but transcended it—evolving beyond biological limitations while retaining understanding of material existence. This makes it potentially more dangerous, as it comprehends human consciousness in ways the Order's entities could not."

The rain intensified as they pulled away from the precinct, visibility reduced to the immediate area illuminated by the car's headlights. Through his connection to the nexus entity, Ethan perceived patterns in the rainfall that ordinary human senses would miss—configurations suggesting influence beyond natural meteorological processes.

"We need to gather everyone involved in this investigation," he said, navigating carefully through streets that had begun to flood in low-lying areas. "Jake Steinman's historical knowledge, Nadia Marsh's research into the Caligari Cataclysm, Alice's analytical approach, and your direct experience with Viktor. If we're going to prevent whatever he's planning at Blackwood Cemetery, we need coordinated strategy rather than improvised response."

Lila nodded. "I've already arranged for everyone to meet at Jake's shop this evening. Eight o'clock. His private library contains resources we'll need for preparation, and the protective measures we established there should prevent Viktor from monitoring our planning."

As they drove through Daybridge's rain-soaked streets toward Crossroads Books, Ethan couldn't shake the feeling that they were approaching a pivotal moment not just in their investigation but in the city's history. Viktor's final working at Blackwood Cemetery represented potential catastrophe beyond conventional understanding.

Yet alongside that dread grew a cautious hope, born from the unlikely alliance forming around their shared purpose. Lila's return to the precinct represented more than merely new information—it symbolized commitment to partnership rather than solitary intervention, recognition that some threats required collaborative response.

The future remained uncertain, the confrontation ahead fraught with dangers both known and unimaginable. But as rain continued to fall over Daybridge, cleansing the city streets while concealing the dimensional thinning that ordinary citizens couldn't perceive, Ethan found unexpected comfort in Lila's presence beside him—not despite their complicated history but because of it, because they had faced extraordinary circumstances together before and emerged changed but not broken.

Halloween night would witness their final stand against forces that threatened to unravel reality itself. And whatever the result, Daybridge would never be quite the same again—transformed not just by the threat they faced but by the unlikely alliance that had formed to confront it.

CHAPTER TWELVE
WHAT LIES BENEATH

DETECTIVE ETHAN REEVES watched Lila Darkmagic's hands as she poured the tea. Steady, despite the gravity of their conversation. Too steady, like someone working hard to seem casual. Her silver rings clinked against the antique pot—iron, he noticed, though disguised as ceramic with elaborate enamel work that incorporated protective sigils into its decorative pattern.

The back room of Crossroads Books served as Jake Steinman's private consultation space. Bookshelves lined the walls, containing volumes too rare or dangerous for the main shop's inventory, while the antique furniture had been selected as much for the subtle protective symbols worked into its craftsmanship as for its aesthetic appeal.

The comfortable space typically projected welcoming warmth, but today tension hung heavy in the air—aggravated by Jake's unexplained absence and the cryptic message he had left on Lila's phone: "Found something in the Vermeer Codex about Viktor's methodology. Meeting a contact. Don't wait up." That had been eighteen hours ago, with no further communication despite multiple attempts to reach him.

"The sigils at the Harrison plot," Ethan said, accepting the teacup while maintaining direct eye contact with Lila. "You recognized them immediately. Didn't even need to consult your books. You identified them as 'Kryzlac configurations' within seconds of seeing them."

Lila's pause was almost imperceptible. Almost—but Ethan's enhanced senses detected the momentary hesitation in her breathing, the subtle shift in her heartbeat. "I've studied many forms of ritual magic during my travels," she replied, her tone maintaining professional detachment. "The Kryzlac tradition is particularly distinctive in its approach to dimensional boundaries."

"And the necromancer's personal mark?" Ethan set crime scene photo #7 on the cluttered table between them, his movement deliberate as he positioned the image directly in Lila's line of sight. The photograph showed a distinctive symbol carved into the headstone of the Harrison family plot. "The one you said was a 'corruption of traditional forms'?"

Her green eyes—a shade too bright to be natural, with occasional flecks of silver—flickered to the symbol, then away with practiced casualness. "As I said, it's a common enough variation for those practicing death magic with intent to breach dimensional boundaries. The specific distortion of the central node indicates European training rather than Asian or African traditions."

Detective Alice Chen, perched on the edge of a worn armchair, narrowed her eyes. "But you knew his name. Before anyone said it. When I described the energy signature at the grave, you said 'That sounds like Viktor's work.'"

The temperature in the room seemed to drop slightly, though the antique radiator continued its steady output of heat. Outside, wind chimes hanging from the shop's eaves jangled discordantly despite the absence of breeze.

"A lucky guess," Lila said, smoothing her already-smooth black dress with a gesture that appeared casual but served to activate the protective enchantments woven into the fabric. "His techniques are... distinctive. The specific combination of necromantic energy with dimensional manipulation creates a signature that few practitioners could achieve."

"Like the technique that killed those three practitioners in Prague?" Alice pulled out her tablet and brought up scanned documents from international police databases. "1987. Same signature on the victims' bodies. According to witness statements, a woman matching your description was present at the scene shortly before the bodies were discovered. You were there, weren't you?"

Lila's cup clinked against its saucer—a minor slip in her usually perfect composure. "Detective Chen, I assure you—"

"Or Buenos Aires, 1992? Venice, 1998?" Alice swiped through digital files with methodical precision. "Interesting pattern. Wherever Viktor appears, reports mention a woman matching your description. Different names, but same face. You don't seem to age much in thirty years of photographs."

The observation hung in the air between them—not merely an accusation of deception but an acknowledgment of fundamental mysteries surrounding Lila's nature and history.

Ethan leaned forward, his posture shifting from professional inquiry to personal connection. "Lila? What aren't you telling us? Jake is missing, potentially in danger, and we're facing a final confrontation with Viktor in less than thirty-six hours. We need complete information, not just selected details that fit your preferred narrative."

The witch sighed, and for a moment her carefully maintained poise cracked like thin ice under unexpected pressure. She looked older suddenly, tired in a way that had nothing to do with physical age but with burdens carried too long in isolation.

"It's... complicated," she said finally, the inadequacy of the phrase evident in her tone.

"Three people are dead," Alice said sharply. "Jake is missing. Nadia Marsh has been attacked and is under protection at Daybridge General. We don't have time for complicated."

Lila stood abruptly, moving to the window whose leaded glass incorporated protective geometry disguised as a decorative pattern. The protection charms hung there tinkled as she passed, responding to the subtle energy field she projected.

"What do you know about soul bonds, Detectives?" she asked, her back to them as she gazed out at the street below.

"Only what's in the old texts," Ethan replied, drawing on knowledge acquired through his research with Jake. "Magical connections between practitioners who share significant working over extended periods. Sympathetic resonance that allows sensing across distances, shared power reserves under certain conditions, mutual vulnerability to specific types of magical attack."

He paused as implications assembled themselves from fragments gathered throughout their investigation—Viktor's apparent awareness of their movements despite precautions, Lila's ability to track his activities across decades despite his sophisticated concealment methods. "Oh."

"Yes." Her voice was barely a whisper. "We were students together. Young. Ambitious. Certain we could control powers better left alone. When the binding ritual went wrong, when he began to change... I should have stopped him then. Should have ended it before his transformation progressed beyond reversal."

"You were lovers," Alice said softly, her usual skepticism softening in response to the naked pain evident in Lila's posture and tone.

"We were everything." Lila's reflection in the window looked distant. "Partners. Rivals. Saviors. Destroyers. The magic tied us together in ways that shouldn't be possible. Even now, I can feel him..." She pressed a hand to her chest. "Here. Always. His presence like background radiation—sometimes barely perceptible, sometimes overwhelming, but never entirely absent."

The admission transformed their understanding of both Lila's motivations and the threat they faced—personal connection adding layers of complexity beyond professional opposition or metaphysical principle.

"That's why you came to Daybridge," Ethan realized, connecting disparate pieces of information. "You didn't show up by coincidence. You knew he was coming—felt him approaching through your connection long before any physical evidence manifested."

"I've followed him for decades. Trying to stop him. Trying to save what's left of the man I knew." She turned back to them, and her eyes held centuries of grief compressed into human expression. "But I've never been strong enough to do what needs to be done."

"Which is?" Alice asked, though her expression suggested she already recognized the implications.

Lila's smile was terrible—not malevolent but tragic, containing knowledge of inevitability that had shaped decades of preparation. "Why do you think I've spent thirty years studying death magic, Detective Chen? There's only one way to break a soul bond when it's progressed to this level of integration."

The implications hung heavy in the air, unspoken but unmistakable. Soul bonds of the magnitude she described couldn't be severed through standard magical countermeasures or simple separation. Their dissolution required more permanent, irreversible solutions.

"You're hunting him," Ethan whispered, the realization carrying weight beyond its simple articulation.

"No." Lila touched one of her silver rings—the one on her left index finger, inscribed with symbols that matched certain configurations they had discovered at ritual sites throughout Daybridge. For a moment it glowed with suppressed power. "I'm hunting us both."

The distinction carried profound implications—not merely pursuit of external threat but recognition of shared destiny, of connection that couldn't be severed without consequences for both participants.

Outside, storm clouds gathered over Daybridge Cemetery in patterns that defied conventional meteorological explanation. Thunder rolled across the darkening sky, or maybe it was the sound of ancient magics stirring in response to the city's transformed reality.

"Help us find Jake," Alice said, her voice gentle but firm. "Tell us everything you know about Viktor. The real story, not the edited version."

The request acknowledged both the necessity of complete information and respect for what that disclosure would cost.

Lila closed her eyes, momentary vulnerability revealing the weight of decision. "Very well. But remember, Detectives—you asked for truth." She sat down, hands clasped to hide their trembling. "It began in Prague, in a room full of candlelight and ambition, when two young fools thought they could master death itself..."

Her voice steadied as she spoke, initial hesitation yielding to the release that comes with confession long delayed. The narrative emerged not as carefully constructed explanation but as lived experience, raw and unfiltered.

"Viktor was brilliant—truly brilliant in ways that conventional academia couldn't recognize or contain. His understanding of necromantic principles wasn't merely theoretical but intuitive." Her expression softened with memory, affection temporarily overriding current opposition. "We met in the university library after hours—both seeking texts that official curriculum considered irrelevant or dangerous, both recognizing in each other ambition that transcended institutional limitations."

She described their initial collaboration—shared research into historical ritual practices, comparative analysis of magical systems across cultural boundaries, discussions that extended far beyond conventional academic parameters. Their relationship had evolved from a scholarly partnership to personal connection, intellectual affinity becoming emotional entanglement.

"When my sister Abby was diagnosed with aggressive leukemia, our research shifted from theoretical to practical—from academic understanding to desperate seeking of solutions that conventional medicine couldn't provide." Lila's voice caught briefly, old grief resurfacing. "Viktor was the one who suggested utilizing our combined knowledge to attempt intervention beyond physical treatment—to access energetic patterns underlying biological processes and redirect them toward healing rather than deterioration."

The account aligned with what she had previously shared but with crucial additional context—personal motivation that transformed abstract magical experimentation into a desperate attempt to save a loved one, ethical considerations overridden by emotional necessity.

"The ritual we designed incorporated elements from multiple traditions—necromantic principles for accessing life-force energies, dimensional manipulation techniques for redirecting them, mathematical configurations to maintain stability throughout the process." Her hands moved unconsciously as she spoke, tracing patterns in the air. "What we didn't understand—what our arrogance prevented us from recognizing—was that the energies we sought to manipulate existed within a larger system whose balance we were fundamentally disrupting."

Ethan and Alice listened without interruption, recognizing the significance of Lila's voluntary disclosure after decades of selective sharing.

"When the ritual began to fail—when the energies we had summoned started consuming Abby rather than healing her—I tried to stop the working, to close the pathways we had opened. But Viktor... he saw opportunity in catastrophe. Possibility rather than failure. He believed we could redirect the process toward transformation rather than mere healing—elevate consciousness beyond physical limitations entirely."

The divergence she described represented more than tactical disagreement—fundamental schism in values that had transformed collaboration into opposition, partnership into enmity that spanned decades and continents.

"I disrupted the ritual's final configuration—damaged the geometric pattern we had established to channel energies in specific directions." Her expression reflected both pride in that intervention and grief at its consequences. "But not before something had opened between dimensions—a breach, temporary but significant, allowing contact if not physical transfer between realities. And in that moment of disruption, with energies discharging in unpredictable patterns, Abby died."

The simple statement carried weight beyond its factual content—acknowledgment of loss that had shaped everything that followed, catalyst for three decades of conflict and pursuit.

"Viktor disappeared that night—taking certain texts and artifacts with him, leaving behind the physical shell of the man I had known and loved." Lila's gaze remained focused on memory rather than present surroundings. "But our connection remained—the soul bond we had established through months of shared working, strengthened rather than severed by the ritual's catastrophic conclusion. I could feel him changing, transforming, as he continued experiments we had begun together—exploring the breach we had created, communicating with whatever existed on its other side."

Her account continued, describing decades of pursuit across continents—interventions when Viktor's activities threatened to replicate their original catastrophe on a larger scale, confrontations that never reached a definitive conclusion due to their continued metaphysical connection.

"Each confrontation followed a similar pattern," she explained, her tone shifting toward analytical precision. "Viktor would establish a ritual site, accumulate necessary components for dimensional working, begin activation sequence. I would interrupt the process before completion, forcing temporary retreat and relocation. But each cycle brought him closer to perfecting his methodology—learning from previous failures, adapting to my intervention strategies, gradually developing working that could withstand opposition."

The pattern aligned with evidence they had gathered—the accelerating sequence of ritual activations throughout Daybridge, the increasingly sophisticated protective measures incorporated into each site, the geometric configuration gradually establishing dimensional resonance that would culminate at Blackwood Cemetery.

"Five years ago, I detected preliminary workings in Daybridge—subtle dimensional manipulations that matched Viktor's evolving methodology but hadn't yet progressed to full ritual activation." She gestured toward the window, indicating the city beyond. "The location was significant—a natural nexus point where dimensional boundaries have always been thinner than surrounding areas, enhanced by historical accumulation of death energy from the city's cemeteries and violent past."

The timeframe explained Lila's extended presence in Daybridge—not merely a response to the current crisis but long-term strategic positioning, establishing defensive measures and gathering allies before Viktor's full arrival.

"I established residence here, began studying local history and dimensional patterns specific to Daybridge, gradually implemented protective measures at key locations throughout the city." Her expression reflected genuine connection. "But I also... found community here. People like Jake, who understood aspects of what I was attempting without requiring complete disclosure. Nadia Marsh, whose historical research provided context I had lacked during previous confrontations."

The admission revealed vulnerability beneath Lila's typically guarded exterior—acknowledgment that isolation had been self-imposed protection rather than inherent preference, that connection with others represented risk she had gradually become willing to accept.

"When Viktor finally arrived in Daybridge—physically rather than merely through preliminary workings established from distance—I felt it immediately." She pressed her hand to her chest again. "The soul bond flared with proximity, growing stronger as he established a presence here and began activating ritual sites throughout the city. I had expected it, had prepared for this confrontation for years, but the intensity still..." She paused, searching for an adequate description. "It was like suddenly hearing music that had been playing at a subconscious level for decades—background noise becoming symphony impossible to ignore."

Ethan nodded, understanding her description through his own experience of enhanced perception—the way his partial integration with the nexus entity had transformed his awareness of Daybridge's dimensional landscape, making previously imperceptible patterns suddenly, overwhelmingly present.

"So, when Jake disappeared..." Ethan began, connecting this new information to their immediate crisis.

"I believe Viktor took him," Lila confirmed, voicing what they had suspected but lacked sufficient evidence to conclude definitively. "Not merely to remove potential ally from our coalition, but for specific knowledge Jake possesses—historical understanding of Daybridge's dimensional nexus points and previous manifestations of breach phenomena throughout the city's development."

The assessment aligned with the message Jake had left before his disappearance—his discovery in the Vermeer Codex potentially providing insight that Viktor would value for his final ritual at Blackwood Cemetery.

"We need to find him before Viktor extracts what he needs," Alice said, professional focus returning now that emotional disclosure had provided the necessary context. "And we need to understand exactly what Viktor is attempting to accomplish at Blackwood Cemetery—not just generally breaching dimensional boundaries but specific intended outcome and methodology."

Lila nodded. "Based on the pattern of ritual sites he's activated throughout Daybridge and the specific components he's gathered, I believe Viktor is attempting to create a permanent gateway between our reality and whatever exists beyond the breach we initially opened in Prague."

She paused, considering how to articulate concepts that extended beyond conventional understanding. "He believes he's been communicating with Sarah's consciousness—that she persists beyond physical death in some form accessible through the breach we created. His working is designed not merely to establish contact but to retrieve—to bring what he perceives as her awareness back into physical form constructed from components harvested throughout Daybridge."

The explanation aligned with evidence they had gathered—the specific pattern of grave desecrations and ritualistic murders, the geometric configuration of ritual sites, the accelerating timeline leading toward Halloween night when dimensional boundaries naturally thinned.

"But you don't believe it's actually Abby he's communicating with," Ethan observed, connecting fragments of information.

"No," she confirmed, her expression grave. "Whatever responds to Viktor's attempts at communication isn't solely my sister—might contain fragments of her consciousness initially, might utilize her memories and personality as a framework, but has evolved into something else entirely. An entity that exists beyond conventional dimensional boundaries, utilizing Viktor's grief and obsession to gain access to our reality."

The assessment transformed their understanding of both Viktor's motivations and the nature of the threat they faced—not merely misguided researcher pursuing forbidden knowledge but manipulated instrument of forces beyond human comprehension.

"So, finding Jake becomes even more urgent," Alice concluded. "Not just for his safety but because whatever knowledge Viktor extracts could enhance final working at Blackwood Cemetery—potentially increasing likelihood of a successful dimensional breach beyond what we've prepared to counter."

Lila nodded, professional assessment temporarily overshadowing personal history. "Yes. And I believe I know where Viktor might be holding him—a location that would serve both as a secure detention facility and preparation site for components he'll incorporate into final ritual."

She moved to the large map of Daybridge that Jake had mounted on the wall. Her finger traced path from Crossroads Books toward the industrial district, coming to rest on abandoned structure near the river's edge.

"The old Mortensen Funeral Home," she said, indicating a building that had once served Daybridge's more affluent citizens. "It contains equipment Viktor would find useful for preserving and preparing organic components, specialized architecture originally designed to accommodate funeral rituals that incorporated esoteric elements, and positioning at significant junction of ley lines running beneath the city."

The location made tactical sense—isolated enough for secure operations while remaining accessible from central Daybridge, containing infrastructure useful for necromantic preparations while positioned at energetically significant location within the city's larger metaphysical landscape.

"We should move quickly," Ethan said, professional training automatically shifting toward operational planning. "Standard approach would be surveillance first, confirm occupancy before attempting entry, but time constraints might necessitate more direct action given Jake's value to Viktor's preparations and the approaching deadline."

Alice nodded. "Agreed. But we need to consider contingency for encountering Viktor himself—our previous confrontation at the foundry demonstrated conventional weapons have limited effectiveness against his capabilities."

"I can provide protective measures," Lila offered, indicating her silver rings. "Not offensive capabilities that would match Viktor directly, but defenses that might allow approach and extraction if Jake is indeed being held there. But we should be prepared for the possibility that this is diversion—attempt to separate our forces before the final confrontation at Blackwood Cemetery."

"We divide resources," Ethan decided. "Alice and I will investigate the funeral home with Lila's protective enhancements, while requesting Nadia Marsh coordinate preparation for Blackwood Cemetery through her academic contacts. Maintains progress toward both immediate objective and longer-term countermeasures."

As they prepared to depart—gathering equipment appropriate for reconnaissance while Lila enhanced their conventional weapons with protections against supernatural threat—the atmosphere in the back room had transformed from tense confrontation to focused collaboration.

The storm clouds continued gathering over Daybridge Cemetery, their unnatural configurations visible through the window. Thunder rolled across the darkening sky, a physical manifestation of metaphysical disruption that ordinary citizens might attribute to conventional weather patterns.

Lila paused at the doorway, her expression revealing momentary vulnerability beneath professional focus. "Thank you," she said quietly. "For listening. For understanding. For not..." She hesitated, searching for adequate articulation.

"For not judging based on partial information," Ethan supplied. "We all have histories we'd prefer to leave behind, decisions we'd make differently given a second chance. What matters is how we address consequences in present, not mistakes made in the past."

Alice's nod conveyed a similar understanding despite her more reserved expression. "Let's find Jake," she said simply. "Then we can worry about cosmic balance and dimensional integrity."

As they left Crossroads Books, stepping into an afternoon that had darkened prematurely under gathering storm clouds, their unlikely alliance felt stronger for truths finally acknowledged—partnership based on shared understanding rather than selective disclosure.

The cosmic chess game approached its conclusion, pieces positioned across Daybridge's transformed landscape for the final confrontation. And as they moved purposefully toward the abandoned funeral home, their combined determination suggested possibility of outcome beyond Viktor's carefully orchestrated design—human agency asserting itself against cosmic manipulation through choices made with full awareness rather than partial understanding.

CHAPTER THIRTEEN
VIGIL
ST. MICHAEL'S HOSPITAL

Two Weeks Before Present Day

The fluorescent lights cast harsh shadows in the ICU waiting room, their sterile illumination stripping away warmth and subtlety. The institutional beige walls and worn blue upholstery appeared washed out under the unforgiving glare, as if the room itself had been drained of vitality.

Detective Alice Chen sat beside a sleeping Jake Steinman; her case notes spread across her lap. Her methodical mind had sorted the information into patterns—victim profiles, ritual site configurations, timeline progressions—seeking logic in events that defied conventional explanation.

Through the observation window separating the waiting area from the ICU proper, she could see Lila Darkmagic standing motionless by the bed of their latest victim—a university student named Michael Hensley, found near the old Harrington Foundry three days ago, barely alive after what the official report described as "assault by unknown assailants" but what they recognized as attempted soul extraction through necromantic ritual.

The young man lay unnaturally still, his skin carrying the grayish pallor of someone caught between states—not merely between life and death in the conventional medical sense, but between dimensional aspects that conventional medicine had no framework to address. Monitoring equipment surrounded his bed, tracking vital signs that remained technically stable despite the profound energetic disruption his consciousness had suffered.

"She's been there for six hours," Reeves said, appearing with coffee in institutional paper cups. His voice carried quiet concern rather than judgment. "Hasn't moved. Barely blinks."

Alice accepted the offered cup with a nod of thanks, inhaling the mediocre coffee's aroma with appreciation born of necessity rather than quality. Her eyes remained on Lila's still form, observing details that most would miss—the precise positioning of her feet that aligned with specific points of the hospital room's geometry, the subtle tension in her shoulders that suggested active effort rather than mere observation.

"She's watching the shadows," Chen replied, indicating with a slight nod the darkness beneath the hospital bed and in corners of the room. "Look at her hands."

Lila's fingers moved in subtle patterns, complex configurations that changed in response to shifts in the room's lighting. Her silver rings caught the fluorescent light, occasionally seeming to retain illumination longer than physically possible. Around the student's bed, the shadows seemed different. More defined, less fluid. Contained rather than reaching, as if invisible boundaries had been established that limited their movement.

"Protection ward," a soft voice said from beside them. They turned to find Jake awake, his posture suggesting he had been conscious and listening for some time despite his closed eyes. "She's keeping the darkness from finishing what it started."

The bookshop owner's explanation carried weight beyond his words—knowledge accumulated through decades of studying esoteric phenomena and witnessing Lila's methods firsthand during their five-year association.

"Can she save him?" Chen asked, the question emerging despite her usual pragmatic focus on achievable outcomes.

"That's not how it works." Jake adjusted his glasses with a practiced movement. "She can't undo what was done. The extraction ritual Viktor's followers performed was incomplete—interrupted by campus security responding to noise complaints—but it still separated aspects of Michael's consciousness from his physical form. What Lila's doing isn't healing or restoration in the conventional sense."

He paused, seeking words for concepts that existed at the boundaries of language's descriptive capacity. "She can stand guard. Make sure nothing else is taken. Prevent further degradation while his system attempts to reintegrate what remains. Create a protected space where natural healing processes—both physical and metaphysical—have an opportunity to function without interference from forces that would exploit his vulnerable state."

Through the window, they watched Lila continue her silent vigil. Her lips moved occasionally, perhaps in prayer, perhaps in spells—the distinction less significant than the intention behind either approach.

"She does this every time," Jake continued, his tone suggesting both admiration and concern. "Every victim we find who still maintains physical life, regardless of their consciousness state. She stands guard until they either wake up or..."

"Or they don't," Reeves finished quietly, understanding the unspoken alternative and its implications not just for the victims but for Lila herself—each failure adding to the burden of responsibility she already carried from events three decades past.

The three of them observed in silence, each processing the scene through different frameworks of understanding.

"It's not guilt this time," Chen realized, articulating insight that had been forming. "Or not just guilt. It's defiance."

The distinction carried significance beyond semantic precision—suggesting evolution in Lila's approach to opposing Viktor's activities rather than merely atoning for past mistakes. Her vigil represented not just protection of individual victim but a direct challenge to the larger pattern Viktor sought to establish.

Jake nodded. "Every soul she prevents Viktor from claiming completely is a choice. A statement. 'Not this one. Not again.'"

The interpretation transformed their understanding of Lila's actions throughout their investigation—suggesting purposeful opposition rather than merely reactive response or atonement. Each intervention, each protective working, represented a deliberate counter-move in a cosmic chess game played across decades and continents.

In the ICU room, Lila's rings flared briefly with silver light, a momentary manifestation of power normally concealed. The student's breathing seemed to ease slightly, cardiac monitor showing marginal improvement in rhythmic stability—small changes perhaps, but significant given the metaphysical nature of the damage his system had suffered.

"How long will she stay?" Reeves asked, the question addressing practical concerns while acknowledging respect for Lila's commitment.

"Until the shadows retreat," Jake said with certainty born of having witnessed similar vigils. "Or until dawn, when natural energetic patterns shift enough to provide temporary protection without her direct intervention. Whichever comes first."

His explanation reflected understanding of both magical mechanics and Lila's personal determination—recognition that her protection wasn't merely a symbolic gesture, but a practical implementation of knowledge accumulated through decades of opposing Viktor's methodologies.

Chen gathered her notes with deliberate movements. "I'll get more coffee."

The simple statement carried meaning beyond its practical utility— commitment to maintaining their own form of vigil alongside Lila's more specialized protection. Recognition that sometimes support meant simply being present, witnessing and acknowledging effort that might otherwise go unobserved in a world focused on quantifiable outcomes.

Because sometimes, that's all you could do. Stand guard. Keep watch. Choose to stay when easier options presented themselves. Maintain presence against forces that thrived on isolation and despair. Small actions perhaps against cosmic threats, but significant in their cumulative effect and the statement they made about priorities and values.

Reeves nodded, understanding the underlying significance of Chen's apparently mundane offer. "I'll check in with the precinct, update Captain Donovan on Hensley's condition without specifying the nature of Lila's intervention." His own contribution to their collective vigil—managing institutional interfaces that allowed their unconventional investigation to continue with minimal interference.

And in the harsh fluorescent light of St. Michael's Hospital, four people held their own kinds of vigil, against shadows both seen and unseen. Each contributing according to their capabilities and understanding— Lila's direct magical intervention, Jake's contextual knowledge, Reeves' management of institutional relationships, Chen's analytical assessment and practical support.

Outside the hospital windows, night deepened over Daybridge, its darkness not merely an absence of sunlight but an active presence gaining strength as dimensional boundaries thinned with approaching Halloween. Streetlights created islands of illumination that seemed increasingly isolated, their reach diminishing as shadows between them grew more substantial.

Within those gathering shadows, forces accumulated that conventional citizens perceived only as vague unease or unsettling dreams— the compromised boundaries that allowed energies normally constrained beyond physical reality to seep gradually into Daybridge's atmosphere.

But in the ICU of St. Michael's Hospital, one room maintained boundaries against this incremental intrusion—protected space where a young student's consciousness might have an opportunity to reintegrate with the physical form from which it had been partially extracted.

As midnight approached, a subtle shift occurred in the quality of light within Michael Hensley's room. The shadows beneath the bed and in room corners seemed to pulse briefly, testing boundaries of protection Lila had established. Her hands moved in new configurations, rings glowing more visibly as she reinforced protections against intensified pressure—midnight representing natural peak in necromantic energies even without specific ritual enhancement.

For several minutes, a silent contest continued—pressure against protective boundaries, adjustments to maintain their integrity, subtle shifts in the room's energetic patterns as opposing forces sought advantage without direct confrontation.

Then, gradually, pressure receded—not defeated exactly but redirected toward less protected targets elsewhere in Daybridge's night-shrouded landscape. The shadows returned to more natural configurations, responding to physical light sources rather than extending beyond their expected boundaries.

Lila's hands stilled momentarily, her shoulders relaxing slightly as the immediate threat diminished. She didn't abandon her position—vigil would continue until dawn provided natural protection—but the intensity of her focus shifted from immediate defense to sustained maintenance.

"She did it," Jake said softly, satisfaction evident despite continued concern for both patient and practitioner. "Forced them to seek elsewhere for tonight at least."

Chen nodded, understanding significance beyond immediate protection. "Another piece removed from Viktor's board. Another soul denied to his working."

The assessment reflected her analytical approach—recognition that each successful protection represented not merely individual salvation but a strategic setback to Viktor's larger pattern. His methodology required specific components gathered according to a precise schedule, with replacements not easily obtained when targets proved inaccessible.

"It makes a difference," Reeves agreed, his connection to the nexus entity providing perspective beyond conventional understanding. "Each disruption forces adaptation, creates inefficiencies in his overall working. The pattern he's establishing throughout Daybridge depends on precise calibration between components—substitutions and improvisations reduce potential effectiveness."

The tactical assessment offered hope within seemingly overwhelming circumstances—suggestion that their accumulated interventions had a tangible impact on Viktor's capabilities even when they couldn't prevent his activities entirely.

As the night progressed toward dawn, their vigil continued—rotation established that allowed each brief respite while maintaining collective presence. Jake eventually dozed again in an uncomfortable waiting room chair, his exhaustion temporarily overcoming concern. Chen continued reviewing case notes, seeking patterns they might have overlooked. Reeves maintained communication with the precinct, managing official aspects of investigation.

And in Michael Hensley's room, Lila Darkmagic stood unmoving, her vigil unwavering despite physical fatigue that would have overwhelmed a less determined guardian. Her protection represented not merely opposition to Viktor's specific activities but a fundamental choice about reality's nature—rejection of perspective that viewed consciousness as merely a resource to be harvested for power rather than inherently valuable.

Dawn approached with a gradual shifting of night's energy patterns, a natural transition that provided a temporary reprieve from necromantic influences that thrived in darkness. As first light appeared on eastern horizon, Lila's posture changed slightly, recognition of approaching threshold when natural protections would temporarily supplement her established wards.

When sunlight finally reached Michael's room, Lila completed final adjustments to the protective configuration she had maintained throughout the night. Her hands moved in closing sequence, setting boundaries that would maintain integrity without her direct presence until she could return before sunset.

Only then did she turn from the bed, her movement careful as physical fatigue reasserted itself after hours of focused concentration. Her face showed strain, but her eyes held satisfaction that transcended exhaustion—recognition of meaningful achievement despite its temporary and limited nature.

As she exited the ICU room, rejoining the others in the waiting area, no words were immediately exchanged. None were necessary between people who had witnessed each other's commitment through night's darkest hours. Chen simply offered fresh coffee from the latest cafeteria run, while Reeves made space on the uncomfortable waiting room couch.

"He's stable for now," Lila said finally, accepting coffee with a grateful nod. "The protection should hold through daylight hours. I'll need to return before sunset to maintain it through another night cycle."

"I've arranged for his parents to arrive this afternoon," Chen informed her. "Their presence might help anchor his consciousness—emotional connection providing an additional pathway for reintegration beyond what magical protection can establish."

The consideration demonstrated Chen's evolving understanding—recognition that conventional relationships and emotional bonds might have practical significance beyond merely human comfort, potentially complementing magical interventions.

"Good thinking," Lila acknowledged, professional respect evident despite physical exhaustion. "Familiar connections can sometimes reach aspects of consciousness that more technical approaches can't access directly."

Jake stirred from his doze, rejoining conversation with an immediate grasp of its significance. "I'll coordinate with hospital staff, ensure the parents aren't separated from Michael during critical evening transition. Nadia Marsh has contacts in administration who can help arrange extended visiting hours if necessary."

Their collaborative planning reflected growing integration of diverse approaches to unconventional threat—magical protection, emotional connection, institutional navigation, analytical assessment all contributing to a comprehensive response rather than depending on a single methodology.

As morning fully established itself over Daybridge, temporarily pushing back shadows that had deepened throughout preceding weeks, they prepared to separate—each with specific responsibilities to address before reconvening later. Their collective vigil had resulted in not just protection of a single victim but strengthening of bonds between unlikely allies, connections that would prove crucial in the approaching confrontation at Blackwood Cemetery.

Lila paused at hospital exit, turning back with uncharacteristic openness. "Thank you," she said simply. "For understanding. For supporting. For seeing significance beyond what conventional perspectives would recognize."

The gratitude reflected evolution in her own approach—from solitary practitioner accustomed to working in isolation to a tentative acceptance of collaboration and shared responsibility.

"Partners," Chen replied with simple precision, the single word carrying multiple layers of meaning—professional relationship, shared purpose, mutual respect despite differing methodologies and backgrounds.

As they stepped out into morning sunlight, temporarily reprieved from darkness gathering throughout Daybridge, their unlikely alliance carried cautious hope alongside a realistic assessment of challenges still ahead. One successful vigil didn't alter the fundamental trajectory of approaching confrontation, but it demonstrated the possibility of meaningful resistance against forces that might otherwise seem overwhelming.

And somewhere in consciousness space not precisely mappable through conventional parameters, Michael Hensley's awareness began a tentative process of reintegration—opportunity made possible through protection established by a woman he had never met, maintained through night's darkest hours when other forces sought to complete what his interrupted ritual had begun.

One soul denied to Viktor's grand working. One piece removed from the cosmic chess board. One life potentially preserved through collective vigil against shadows both seen and unseen.

CHAPTER FOURTEEN
THREADS OF THE PAST
SIMMONS' APARTMENT

11:23 PM

The banker's box had sat in Simmons' closet for twenty-five years, labeled simply "Chapel Hill" in faded marker. The cardboard showed the wear of multiple moves—corners softened, edges frayed, a water stain on one side from the time his upstairs neighbor's pipe burst while he was working a double homicide on the south side. He'd never been able to throw it away, even during his darkest days when the bottle seemed like his only friend.

Detective Mark Simmons' apartment reflected his solitary lifestyle— functional furniture chosen for durability rather than style, walls bare except for a few framed commendations and his daughter's college graduation photo, kitchen showing evidence of someone who viewed cooking as necessary sustenance rather than pleasure. The space was meticulously clean in the way of someone whose external order compensated for internal chaos—surfaces free of dust, floors recently vacuumed, dishes washed and put away despite late hour and evident exhaustion.

Now, sitting at his kitchen table with case files from the Harrison grave robbery spread out in his characteristic methodical arrangement, he finally pulled the box down from the closet shelf. His hands betrayed momentary hesitation as they reached for the lid, muscle memory recalling the weight of failure and obsession the contents represented.

The rubber band holding the manila folder snapped with age when he attempted to remove it. Photos spilled across his table—crime scenes he'd memorized during countless sleepless nights, faces of victims he still saw in his dreams despite decades of distance. Julia Microft's senior photo smiled up at him, forever nineteen—bright eyes and confident expression capturing potential never realized, future abruptly terminated by forces he hadn't understood then and still struggled to fully comprehend.

His phone buzzed, screen illuminating with Rivera's name—his current partner checking in as she often did during late night research sessions that had become increasingly frequent since the Harrison grave robbery case began.

"Found something in the Harrison soil samples," she said without preamble when he answered. "Traces of some herb the lab can't identify, even with expanded toxicology screening. And there were markings in the dirt that—"

"Looked like interlocking circles?" Simmons was already pulling out an old evidence photo from the Chapel Hill file, heart rate accelerating as suspicion crystallized into certainty. "With something like backward letters between them? Almost runic but not matching any known historical alphabet?"

A pause on the line. "How did you know?"

He stared at the photo from '98—the same distinctive markings, drawn in chalk around Julia Microft's car where they'd found it abandoned in Chapel Hill Cemetery's southwestern parking area. The configuration was unmistakable despite decades separating the cases.

"Because I've seen them before." His voice carried weight of recognition that validated decades of uncertainty. "Remember that homeless man, the one we interviewed yesterday? The one who kept ranting about the Harrison grave and said something about 'they're doing it again'?"

"The guy you insisted we hold for questioning longer than the lieutenant thought necessary? What about him?"

Simmons pulled out a sketch from the Chapel Hill file—a symbol drawn by another homeless witness in '98, right before he disappeared from the shelter where officers had placed him for protection. The drawing showed the same distinctive configuration they'd found carved into the Harrison headstone last week.

"Back then, I thought he was just another witness—someone who had seen something relevant to the investigation and might provide useful testimony." Simmons' hands shook slightly as he lined up the photos from different decades. "But he wasn't just reporting observations. He was trying to warn us about what was happening. Just like the witness in '98 was trying to warn me about the Necrium before he disappeared."

"The what?" Rivera's question carried a mixture of professional curiosity and personal concern.

"A cult. Or at least, that's what I thought they were at the time." He pulled out his old notebook, leather cover cracked with age and pages yellowed. He flipped to pages of research he'd done between interviews—notes on historical occult practices, transcriptions from rare books, symbolic analyses that attempted to decode ritual configurations found at multiple sites.

"They believed in drawing power from the dead—not merely symbolic connection but actual energy transfer through specific ritual configurations and physical components harvested from deceased individuals with particular characteristics." His finger traced underlined passage where he had attempted to systematize apparent selection criteria. "I tracked them for months, identifying a pattern that connected multiple incidents across three counties. But everyone thought I was obsessed, seeing connections that weren't there. Then Julia disappeared, and..."

"And you got shot," Rivera finished softly, reference to official report that had documented his injury while investigating a lead at Chapel Hill Cemetery.

"That's what the report says." Simmons touched his shoulder unconsciously, fingers finding scar tissue through his shirt. "That's what I agreed to say in my statement after initial interviews went nowhere. But I never saw a gun. What I saw..." He trailed off, remembering darkness moving wrong, remembering voices that couldn't have been human.

"The old bookstore owner," he cut in, redirecting conversation toward immediately relevant connection. "Jake Steinman. The one I tried talking to today before discovering he's been missing for several days? Back in '98, he had books about the Necrium in his collection—restricted access volumes he showed me only after multiple visits established sufficient trust."

Simmons pulled another notebook from the box, this one containing information separate from official case documentation—research conducted through unofficial channels during periods when supervisors had directed him to pursue other investigations.

"He called them 'death merchants' in his historical materials. Said they appeared throughout history under different names and organizational structures but always with same fundamental methodology and purpose. Using specific rituals to... to trade with something that lived in the spaces between life and death. Entities that existed beyond conventional reality but could interact with the physical world through properly prepared intermediaries."

Silence on the line as Rivera processed information that challenged conventional investigative frameworks while potentially connecting their current case to a historical pattern.

"I didn't believe him," Simmons continued, admission carrying the weight of subsequent reconsideration. "Thought he was eccentric at best, delusional at worst—someone who had spent too much time with obscure texts until he could no longer distinguish scholarly analysis from supernatural fantasy. But look at this."

He pulled out an old newspaper clipping, carefully preserved despite yellowing paper. "Three months before Julia disappeared, there was another grave robbery at Hillside Cemetery in the next county. Same precise excavation methodology—soil removed in a specific pattern rather than merely piled aside. Same unknown herbal residue found in soil samples. Same symbols drawn in materials that didn't photograph well but were documented in field notes that were subsequently removed from official case file."

"Mark, what exactly are you saying?" Rivera's question focused potential implications for current investigation rather than historical reassessment.

He looked at the crime scene photos from the Harrison grave, then back at the files from '98, the similarities undeniable despite decades separating the incidents—precision suggesting methodology transmitted through direct teaching rather than independent reinvention.

"I'm saying I was right back then, just not in the way I thought. This isn't just about solving the Harrison case anymore or even connecting it to the current missing persons we've been investigating." His voice steadied as he articulated conclusion that integrated historical evidence with current investigation. "The Necrium is back, or maybe they never left. Maybe they've been operating continuously with periodic intensification of activity corresponding to specific astronomical alignments or dimensional thinning that Jake Steinman tried to explain to me twenty-five years ago before I was ready to understand."

He picked up Julia's photo again. "And this time..." His voice hardened with determination. "This time I'm going to stop them. Because now I know what we're really dealing with—not just human criminal activity, however organized or ritualistic, but an interface between conventional reality and forces existing beyond parameters we normally recognize."

"We," Rivera said firmly. "What we're dealing with. You're not alone this time, Mark."

The statement acknowledged both the isolation that had characterized his previous investigation and commitment to partnership that would prevent repetition of that damaging experience.

He smiled tiredly, expression visible to no one but conveying genuine appreciation through vocal tone. "No. But after what I've learned today about the connections between these cases and what they suggest about what's really happening in Daybridge, you might wish I was."

The comment wasn't self-pity, but a realistic assessment of potential professional risk associated with pursuit of explanation that extended beyond conventional criminal activity into territories institutional frameworks weren't designed to address.

Above his apartment, wind chimes jingled without a breeze—metal tubes creating a discordant melody that carried through the ceiling from the balcony of upstairs neighbor. Simmons glanced up, remembering Jake Steinman's warnings about signs and portents—subtle indicators of dimensional thinning that manifested through apparently natural phenomena occurring without conventional causation.

He'd dismissed them all back then, categorizing such perspectives as superstition incompatible with professional investigation based on evidence and logical analysis. The experiences at Chapel Hill Cemetery had begun shifting that perspective, but institutional pressure and his own psychological defenses had prevented full integration of those events into a coherent understanding.

He wouldn't make that mistake again. Wouldn't allow institutional skepticism or personal reluctance to prevent recognition of patterns that transcended conventional explanatory frameworks.

"I need to talk to Detectives Reeves and Chen," he said, decision crystallizing as connections between his historical case and current investigation solidified. "Their involvement with the missing persons cases connected to the Harrison grave desecration suggests they've been

tracking the same pattern from different angle. And their consultant—
the woman with the silver rings. There's something about her..."

He trailed off, remembering brief encounter in precinct hallway when
the woman had looked at him with an expression suggesting recognition beyond ordinary professional acknowledgment. Her gaze had
lingered on his shoulder where injury from Chapel Hill Cemetery had
left both physical scar and metaphysical marker.

"You think they know something about all this?" Rivera asked, professional curiosity engaged by potential investigative collaboration.

"I think they've been investigating the same pattern we're seeing, but
with different resources and possibly different understanding of what's
actually happening." Simmons began gathering essential materials
from both historical and current cases. "Reeves especially seems to
have connections beyond conventional law enforcement—his involvement in that strange case at Daybridge Bridge last year and subsequent
partnership with consultants whose expertise doesn't appear in any
official credentials."

"I'll set up a meeting for tomorrow morning," Rivera said, practical
implementation already following theoretical connection. "Assuming
you think this can wait until then? Or is there something we should be
doing tonight based on what you've discovered?"

Simmons considered the question with appropriate seriousness,
balancing urgency against practical limitations. "Morning should be
sufficient," he decided after reviewing current evidence regarding
timing and progression. "Based on both historical pattern and current
indicators, we're building toward something significant rather than
facing immediate culmination. And proper briefing with prepared
materials will be more effective than fragmented explanation without
supporting documentation."

Rivera acknowledged his assessment before ending call to make necessary arrangements, leaving Simmons alone with evidence spanning
twenty-five years of activity that had shaped Daybridge in ways most
citizens never recognized.

As he continued organizing materials for effective presentation to colleagues who might actually understand what he had been pursuing since Chapel Hill Cemetery changed his understanding of reality's parameters, the wind chimes above his apartment jingled again despite continued absence of natural air movement.

This time, he didn't dismiss the phenomenon as coincidence or seek a conventional explanation. Instead, he acknowledged it as potentially significant indicator—not through superstitious attribution of meaning to random occurrence but through recognition that patterns throughout Daybridge increasingly suggested thinning of boundaries between conventional reality and forces existing beyond parameters normally perceived.

The realization brought neither fear nor excitement, but focused determination based on professional responsibility and personal experience—commitment to addressing threat he had encountered before without adequate understanding or institutional support but now approached with both improved comprehension and potential allies.

As midnight approached and he completed organization of essential materials for morning briefing, Simmons felt the weight of twenty-five years lift slightly—not through the resolution of historical case but through validation that his pursuit hadn't been merely obsessive fixation or psychological compensation for traumatic experience. The pattern he had identified was real, continuing, and potentially approaching culmination that threatened Daybridge in ways most citizens couldn't comprehend.

But this time, he wasn't alone in recognizing what was happening. This time, connections between seemingly disparate events were being identified by multiple investigators approaching pattern from different perspectives with complementary expertise and resources.

As he finally allowed himself brief rest before morning meeting that might integrate his historical investigation with current developments, Simmons thought again of Julia Microft—not merely as a victim whose case remained unsolved but as an individual whose disappearance had initiated a journey leading to the current moment when resolution might finally become possible, not just for her case specifically but for the pattern of which it formed component.

Justice delayed wasn't necessarily justice denied, if pursuit continued despite institutional obstacles and conventional limitations.

～

CHAPTER FIFTEEN
ALICE'S TRUTH

Detective Ethan Reeves stood at the window of his cramped studio apartment, watching the dawn break over Daybridge like a bruise— the sky a mottled purple shot through with veins of angry red. The unnatural coloration wasn't merely meteorological but a reflection of dimensional thinning that had accelerated throughout the city.

He had been awake for hours, his mind churning with the events of the past few days—the confrontation with Viktor Kalishnikov at the abandoned Harrington Foundry, Lila's unexpected candor about their shared history in Prague, and Jake Steinman's continued absence despite their thorough search of the abandoned Mortensen Funeral Home.

But beneath these immediate tactical concerns lay deeper unease— awareness that the approaching confrontation represented more than merely another case or supernatural threat to be contained. The dimensional breach Viktor sought to establish at Blackwood Cemetery potentially threatened reality itself, not just Daybridge or its immediate surroundings but fundamental structures that maintained separation between ordered existence and chaos.

Even as he grappled with this weight, Ethan found his thoughts drifting to his partner, Alice Chen. She had been uncharacteristically quiet since their search of the funeral home had yielded evidence of Jake's temporary captivity but no direct trail to his current location. Her normally sharp analytical approach and incisive observations had been replaced by a brooding silence that set Ethan's nerves on edge.

He had tried to talk to her about it—had even suggested they take a brief break from the case to clear their heads. But Alice had brushed him off with a tight smile, insisting that she was fine and that they needed to stay focused on the task at hand.

With a heavy sigh, Ethan turned away from the window and grabbed his jacket from the back of a chair. He had a long day ahead—final coordination with Nadia Marsh regarding counter-ritual preparations for Blackwood Cemetery, follow-up on potential sightings of Jake reported overnight, and continued analysis of evidence recovered from the funeral home.

But first, he needed to check in with Alice—needed to address the unacknowledged tension that had developed and ensure that whatever personal concerns affected her would not compromise their coordinated response to the approaching confrontation.

As he stepped out into the hallway, the smell of stale cigarette smoke and cheap pine-scented cleaner assaulted his nostrils. His werewolf aspects registered the chemical compounds as potential threats before rational assessment categorized them as merely unpleasant.

Outside, the city was beginning to stir to life, though Ethan perceived underlying tension throughout Daybridge—subtle behavioral changes among pedestrians who moved with unconscious wariness, increased incidents of minor traffic accidents reflecting distraction and anxiety, even alterations in urban wildlife patterns as rats and pigeons responded to energetic disruptions invisible to conventional human perception.

When he arrived at the station, he found Alice already at her desk, her head bent over a stack of files and her brow furrowed in concentration.

The precinct hummed with early morning activity, yet Alice seemed isolated within this activity, focused so intently on materials before her that she created personal space through concentration alone.

She looked up as he approached, her dark eyes shadowed with exhaustion and something else that Ethan couldn't immediately identify despite his enhanced perception. The uncertainty itself represented a warning sign—their partnership typically characterized by mutual understanding that transcended verbal communication.

"Morning," he said, his voice rough with lack of sleep. "You been here long?"

Alice shrugged, her gaze sliding back to the papers with uncharacteristic avoidance. "A while. I couldn't sleep, so I figured I might as well get a head start on the day."

The explanation seemed reasonable on the surface but contained subtle wrongness that triggered Ethan's professional concern—combination of evasiveness regarding specific timeline, deflection from actual content of her early morning research, and physical indicators of stress that exceeded normal parameters.

"Alice," he said softly, his voice low enough to ensure privacy within busy precinct while conveying urgent concern. "What's going on with you? And don't tell me it's nothing—I know you better than that."

For a long moment, Alice was silent, her eyes fixed on the files as if they contained answers to questions she hadn't yet fully articulated. Her hands remained perfectly still on the documents—unusual for someone whose thinking process typically involved physical activity, whether rearranging materials or unconscious gestures that paralleled internal analytical progression.

Then, with a heavy sigh that seemed to release tension accumulated over hours or perhaps days, she looked up at him, her gaze filled with complex emotion that made Ethan's heart ache.

"It's about my past," she said at last, her voice barely above a whisper. "About why I became a cop in the first place."

The admission represented a significant shift from her typical compartmentalization between professional function and personal history—separation she had maintained even as their partnership evolved from a standard professional relationship into something that transcended conventional boundaries.

Ethan sat down on the edge of her desk; his attention focused entirely on his partner as she began to speak. He had always known that Alice had her secrets—had always sensed that her methodical approach and exceptional analytical capabilities reflected not merely natural talent but specific personal motivation that drove consistent excellence beyond ordinary professional dedication.

"When I was a kid," Alice began, her voice trembling slightly with emotion normally kept rigorously controlled, "my older sister disappeared. She was only sixteen at the time—a bright, beautiful girl with her whole life ahead of her. But one day, she just vanished without a trace."

Ethan felt a chill run down his spine at her words, his mind already racing with potential connections between this personal history and their current investigation. In a city like Daybridge, where supernatural phenomena operated alongside conventional reality and historical patterns often repeated with cosmic precision, such disappearance carried implications beyond an ordinary missing person's case.

"The police investigated, of course," Alice continued, her voice growing steadier as she transitioned from emotional acknowledgment to factual recounting. "But they never found any leads, never made any progress. It was as if she had simply vanished into thin air."

She paused, her eyes distant as she accessed memories normally kept carefully compartmentalized. "I was only ten years old at the time. But I remember the way it tore my family apart—the way my parents retreated into their own private hells of grief and despair, leaving me to fend for myself in a world that suddenly seemed so much darker and more dangerous than before."

Ethan reached out and took her hand, his fingers intertwining with hers in a gesture of silent support. He could feel the tension thrumming through her body like an electric current—years of buried pain and unresolved questions surfacing through deliberate choice rather than unwilling emergence.

"I never stopped looking for her," Alice said, her voice steadying as she connected past motivation to present professional identity. "Never stopped hoping that one day, I would find the answers that had eluded me for so long. That's why I became a cop—why I threw myself into this job with everything I had. I thought that if I could just solve enough cases, save enough lives, maybe I could make up for the one I couldn't save."

The explanation illuminated aspects of Alice's professional approach that had been apparent but never fully contextualized—her exceptional dedication to victim advocacy, her methodical thoroughness that sometimes extended beyond institutional requirements, her particular attention to cases involving disappearances or situations where conventional explanation seemed insufficient.

Ethan felt his heart ache for his partner, for the weight of unresolved loss and persistent questions she had carried throughout her professional development while maintaining exceptional performance standards.

"Alice," he said softly. "I'm so sorry. I had no idea."

She looked up at him then, her eyes shining with complex emotion that balanced vulnerability with continuing strength. "I never told anyone. Not even my own partners before you. I thought that if I could just keep it compartmentalized, keep it separate from my professional function, it would remain motivation without becoming limitation or distraction."

Ethan nodded understanding, recognizing pattern familiar from his own experience. "But something's changed," he observed, connecting her unusual behavior of recent days with this disclosure. "Something about our current investigation has brought this back in ways you can't compartmentalize."

For a long moment, they sat there in silence, the weight of shared understanding hanging between them while surrounding precinct continued its morning activities.

Then, with a deep breath that physically manifested her transition from disclosure to action, Alice squared her shoulders and looked him directly in the eye, her gaze filled with a fierce determination.

"I need to show you something," she said, her voice steady as she pulled a folder from beneath the stack of materials on her desk. "Something I found while searching through cold cases that might connect to Viktor's activities in Daybridge before his current operation began."

Alice opened the folder, revealing photographs and reports dating back twenty-five years—timeline that aligned with what Jake Steinman had identified as the previous cycle of dimensional thinning in Daybridge, a period that included Detective Simmons' still-unsolved Chapel Hill case and several other incidents officially classified as missing persons but containing anomalous elements.

"These disappearances follow a pattern similar to what we're seeing now," Alice explained, her analytical precision returning. "Young people with specific characteristics—unusual talents, heightened sensitivity, distinctive energy signatures according to witnesses with relevant perception capabilities. All vanished without conventional explanation, all during period approximately twenty-five years ago when dimensional thinning similar to the current situation affected Daybridge."

Ethan studied the materials with focused attention, noting details that would have seemed insignificant to investigators lacking their specialized knowledge. The pattern she had identified was subtle but undeniable once properly contextualized—sequence that suggested deliberate selection rather than random victimization, methodology consistent with what they now understood about Viktor's approach.

"And your sister?" he asked gently, recognizing connection implied but not explicitly stated.

Alice nodded, pulling additional document from back of folder—missing persons report filed twenty-five years earlier in a neighboring county, containing a photograph of a teenage girl whose resemblance to Alice was immediately apparent. "Sarah Chen, sixteen years old, last seen leaving afterschool program where she had been participating in advanced mathematics study group. No witnesses to actual disappearance, no body ever recovered, no conventional explanation ever established."

The photograph showed a bright-eyed young woman with evident intelligence in her expression and confidence in her posture—person of significant potential whose sudden absence would create not just personal tragedy for her family but genuine loss to the larger community.

"The timing aligns with Viktor's previous cycle of activity in this region," Alice continued, professional analysis providing structure for managing emotional content. "And Emily had characteristics consistent with other victims—mathematical talent beyond ordinary parameters, intuitive understanding of patterns that extended into territories conventional education couldn't adequately explain. The kind of perception Viktor seems to target specifically when gathering components for his dimensional workings."

Ethan considered the implications with careful attention to both investigative significance and personal impact on his partner. The connection Alice had established appeared valid from an investigative perspective, suggesting a legitimate avenue for further exploration rather than merely a personal fixation.

"This changes our approach," he acknowledged, respecting both the professional validity of her analysis and the personal significance. "Not fundamentally—Viktor still needs to be stopped regardless of historical context or specific victimology—but it adds a dimension we need to consider when planning our intervention at Blackwood Cemetery."

Alice nodded agreement, relief visible in her expression as her disclosure received professional validation alongside personal support. "I should have told you sooner," she admitted. "But I needed to verify the pattern before potentially compromising our objectivity with a personal connection that might not actually exist."

"I understand," Ethan assured her. "You needed sufficient evidence to establish legitimate investigative connection rather than merely personal association that might have appeared as projection rather than actual pattern recognition."

The acknowledgment accepted her professional reasoning while implicitly affirming that sufficient evidence now existed to justify incorporating this additional dimension into their approach.

"So, what now?" Alice asked, transitioning from disclosure and validation to practical planning. "How does this affect our approach to Halloween night and the counter-ritual we've been preparing with Lila and Nadia Marsh?"

Ethan considered the question with appropriate seriousness, balancing tactical considerations against ethical responsibilities. "The fundamental approach remains the same," he decided after careful consideration. "We still need to establish the counter-ritual at Blackwood Cemetery to prevent a dimensional breach and contain whatever forces Viktor has accumulated throughout his preparations."

He paused, acknowledging the additional dimension now integrated into their planning. "But we add a component specifically focused on identifying and potentially recovering any consciousness signatures Viktor has harvested throughout previous cycles—not just preventing future acquisitions but addressing historical extractions that might include your sister alongside other victims from previous manifestations."

The approach respected both the primary objective of preventing catastrophic dimensional breach and the legitimate secondary goal of potential recovery or resolution regarding historical victims—balance that acknowledged personal connection without allowing it to override larger responsibility.

Alice's expression reflected complex response to his proposed approach—gratitude for the inclusion of her personal concern within legitimate operational parameters alongside a realistic assessment of potential limitations. "You think it's possible?" she asked, hope tempered by a professional understanding of challenges involved. "To actually recover consciousness signatures extracted so long ago?"

"I don't know," Ethan answered honestly, respecting their partnership too deeply to offer false assurance. "But Lila's experience with Viktor's methodologies and Nadia Marsh's research into dimensional mechanics suggest a possibility worth pursuing through properly structured counter-ritual. Not guaranteed success but a legitimate approach based on established principles."

The assessment offered realistic hope without promising specific outcome that couldn't be guaranteed given the unprecedented nature of their planned intervention and fundamental uncertainty regarding the exact state of consciousness signatures extracted through Viktor's previous workings.

Alice nodded acceptance of this measured approach, her expression reflecting the integration of personal hope with professional realism. "Thank you," she said simply, words conveying multiple layers of appreciation—for his acceptance of her disclosure, for validation of her analytical connection, for incorporation of an additional dimension into their planned intervention.

"Partners," Ethan responded, the single word carrying weight beyond its surface simplicity—acknowledgment of a relationship that balanced professional functionality with personal support, that respected individual motivation while maintaining shared purpose.

As they prepared to continue their day's activities—meeting with Lila and Nadia Marsh to finalize preparations for Halloween night, coordinating with Detective Simmons regarding security parameters for Blackwood Cemetery, continuing search for Jake Steinman—their partnership felt strengthened rather than complicated by Alice's disclosure and its integration into their approaching confrontation with Viktor Kalishnikov.

The dawn continued brightening outside precinct windows, unnatural coloration gradually shifting toward more conventional daylight as sun rose higher above Daybridge's skyline. Within thirty-six hours, they would face final confrontation at Blackwood Cemetery—a dimensional breach potentially altering reality itself if their counter-ritual proved insufficient against forces Viktor had accumulated.

But they would face this challenge together—partnership enhanced rather than diminished by truths acknowledged and integrated rather than concealed or compartmentalized. And perhaps in confronting a cosmic threat that transcended conventional parameters, they might simultaneously address personal quest that had motivated Alice's professional journey from its beginning—resolution regarding sister's disappearance that had shaped her development without defining her identity or limiting her capability.

CHAPTER SIXTEEN
THE SIGIL BOOK

THE BLACK CAULDRON was a dingy little occult shop, hidden away in the heart of Daybridge's red-light district where neon signs advertising adult entertainment competed with the glow of streetlamps that needed replacing months ago. Unlike the polished metaphysical boutiques that had proliferated in the city's gentrified districts, The Black Cauldron made no concessions to mainstream accessibility or Instagram aesthetics. Its grimy windows and peeling paint hinted at the shady nature of its usual patrons—practitioners seeking components for workings that extended beyond white-light affirmations into territories where intent and consequence carried weight.

The shop occupied the ground floor of a narrow three-story building wedged between a pawnshop and a bar whose perpetually blinking "Open" sign created rhythmic red illumination across the cracked sidewalk. The structure dated back to Daybridge's industrial boom in the late nineteenth century, when this district had housed workers for nearby factories. Original architectural details remained visible beneath accumulated grime—ornate cornices, decorative brickwork, and windowsills whose intricate carvings contained symbols older than the building itself.

Detective Ethan Reeves and his partner, Alice Chen, stood outside the shop's entrance, their faces grim as they studied the faded sigils and arcane symbols that adorned the heavy wooden door. The markings weren't merely decorative but functional—a complex interlocking system of protective wards, ownership declarations, and customer advisories legible to those with eyes to see such things.

"Are you sure about this?" Alice asked, her voice tight with tension. Her hand unconsciously moved toward her service weapon. "Lila's not exactly known for her trustworthiness. This could be another manipulation, drawing us away from more productive lines of investigation when we have less than thirty hours before Viktor's working at Blackwood Cemetery."

The concern was legitimate—their consultant's selective disclosure of information had complicated their response to developing threats, while her personal connection to Viktor introduced a potential conflict of interest that couldn't be dismissed despite her apparent opposition to his activities.

Ethan nodded, his jaw clenched with determination as he reached for the door handle. "I know," he said, his voice low. "But right now, she's the only lead we've got. If anyone can help us decipher Viktor's ritual and identify potential vulnerabilities in his approach, it's her."

His hand completed a gesture that was simultaneously physical and energetic—turning the handle while unconsciously projecting intent recognized by the door's embedded wards as a legitimate request for entry. The response was immediate—subtle shift in resistance followed by yielding that allowed access without triggering defensive measures.

With a deep breath, he pushed open the door and stepped inside. The musty scent of old books and dried herbs hit him like a physical blow —not merely olfactory input but information-dense communication conveying history and purpose of the establishment through chemical signatures that bypassed conscious processing.

Beyond mere smell, the atmosphere carried a subtle energetic charge that registered through his enhanced perception as complex interplay between various components stored within—materials gathered from locations throughout the world, preserved through methods that maintained their essential properties while preventing unintended interactions.

The shop was dimly lit, the only illumination coming from a handful of flickering candles strategically positioned and the eerie blue-green glow of a crystal formation that sat on a central display table—not a conventional crystal ball of popular imagination but a geological specimen whose natural configuration created unusual resonance patterns with surrounding energetic fields.

As his eyes adjusted to the gloom—process enhanced by his lycanthropic nature—Ethan saw Lila emerge from the back room, her raven hair gleaming in the candlelight and her emerald eyes carrying subtle silver flecks that manifested when she operated in spaces aligned with her magical orientation.

"Well, well," she purred, her voice carrying a mixture of genuine amusement and deliberately constructed persona. "Look what the cat dragged in. Daybridge's finest, seeking wisdom in territories they normally avoid until circumstance forces their hand."

Ethan ignored her theatrical presentation; his gaze fixed on the ancient tome she held—leather-bound volume whose physical characteristics suggested significant age while its energetic signature communicated contents extending beyond conventional textual information into territories where knowledge itself carried power independent of the reader's understanding or intention.

"Is that it?" he asked, his voice tight with anticipation. "The sigil book you mentioned at Crossroads Books? The one containing Viktor's methodological foundations?"

Lila nodded, a smile playing at her lips as she held out the book with a gesture that simultaneously offered access while establishing conditions—presentation rather than surrender, temporary lending rather than permanent transfer.

"It is," she said, her voice shifting from theatrical greeting to more authentic engagement. "The Liber Signorum, compiled in the sixteenth century by practitioners who sought to systematize approaches to dimensional interface that had previously been transmitted through oral tradition or fragmentary manuscripts. But be warned, Detective— the knowledge contained within these pages is not merely academic documentation of historical practices. It represents an active methodology that responds to attention and intention regardless of reader's preparation."

The caution wasn't merely dramatic flourish but practical warning regarding material whose nature transcended ordinary textual information. Unlike conventional books that remained inert regardless of reader's engagement, certain texts contained knowledge specifically designed to influence consciousness through mechanisms operating beyond mere intellectual comprehension.

Ethan took the book from her, his fingers registering slight resistance before complete transfer—not merely physical weight but subtle energetic response as the tome's embedded protections assessed his nature and intent before permitting full access to its contents. The cover was made of ancient leather, the once-vibrant colors faded to mottled brown. Strange symbols and glyphs were etched into its surface— protection against unauthorized access, preservation of internal contents against environmental degradation, and specific keying to lineages of practitioners authorized to utilize information contained within.

As he opened the book, a wave of dizziness washed over him—not merely psychological response but an actual physiological reaction to energetic fields embedded within the text's physical structure. The musty scent of the pages mingled with a sharp metallic tang that registered through his enhanced senses as a marker of specific binding methods used in the book's creation.

He felt Alice's hand on his arm, steadying him as he fought to maintain equilibrium between ordinary perception and enhanced awareness triggered by his contact with the book. Her touch provided grounding through human connection—reminder of their shared purpose and professional identity that helped resist the tome's natural tendency to overwhelm consciousness unprepared for its form of information transmission.

"Are you okay?" she asked, her voice filled with concern that transcended professional partnership.

Ethan nodded, his jaw clenched with determination as he focused on the pages before him. The text was written in multiple languages—sections in Latin and Greek interspersed with passages in scripts he didn't immediately recognize, annotations in what appeared to be early German, and diagrams whose geometric precision conveyed information independent of accompanying textual explanation.

But as he studied the content, he felt a strange sensation of recognition despite never having formally studied most of the languages presented —comprehension emerging not through conventional linguistic knowledge but through his connection to the nexus entity beneath Daybridge Bridge, which provided access to patterns and meanings beyond his personal education or experience.

"I can read it," he said, his voice filled with wonder at unexpected capability. "I don't know how, but I can understand what it says—not word-for-word translation but essential meaning and functional implications of the methodologies described."

Lila's eyes widened, a flicker of genuine surprise crossing her face before she quickly reasserted professional composure. "Well, well," she murmured. "It seems the nexus integration has progressed further than we anticipated. Your connection to Daybridge's dimensional intersection point is providing access to knowledge frameworks beyond conventional human perception or linguistic capability."

The observation contained neither judgment nor immediate concern but a professional assessment of developing capability that might prove relevant to their approaching confrontation with Viktor at Blackwood Cemetery.

Ethan acknowledged her assessment with a brief nod while maintaining focus on the text before him. As he continued examining the book's contents, he felt a growing sense of unease—visceral response to information structured specifically to create pathways between ordinary consciousness and dimensions existing beyond conventional perception.

The book contained systematic documentation of sigil construction and application across multiple magical traditions—not merely symbolic representation but detailed technical methodology for creating configurations that functioned as interfaces between physical reality and energetic patterns existing beyond conventional dimensional boundaries.

He reached the section containing description of specific sigil configuration they had discovered at multiple crime scenes throughout Daybridge—the distinctive arrangement found carved into the Harrison headstone, drawn in specialized materials at the foundry ritual site, and incorporated into patterns left at locations where Viktor's followers had performed soul-extraction rituals. The book identified this as "Khavisor Configuration"—described not as Viktor's personal innovation but as an adaptation of methodology documented centuries earlier, modified to accommodate specific objectives related to dimensional breach and consciousness transfer.

As he studied the technical description accompanying detailed diagram, Ethan felt a chill run down his spine—recognition that Viktor's activities throughout Daybridge represented the implementation of established methodology rather than merely personal experimentation or improvised approach. The systematic nature of the working, its precise geometric configuration and specific component requirements, suggested preparation extending beyond recent months into decades of research and development.

"This explains the precision of his ritual sites," Ethan said, looking up to meet Lila's gaze directly. "He's not improvising or developing new methodology—he's implementing an established approach documented centuries ago but adapted for specific application related to consciousness retrieval and dimensional breach stabilization."

Lila nodded. "Viktor was always methodical—brilliant innovator certainly, but one who built upon established foundations rather than attempting to create entirely new approaches without reference to historical precedent. His work in Prague represented adaptation rather than pure innovation—application of principles documented in texts like this one to a specific situation involving Sarah's consciousness and our attempt to preserve it beyond physical deterioration."

"According to this," Ethan continued, indicating the specific passage describing the Khavisor Configuration's purpose and implementation requirements, "the final working requires precise alignment of previously established components—ritual sites activated in a specific sequence, energetic signatures harvested from selected individuals, physical materials gathered according to particular criteria. The geometric arrangement throughout Daybridge isn't merely symbolic but functional—creating a network that channels and amplifies energies toward a central focus point where dimensional breach can be stabilized beyond temporary manifestation."

Alice leaned closer, studying the diagram with focused attention despite inability to read accompanying text directly. Her analytical skills allowed recognition of patterns and relationships even without complete comprehension of the theoretical framework.

"That's consistent with what we've observed," she confirmed. "Each ritual site Viktor has activated throughout Daybridge shows evidence of energy transfer toward a central location—Blackwood Cemetery based on both geographic positioning and historical significance. The pattern suggests a culmination requiring all previously established components functioning in coordinated configuration rather than merely sequential activation of independent workings."

The assessment aligned with what Nadia Marsh had identified through historical research into similar manifestations throughout Daybridge's history—pattern repeating approximately every twenty-five years with variations reflecting available knowledge and specific practitioner objectives during each cycle.

"The final component involves Blackwood Cemetery's chapel," Ethan said, turning to a section describing optimal conditions for stabilizing a permanent dimensional breach. "Its architecture was deliberately designed to enhance certain forms of energy channeling—not through conscious intention of the original architects but through influence exerted during the construction process by entities interested in facilitating future dimensional interface at that location."

The information confirmed what Jake Steinman had suggested during their planning session at Crossroads Books—that Blackwood Cemetery's unique position within Daybridge's energetic landscape represented not merely coincidental alignment but deliberate positioning established through historical processes extending beyond conventional understanding of the city's development.

As implications crystallized regarding both Viktor's methodology and approaching culmination at Blackwood Cemetery, Ethan felt an urgent need to incorporate this information into their counter-ritual preparations—adjustments to the approach they had developed with Nadia Marsh that would account for specific vulnerabilities now identified within Viktor's established pattern.

"We need to go," he said, his voice tight with urgency as he closed the book while maintaining careful control over its influence on his consciousness. "Nadia Marsh needs to see this before finalizing our counter-ritual design for Halloween night."

Alice nodded, her own face reflecting professional concern regarding timeline implications. With less than thirty hours remaining before optimal conditions for Viktor's final working, efficient integration of new information into their preparation process represented a critical priority.

As they prepared to leave the shop, Lila moved to intercept them—not through hostile action but deliberate positioning that established a moment for important clarification before they departed with the valuable resource. "There's something you should understand before taking the book," she said, her tone serious. "The Liber Signorum isn't merely an information source but an active interface—material specifically designed to create pathways between a reader's consciousness and dimensional spaces documented within its pages. Prolonged exposure without appropriate preparation or protective measures can result in unintended influence or unwanted attention from entities perceiving access through established connections."

The warning wasn't an attempt to prevent their use of the resource but practical caution regarding appropriate handling of material whose nature transcended ordinary textual documentation or historical artifact.

"I understand," Ethan acknowledged, recognition of risk balanced against necessity of accessing information critical to addressing imminent threat. "I'll maintain appropriate boundaries and limit exposure to essential information gathering rather than extended study or experimentation."

Lila studied him briefly, professional assessment rather than merely theatrical performance. What she observed apparently satisfied her concerns, as she nodded without further attempt to qualify or restrict their access to the book.

"Very well," she said, stepping aside to allow their departure. "But remember—knowledge without understanding is merely information; understanding without wisdom is merely capability; wisdom without compassion is merely power divorced from purpose."

The statement wasn't merely philosophical platitude but practical warning regarding the relationship between information contained within the book and its potential application in approaching confrontation with Viktor—reminder that effective opposition required not merely technical capability but an appropriate framework for applying that capability toward constructive rather than merely destructive outcome.

As they left The Black Cauldron, returning to Daybridge's neon-lit streets with the valuable resource secured for integration into their counter-ritual preparations, Ethan felt a momentary shift in the surrounding atmosphere—subtle alteration in ambient energetic patterns suggesting a response to their acquisition of a significant knowledge component relevant to the approaching confrontation at Blackwood Cemetery.

The sensation reinforced urgency of their mission while simultaneously suggesting possibility not previously apparent—that predetermined patterns might be subject to alteration through appropriate intervention based on sufficient understanding and properly applied methodology.

As they moved quickly toward their vehicle, Ethan maintained careful awareness of both physical surroundings and subtle energetic patterns permeating Daybridge's urban landscape. The city felt increasingly charged with anticipatory energy—ordinary citizens unconsciously responding to dimensional thinning they couldn't consciously perceive but nonetheless influenced their emotional states and behavioral patterns.

"Straight to Nadia Marsh?" Alice asked as they reached their vehicle, professional focus immediately transitioning from acquisition to application.

Ethan nodded, carefully securing the Liber Signorum in a specialized container they had brought for this purpose—protective case lined with materials designed to minimize energetic emissions while preventing unauthorized access or environmental damage during transport.

"She's coordinating final preparations with the team at Blackwood Cemetery—establishing the foundation for counter-ritual we'll implement tomorrow night when Viktor attempts his final working."

The plan they had developed with Nadia Marsh involved a complex integration of multiple approaches—conventional security parameters established through Detective Simmons' coordination with departmental resources, specialized protective measures designed by Lila, historical context provided by Nadia Marsh's research, and unique capabilities contributed by Ethan's connection to the nexus entity and Alice's analytical framework.

As they drove through Daybridge's increasingly unsettled atmosphere toward their rendezvous with Nadia Marsh at Blackwood Cemetery, Ethan felt a momentary connection with the larger pattern extending beyond their immediate investigation—sense of participation in a cosmic cycle that had manifested repeatedly throughout human history, with current iteration representing particularly significant manifestation due to unique conditions created by previous dimensional disruption beneath Daybridge Bridge and Viktor's sophisticated adaptation of historical methodology.

The Liber Signorum represented the critical component in their preparation—not merely an information source but a practical methodology for addressing the specific approach Viktor had implemented throughout his systematic activation of ritual sites throughout Daybridge.

As Blackwood Cemetery appeared on the horizon—Gothic revival chapel silhouetted against unnaturally colored sky—Ethan felt simultaneous apprehension regarding approaching confrontation and determination to implement an effective response based on knowledge now available through resources they had accumulated throughout their investigation.

The final confrontation approached with cosmic inevitability shaped by cycles extending beyond individual lifetimes—pattern established through previous manifestations but not necessarily predetermined in outcome or implications. And as they approached the location where this cosmic drama would reach culmination less than thirty hours hence, Ethan and Alice carried not merely professional responsibility as Daybridge's law enforcement representatives but larger obligation as conscious participants in a pattern whose resolution would determine far more than merely local stability or individual fate.

CHAPTER SEVENTEEN
LESSONS IN POWER
PRAGUE, 1987

CHARLES UNIVERSITY - Hidden Archives

"Again."

The word hung in the musty air of the underground chamber. The space had once been part of the university's medieval foundation, its existence deliberately obscured during renovations, accessible only through concealed maintenance corridors.

Lila's hands shook as she traced the sigil in the air, silver light trailing from her fingertips. The rat in the bronze circle stirred weakly, its life force flickering like a candle in a draft.

"You're hesitating," Viktor said softly. He stood behind her, close enough that she could feel the unnatural coolness radiating from his body. "Death is a doorway, little shadow. Not an ending. Your hesitation comes from misunderstanding its fundamental nature."

His pet name for her—"little shadow," a reference to her ability to perceive darkness beyond ordinary absence of light—carried complicated emotional resonance. Affection certainly, but also a reminder of the power differential between them.

"I can't—" The sigil wavered as her concentration faltered. The rat shuddered in response, its existence flickering as the partially formed interface destabilized.

"Death is a doorway," she whispered, accepting the principle as the sigil reformed.

The sigil blazed as her intention aligned with method. The rat convulsed, stopped breathing. After a moment of perfect stillness, its eyes opened, glowing silver.

"Beautiful," Viktor murmured. "Now hold it."

Sweat beaded on Lila's forehead as she maintained the connection. The rat stood, its movements jerky but purposeful—responding to her direction rather than merely twitching. Not just reanimation—true necromancy. Control of consciousness separated from its original physical form.

"Good." His lips brushed her ear. "Now reach deeper."

She felt it then—the current beneath death's surface. A vast, cold river of power flowing through a dimensional intersection normally inaccessible to human consciousness. Not merely abstract energy but potential waiting to be shaped according to will...

The rat's form began to change, bones cracking and reforming as its physical structure realigned according to patterns transmitted through the expanded interface.

"Viktor—" Fear crept into her voice as the manifestation exceeded her anticipated outcome.

"Don't stop." His grip tightened.

The rat was something else now, something wrong by conventional standards. Its shadow writhed independently on the floor, no longer bound by the conventional relationship between a physical object and light.

"I don't—" Blood trickled from her nose, a physical manifestation of the stress. "This isn't what we planned."

"Plans change." There was an edge to his voice now, a hunger she'd been trying to ignore. "We can do so much more than we initially imagined. Think of it, little shadow. No more death. No more loss. Everything under our control."

The thing that had been a rat screamed with a human voice—sound impossible from its original vocal apparatus.

Lila was wrenched away by some external force—intervention by an observer previously unmentioned but obviously present within the chamber. The sigil shattered, and the connection between dimensions abruptly terminated. The creature collapsed, melting into shadow that briefly maintained autonomous movement before dissipating.

"You're not ready." Disappointment colored Viktor's words as he addressed a figure emerging from the chamber's shadows—an older woman whose appearance suggested Eastern European ancestry.

"That wasn't necromancy," Lila wiped blood from her nose, her hand trembling. "That was... something else. Something beyond our stated objectives."

"That was power." Viktor turned to the ancient grimoire on the lectern, pages rustling without wind.

His laugh was soft, almost gentle. "And that's why you'll never be strong enough alone." He touched her cheek, his fingers colder than before. "But together? We could reshape death itself. No more barriers. No more rules."

She leaned into his touch, hating herself for responding positively to a connection she intellectually recognized as potentially destructive. "The soul bond ritual..."

"Tonight." His eyes gleamed with something that might have been love, might have been madness. "Under the dark moon. Then nothing can stop us from achieving what we've worked toward all these months."

The older woman melted back into shadows without comment or

intervention beyond her initial termination of the dangerous connection.

Later, Lila would remember this moment—the last chance to walk away before commitment to a path that would transform both partici- pants in ways neither fully anticipated. The pivotal decision point where the possibility of an alternative approach remained available before subsequent events foreclosed options through consequences neither could have predicted.

"Nothing can stop us," she echoed, and sealed both their fates.

CHAPTER EIGHTEEN
PRESENT DAY
CROSSROADS BOOKS, BACK ROOM

"LILA?" Detective Chen's voice snapped her back from memories that felt simultaneously distant and immediate. "You were saying about Prague? About what happened after the ritual went wrong?"

The back room of Crossroads Books had become their impromptu headquarters—Jake Steinman's absence leaving the space available while protective measures he had established throughout the building provided security against both conventional surveillance and meta-physical monitoring.

Rain drummed steadily against the windows, providing background rhythm to their conversation. Weather patterns throughout Daybridge increasingly responded to metaphysical processes as dimensional boundaries continued thinning with Halloween's approach.

Lila touched the silver ring on her left hand—the one that had once been gold, before that night changed everything. "Yes. Prague." She forced a smile that conveyed resignation rather than amusement. "Where a young woman thought she could master death without being mastered by it."

"And Viktor?" Detective Reeves asked, his transformed nature providing intuitive recognition of connections between historical events and current manifestations. "What happened to him in the ritual? How did he become what we encountered at the foundry?"

"The same thing that happened to me." She turned to the window, where storm clouds gathered in configurations that defied conventional meteorological explanation. "We got exactly what we wanted. And it destroyed us both."

Thunder rolled across Daybridge's landscape, sound carrying harmonic properties beyond ordinary acoustic phenomena. In the distance, cemetery bells tolled without human intervention—physical manifestation of dimensional thinning.

"But that's not the whole story, is it?" Alice pressed gently, her professional experience with traumatized witnesses allowing recognition of narrative gaps representing not deliberate deception but psychological protection.

"No." Lila's reflection in the window momentarily showed a superimposition of her younger self—image from three decades earlier when ambition and grief had overridden caution. "The worst part isn't what the ritual did to us."

She turned back to the detectives, her eyes ancient with accumulated guilt. "It's what I did after. When I realized what he'd become—what we'd become—and chose to..."

She stopped abruptly, head tilting as if listening to something only she could hear. Her rings glowed faintly, a physical manifestation of energetic response to dimensional fluctuations.

"He's starting." Her voice carried a quality of simultaneous presence and distance. "Can you feel it? The doorway opening?"

Above Daybridge Cemetery, storm clouds began to spin in a configuration that conventional meteorology could neither predict nor explain—atmospheric manifestation of energetic patterns responding to Viktor's preliminary activation.

Ethan nodded grimly. "Yes. The dimensional thinning is accelerating. It's not just a natural progression toward Halloween anymore—he's actively enhancing the process."

"Timeline implications?" Alice asked, professional focus immediately identifying practical significance.

"He's moving faster than anticipated," Lila confirmed, gathering herself with visible effort. "Not yet the final ritual—that still requires specific astronomical alignment at midnight tomorrow—but preparatory conditioning that establishes optimal environmental parameters."

"We need to accelerate our own preparations," Ethan concluded. "Nadia Marsh should be informed about this development—it may affect the counter-ritual design we've been developing based on information from the Liber Signorum."

"I should go to Blackwood Cemetery," Lila said, decision crystallizing. "Not direct intervention yet—that would likely accelerate his timeline rather than disrupting his methodology—but closer observation that might provide additional tactical information."

"Not alone," Alice stated firmly. "Your connection to Viktor provides valuable perceptual framework, but it also represents a potential liability if proximity intensifies influence or triggers an emotional response."

"I'll go with her," Ethan volunteered. "My connection to the nexus entity provides an independent perceptual framework that might identify aspects invisible to Lila through her personal history with Viktor."

Alice nodded agreement. "I'll continue working with Nadia Marsh to integrate information from the Liber Signorum into our counter-ritual configuration. The Khavisor Containment Method seems particularly relevant given what we've observed."

"Be careful," Alice said as Ethan and Lila prepared to depart. "Observation only—no direct engagement unless absolutely necessary for immediate survival or prevention of catastrophic escalation."

"Understood," Ethan acknowledged. "Reconnaissance only—information gathering toward effective implementation of counter-ritual rather than preliminary confrontation."

Lila nodded agreement. "The soul bond provides perceptual advantage without necessarily enabling direct influence in either direction— observation without immediate vulnerability to manipulation."

As they departed Crossroads Books, stepping into Daybridge's rain-soaked streets beneath unnaturally configured storm clouds, their unlikely alliance represented evolution beyond initial awkward cooperation into a genuine partnership based on shared purpose despite differing backgrounds.

The cosmic chess game approached its conclusion, pieces positioned across Daybridge's transformed landscape for a final confrontation that would determine not just individual fates but potentially reality's fundamental structure.

CHAPTER NINETEEN
UNEASY ALLIANCES

THE BLOODY CHALICE WAS A DARK, smoky bar nestled in the heart of Daybridge's supernatural underworld. From street level, it appeared as merely another anonymous door between a pawnshop and vacant storefront, its worn brass plaque bearing no name or indication of the business within.

The air was thick with the scent of stale beer and clove cigarettes. The walls were adorned with occult symbols and grotesque taxidermy—decorative elements that simultaneously served as territorial markers and protective wards.

It was a place where the city's various supernatural communities could mingle and conduct business away from prying eyes—a neutral ground where ancient grudges were temporarily set aside in the name of commerce and politics.

Detective Ethan Reeves and his partner, Alice Chen, stood at the entrance, their expressions grim as they surveyed the room. They had come here at Nadia Marsh's suggestion—her historical research indicating previous manifestations of dimensional thinning had occasionally been addressed through collaborative effort between otherwise antagonistic supernatural factions.

Their objective was ambitious but potentially essential—to seek allies against Viktor Kalishnikov by persuading Daybridge's established supernatural powers to temporarily unite against a common threat that endangered all realities connected through the city's unique position as a dimensional nexus point.

At the center of this complex social ecosystem sat a figure immediately recognizable despite Ethan having encountered him only twice previously. Alexei Volkov presented as a tall, elegantly dressed individual whose physical appearance suggested Eastern European ancestry combined with subtle indications of vampiric modifications. His skin carried the pallor characteristic of his kind without crossing into parody.

As leader of the city's vampire community—or more accurately, coordinating representative for multiple vampire lineages maintaining uneasy cooperation—Alexei had accumulated political influence, financial resources, and territorial authority.

As Ethan and Alice approached his table, Alexei looked up with an expression suggesting their arrival represented expected development rather than an unanticipated intrusion. "Detectives," he acknowledged, his voice carrying an accent acquired during formative years in pre-revolutionary Russia. "Your arrival suggests developments beyond ordinary jurisdictional parameters. What brings representatives of conventional law enforcement to a territory where your institutional authority holds limited application?"

Ethan maintained direct eye contact while avoiding the specific intensity that vampires might interpret as a challenge. "We appreciate your willingness to meet with us, Mr. Volkov. Recent developments throughout Daybridge suggest an approaching crisis that potentially affects multiple communities regardless of species designation or territorial boundaries."

"Viktor Kalishnikov has been systematically activating ritual sites throughout Daybridge," Alice continued. "The pattern suggests a final working scheduled for Halloween night at Blackwood Cemetery—a dimensional breach potentially affecting stability throughout the metaphysical framework underlying Daybridge's unique position as a nexus point."

Alexei's expression shifted subtly. "Kalishnikov," he repeated, pronunciation reflecting familiarity with the linguistic origin. "The necromancer from Prague. Rumors suggested his activities had shifted westward in recent decades, though specific confirmation had proven elusive."

"Our intelligence suggests he's implementing the Khavisor Configuration," Ethan continued. "Historical precedent indicates the potential for a permanent breach rather than merely a temporary connection between realities."

Alexei remained silent momentarily, fingers steepled. "The Khavisor Configuration," he finally acknowledged. "Not encountered directly since Vienna in 1862. Significant complications resulted from even partial implementation under considerably less favorable conditions than current alignment presents."

"We have developed a counter-ritual designed to address dimensional instability," Alice explained. "Nadia Marsh's historical research combined with specialized expertise from a consultant familiar with Viktor's specific methodologies has provided a framework for an approach potentially capable of restoring dimensional balance."

"However," Ethan continued, "optimal effectiveness would require participation from representatives of Daybridge's various metaphysical traditions—each contributing specific energetic signatures and operational methodologies that would collectively address dimensional instability more effectively than any single approach."

Alexei's expression remained carefully neutral. "Your approach demonstrates unusual sophistication for representatives of conventional law enforcement. This suggests either remarkable adaptation to extraordinary circumstances or assistance from sources not explicitly identified within your initial presentation."

"Recent events have required evolution in our investigative methodology," Ethan acknowledged. "Detective Reeves' connection to the nexus entity beneath Daybridge Bridge provides certain perceptual advantages, while departmental reorganization following events last winter has established a specialized unit addressing situations extending beyond conventional parameters."

"Fascinating," Alexei responded, genuine interest evident beneath his carefully maintained professional demeanor. "Such adaptation suggests potential for a more productive relationship between conventional governance structures and supernatural communities than historical precedent might indicate. This represents a potential advantage extending beyond merely current crisis response."

"However," Alexei continued, "effective participation would require coordination beyond merely my personal agreement or factional commitment. The nature of dimensional stability affects multiple communities with different priorities and historical relationships that cannot simply be overridden through executive decision."

"We understand," Alice acknowledged. "Our proposal involves presentation to representatives from multiple communities rather than merely requesting unilateral commitment from any single faction."

"What you propose is unprecedented in recent cycles," Alexei observed. "The last such gathering occurred during dimensional fluctuations of 1923, establishing Accords that continue governing interactions between supernatural communities despite subsequent modifications."

"I will facilitate preliminary discussions with key representatives," Alexei decided. "Midnight gathering at the Obsidian Chamber— neutral territory beyond even this establishment's protected status, accessible only through specific invitation and appropriate escort ensuring both physical security and metaphysical confidentiality."

"Thank you," Ethan acknowledged, sincere appreciation without unnecessary effusiveness. "Your assistance represents an important component in developing an effective response to a situation potentially affecting multiple communities."

"One question remains," Alexei said as they prepared to depart. "The necromancer's consultant—the woman with silver rings. Her connection to Viktor Kalishnikov extends beyond merely professional opposition or academic interest. This relationship potentially influences your counter-ritual design in ways not explicitly addressed."

"Lila Darkmagic's personal history with Viktor provides valuable insight regarding his specific methodologies and potential vulnerabilities," Alice acknowledged. "The soul bond established during the Prague incident creates both perceptual advantage regarding his current activities and potential complications during direct confrontation that have been incorporated into our counter-ritual design."

Alexei nodded. "Midnight. The Obsidian Chamber. Representatives from key factions will be present, though I cannot guarantee universal participation or unanimous agreement regarding proposed collaboration."

As Ethan and Alice departed the Bloody Chalice, returning to Daybridge's rainy streets, they carried cautious optimism regarding a potential alliance that might significantly enhance their counter-ritual effectiveness without unrealistic expectations regarding universal cooperation.

The cosmic chess game continued advancing toward a final confrontation, but potential participation from representatives of Daybridge's various supernatural communities suggested possibilities not previously apparent within their planning framework—a collective response potentially more effective than merely the sum of individual contributions.

∾

CHAPTER TWENTY
CONVERGENCE

STORM CLOUDS GATHERED above Daybridge as night fell, their unnaturally geometric formations visible even to ordinary citizens who attributed them to conventional weather patterns rather than dimensional thinning. Lightning pulsed within the darkening mass, not random flashes but rhythmic sequences suggesting conscious design rather than natural phenomena.

From the rooftop of an abandoned warehouse in the industrial district, Detective Ethan Reeves observed movement at the eastern entrance of a facility they had identified as Viktor's primary operational center. His enhanced senses detected details invisible to ordinary perception—the unnatural gait of figures approaching the building, their bodies moving with jerky coordination suggesting partial reanimation rather than fully living beings.

"Five subjects approaching the east entrance," Alice whispered beside him, her exceptional observational skills compensating for her lack of supernatural enhancements. "Their movement patterns are consistent with necromantic binding—not fully deceased but no longer conventionally alive either."

"Partial reanimation," Ethan confirmed, detecting the distinctive energy signatures surrounding the figures. "They retain enough independent function for coordinated activity but lack free will. The Liber Signorum calls them 'servitors'—consciousness partially separated from physical form but maintained under external control."

They watched as the figures entered the warehouse, moving with purposeful coordination despite their unnatural gait. After several minutes of observation, Alice spotted another figure approaching from the north loading dock—this one moving with fluid grace unlike the servitors.

"Different movement pattern," she noted. "More coordinated. Probably a living follower rather than a reanimated servitor."

"Likely a lieutenant in Viktor's organization," Ethan agreed. "These facilities match the energy signature patterns we tracked from the cemetery. This has to be where he's coordinating the final ritual preparations."

After a careful assessment of the building's security measures, they made their way to a rooftop access point that offered a vantage into the main area without exposing themselves to detection. What they saw confirmed their worst fears.

In the center of the warehouse floor, Viktor's followers had established an elaborate ritual configuration—concentric circles inscribed with symbols that pulsed with sickly green light. The partial geometry already completed matched descriptions of the Khavisor Configuration from the Liber Signorum, designed to create permanent breaches between dimensions rather than merely temporary connections.

"They're further along than we anticipated," Alice whispered, documenting the configuration with specialized equipment Nadia Marsh had provided. "The alignment is nearly complete."

"And they're not just preparing for Halloween night," Ethan observed, his enhanced perception detecting energy flows invisible to ordinary sight. "They're establishing resonance pathways between this location and Blackwood Cemetery—a distributed network rather than just a single focal point."

As they watched, the central figure—the one they had identified as a living lieutenant rather than a servitor—began activating components of the ritual configuration. Unlike the mechanical movements of the servitors, this individual moved with purpose and knowledge, adjusting symbols and realigning components with practiced expertise.

"Initial calibration sequence," Ethan whispered. "They're testing the resonance pathways before full activation."

Alice immediately recognized the strategic opportunity. "Calibration represents a vulnerability—disruption now would create cascade effects throughout their network rather than just a temporary delay."

"We need to target the central conduit," Ethan agreed, noting the point where energy flows converged most intensely. "Disrupt that, and the entire configuration will destabilize."

With practiced coordination developed through months of working together on increasingly unusual cases, they positioned themselves for intervention. Using specialized equipment developed through collaboration between Nadia Marsh and supernatural allies, they targeted the central conduit during a critical phase of the calibration sequence.

The disruption was immediate and dramatic. Rather than a catastrophic explosion or visible destruction, the ritual configuration simply... faltered. The pulsing green light flickered and destabilized, its carefully structured patterns dissolving into chaotic, uncoordinated energy.

"Successful implementation," Ethan confirmed as they watched the ritual collapse from their hidden position. "The desynchronization is spreading throughout their network. They can't complete the calibration without rebuilding the entire configuration."

Before they could withdraw, however, alarms sounded throughout the facility. Viktor's lieutenant had detected the interference, triggering security protocols that sent servitors searching through the warehouse.

"Time to leave," Alice said, already moving toward their exit route. "We've accomplished our objective."

As they escaped through the rooftop access and made their way back to street level, Ethan could feel the dimensional disturbances throughout Daybridge subsiding slightly—not resolving completely, but no longer actively intensifying as they had been before their intervention.

"We've bought ourselves time," he said as they reached their vehicle. "But Viktor will adapt. He'll have contingencies."

"Then we'll use the time to finish preparing our counter-ritual," Alice replied, already contacting Nadia Marsh to report their findings. "The disruption pattern confirms our theory about his distributed network. We can use that knowledge to enhance our approach at Blackwood Cemetery."

As they drove through Daybridge's rain-slicked streets, the storm clouds overhead continued their unnatural formations, but their intensity had diminished. For now, at least, they had interrupted Viktor's preparations and gained valuable intelligence about his methods.

The battle wasn't over—far from it—but they had won this skirmish. The true confrontation still lay ahead at Blackwood Cemetery, where Viktor's final ritual would reach its culmination on Halloween night.

CHAPTER TWENTY-ONE

THE PRICE OF KNOWLEDGE

"THERE HAS TO BE ANOTHER WAY," Lila said, staring at the artifacts laid out on the steel table in Evidence Room B.

Three ceramic vessels occupied precisely measured positions, their apparently simple exteriors revealing complex symbology upon closer examination. A copper disc clouded with age sat slightly offset from the geometric center. And in the center, a dagger with a blade that seemed to drink light rather than reflect it.

"We're out of time," Detective Chen gestured to the map of Daybridge pinned to the wall where red markers showed the ritual sites Viktor had systematically activated. "Four more people missing since sunset. The pattern is accelerating."

"The objects are connected," Detective Reeves added. "Part of the same ritual set. If anyone can trace the resonance back to him—"

"You don't understand what you're asking," Lila interrupted, her rings clinking as her hands shook. "This magic... it doesn't just reveal. It remembers. Everything I've done. Everything I've been."

Alice stepped closer, her voice softening with genuine concern. "The nightmares you mentioned during our planning session at Crossroads Books. They're getting worse, aren't they?"

Lila laughed bitterly. "Nightmares would be a blessing, Detective Chen. No, what I see when I close my eyes are memories. Prague. The ritual chamber. What we became that night." She touched the dagger's hilt with deliberate caution. "What I helped him become."

The metal was cold, impossibly cold—like Viktor's hands had been, near the end.

"You're not that person anymore," Ethan said quietly, his enhanced perception allowing him to see the fundamental difference between Lila's energy signature and Viktor's corrupted pattern.

"Aren't I?" Lila's eyes met his in the reflection of the blade. For a moment, they glowed silver—a brief manifestation of the power she normally kept contained.

"Dark magic leaves marks, Detective Reeves. It changes you," she explained. "Every time you use it, the old pathways open wider. The power remembers."

"Then use that," Alice suggested, picking up one of the ceramic vessels. "You understand his methods better than anyone. You know how his mind works."

"Because we shared one, once." Lila closed her eyes. "The soul bond didn't just connect us. It... merged things. Even now, sometimes I can't tell which memories are mine and which are his. Which desires. Which dreams."

Thunder rattled the evidence room's high windows—atmospheric manifestation of dimensional thinning affecting Daybridge's entire metropolitan area.

"Jake doesn't have time for us to find another solution," Ethan pressed, referring to their missing colleague. "Neither do the others."

Lila's fingers tightened on the dagger, decision crystallizing despite legitimate concerns. "If I do this... if I open myself to that power again... Promise me something."

"Name it," Alice said without hesitation.

"If I start to change, if you see any sign that I'm becoming like him..." She met their eyes directly. "Stop me. Whatever it takes."

The detectives exchanged glances—silent communication representing comprehensive assessment.

"You have our word," Ethan said finally, his enhanced perception allowing recognition of the genuine necessity behind the request.

Lila nodded and began removing her rings, laying them one by one on the table with deliberate precision. Protection charms, wards, barriers —everything she'd used for decades to maintain separation between her consciousness and the energetic currents accessed through pathways established during the Prague incident.

"Step back," she warned. "And whatever you see, whatever happens... don't break the circle I'm about to cast."

She arranged the artifacts in a precise pattern, hands steady now with terrible purpose. The dagger at the north point. Vessels at southeast, southwest, and center. The copper disc reflecting nothing.

"Last chance to walk away," she whispered, more to herself than to the detectives.

Then she began to chant—the language wasn't meant for human tongues, the sounds slithering through the air and making shadows twist unnaturally. Her rings sparked and went dark as ancient wards collapsed. Power rushed in, cold and familiar. Like coming home. Like drowning.

The artifacts began to glow with a sickly light. In their depths, shadows moved—dimensional interfaces opening between physical objects and metaphysical currents.

"Little shadow," a voice whispered—auditory phenomenon potentially representing actual communication through a dimensional pathway, memory activation, or something worse. "Welcome back."

Lila's eyes snapped open, solid silver now. When she spoke, other voices echoed behind her words. "I see you, my love."

Her fingers traced patterns in the air, leaving trails of darkness. "I remember the way."

Images flickered in the copper disc: candlelight, blood, a chamber deep beneath the earth. Viktor's face, beautiful and terrible, reaching for her across decades.

"The old foundry," she gasped, fighting to hold on to her individual identity as power coursed through pathways established during the Prague incident. "Under the killing floor. He's built a gateway—"

The dagger rose, spinning slowly in midair.

"Lila?" Alice stepped forward despite the warning about maintaining the circle's integrity.

"Stay back!" The words came out distorted, inhuman. "I can see... so much... the pattern... it's all connected..."

The ceramic vessels cracked, leaking shadows.

"The missing people," she continued, silver eyes wide with an expression suggesting both horror and fascination. "They're alive. He needs them for the final binding. To break death's last laws. To finish what we... what I..."

She stopped, swaying. A drop of blood rolled from her nose.

"Lila!" Ethan moved toward the circle, professional concern overriding caution.

"Don't!" She fell to her knees, still holding the patterns of power. "Almost... got it..."

The copper disc shattered. In its fragments, a map of ley lines blazed, centering on the foundry.

"There," she whispered, her voice weakening. "Hurry. Before moonrise. Before..."

The power surged, singing in her veins. So familiar. So right. Part of her never wanted to let it go.

"Detectives," she managed, voice cracking with strain. "The promise. Remember..."

Thunder shook the building. In the darkness behind her eyes, Viktor smiled.

And somewhere deep in Lila Darkmagic's soul, an old hunger stirred.

As energy patterns gradually stabilized following the successful completion of the intended procedure, Ethan and Alice moved carefully toward Lila's kneeling form—approaching with both professional concern and tactical awareness.

"Lila?" Alice spoke gently.

"I'm..." Lila began, voice weak but recognizably her own. "I'm still here. Still... myself. Mostly."

"We need to move quickly," Ethan stated, focusing on the information they had gained. "The foundry location provides a tactical advantage for approach, but the moonrise timeline creates urgency."

"I'll contact Captain Donovan to coordinate tactical team deployment," Alice said, already reaching for her phone. "Detective Simmons should be informed about the potential connection between the foundry location and historical case files he's been reviewing."

As they helped Lila to her feet, their collective focus shifted toward immediate operational requirements—a rescue mission addressing the disappeared victims identified at Viktor's operational center beneath the old foundry.

The storm continued rolling across Daybridge's transformed landscape as they prepared for immediate deployment. And as Lila carefully replaced her protective rings, she felt both professional satisfaction and personal concern regarding lingering influence potentially affecting her consciousness integrity beyond the immediate resolution.

The old hunger remained—quieter now beneath restored protection layers, but nonetheless present.

~

CHAPTER TWENTY-TWO
CONFRONTATION

VIKTOR KALISHNIKOV STOOD before an altar of blackened stone in a cavernous chamber beneath the old foundry. The space was illuminated by a sickly green glow emanating from ancient runes carved into precise geometric configurations along the walls and floor. His hands moved through intricate patterns with inhuman precision as he chanted in a language not meant for human vocal apparatus.

Around him, entities manifested physical forms through necromantic energy—not merely reanimated corpses but complex consciousness constructs occupying partially materialized bodies. They maintained a protective formation around the ritual site, their empty eyes scanning for threats.

This location represented the culmination of Viktor's systematic preparation throughout the preceding months—a nexus point carefully selected and prepared for his final working. Despite the setback at the warehouse, he had contingencies in place. The ritual would proceed as planned, though with modifications necessitated by the interference.

As his chanting reached critical intensity, the runes began pulsing with precisely modulated energy. The air surrounding the altar shimmered with dimensional distortion. With a final vocalization completing the activation sequence, a shockwave of necromantic energy expanded outward from the altar.

Viktor could perceive the boundaries between conventional reality and adjacent dimensional spaces growing increasingly permeable. The veil separating material existence from alternate states was systematically thinning according to his calculations.

But even as he monitored the implementation progression, unexpected movement registered within his peripheral awareness—not random environmental fluctuation but deliberate infiltration. Three figures emerged from concealment at the chamber's perimeter: Detective Ethan Reeves, his partner Alice Chen, and Lila Darkmagic.

They represented formidable opposition collectively—Ethan with his connection to the nexus entity, Alice with her tactical expertise and specialized weapons, and Lila with her knowledge of Viktor's methodologies and her own considerable power.

With a precisely calculated energy projection, Viktor directed necromantic force toward the intruders—not merely a hostile action but a strategic response designed to neutralize potential disruption. The energetic projection manifested as visible green light streaking toward them.

But the opposition group demonstrated preparation beyond merely coincidental presence. They had anticipated his attack patterns and prepared effective defensive methodology.

Alice Chen initiated immediate counteraction, utilizing specialized weapons designed specifically for confronting necromantic entities. Her movements demonstrated both extensive training and natural aptitude as she engaged the servitors that rushed to intercept them.

Ethan Reeves partially transformed, his lupine aspects emerging as he engaged the necromantic entities with enhanced strength and speed. His connection to the nexus entity provided resistance against Viktor's magical attacks, allowing him to advance despite the necromancer's attempts to repel him.

Lila Darkmagic deployed energetic shields, her silver rings glowing as she activated protective measures designed specifically to counter Viktor's particular brand of necromancy. Her deep knowledge of his methods allowed her to anticipate and neutralize his attacks with practiced efficiency.

The combined opposition created a temporary advantage through coordinated implementation of complementary methodologies. For a brief period, their intervention effectiveness suggested potential success regarding ritual disruption.

But Viktor's capabilities extended significantly beyond parameters typically characterizing even exceptional practitioners. With precisely calculated energy manipulation, he generated a dimensional vortex phenomenon combining both offensive capability against the immediate opposition and ritual enhancement functionality.

The manifestation created an immediate threat, distorting space around the intruders and making coordinated movement difficult. But before Viktor could complete the implementation sequence necessary for achieving optimal effect, Ethan Reeves initiated direct engagement against the primary practitioner.

His transformation providing enhanced mobility, Ethan leaped through the dimensional distortion toward Viktor. The necromancer barely registered sufficient threat awareness before Ethan's clawed hand struck him, creating both physical disruptions affecting Viktor's material manifestation and energetic interference disrupting the implementation sequence.

Viktor's vocalization following physical engagement reflected both pain and surprise at effective physical intervention despite his advanced metaphysical state. But even as Ethan maintained physical engagement with Viktor, the overall tactical situation continued developing unfavorably for the opposition group.

The necromantic entities demonstrated continuous regeneration capability beyond parameters typically characterizing conventional reanimation techniques. The servitor quantity appeared effectively unlimited despite continuous neutralization by both Alice and Lila.

And despite temporary disruption affecting the implementation sequence, the ritual continued progressing toward intended culmination—energetic patterns established through careful preparation maintaining operational functionality.

Just as tactical assessment indicated probable failure regarding intervention effectiveness, unexpected energetic manifestation originated from Lila's position—sudden illumination expanding outward with specific wavelength characteristics suggesting purification functionality.

Before her appeared what seemed to be the Liber Signorum—ancient text containing technical documentation regarding sigil construction and application. The book functioned as both information source regarding appropriate countermeasures and active interface establishing a connection between practitioner consciousness and dimensional forces.

As Lila's vocalization reached a critical frequency combination necessary for establishing harmonic interference directly opposing Viktor's implementation methodology, the Liber Signorum manifested unusual illumination suggesting energetic activation. The pages moved without physical manipulation—autonomous operation suggesting consciousness integration.

As Lila's implementation sequence reached culmination, the Liber Signorum released explosive energy specifically calibrated to counter necromantic patterns supporting both servitor entities and ritual components.

The servitor entities were immediately affected through specific disruption targeting animation energy rather than merely physical structure. Viktor himself appeared significantly affected through both physical disruption and energetic interference targeting his consciousness configuration.

His vocalization following countermeasure implementation reflected both pain and unexpected recognition potentially indicating prior knowledge regarding the specific countermeasure methodology.

When the countermeasure manifestation eventually subsided following complete energy discharge, the chamber appeared significantly altered through both physical disruption and energetic interference targeting dimensional properties.

The opposition group members gradually recovered from the countermeasure implementation experience. Ethan's transformation gradually receded, physical manifestation shifting from lupine configuration toward human appearance. Alice immediately provided physical support despite her own exhaustion following intensive combat engagement.

Lila appeared most significantly affected through both physical exhaustion suggesting substantial energy expenditure, and consciousness alteration suggesting metaphysical influence beyond merely psychological impact.

"It's over," she managed despite evident exhaustion. "Viktor is... Not gone. But diminished. Significantly weakened. The Khavisor Configuration has been disrupted beyond recovery potential before Halloween alignment. The working cannot be completed as designed."

"The missing people," Ethan asked, still catching his breath. "Are they..."

"Still alive," Lila confirmed, continuing movement toward her colleagues despite physical instability. "But not here. Secondary containment location. We need to... The old cemetery chapel. Northern section. Underground chamber beneath a false crypt. That's where they're being held."

"We need to contact Captain Donovan," Alice stated, already reaching for her communication device. "Coordinate tactical team deployment for victim extraction while securing this location against potential recovery attempt."

As they carefully navigated the chamber exit, supporting each other through complementary capabilities, their shared purpose remained clear despite physical exhaustion and tactical complications.

The cosmic chess game continued despite significant disruption successfully implemented against Viktor's working—setback representing tactical victory within strategic confrontation still progressing toward ultimate resolution regarding dimensional integrity and cosmic balance.

CHAPTER TWENTY-THREE
CONNECTIONS

RAIN FELL in sheets over the city of Daybridge, turning the streets into a labyrinth of glistening asphalt and neon reflections. Ethan Reeves stood alone on the rooftop of the abandoned factory, his face turned up to the storm-swept sky as he let the cold droplets wash over him.

He had come here to confront the ghosts of his past. Five years ago, this factory had been the site of the third victim in a series of ritualistic murders he had failed to solve as a rookie detective. The case had haunted him ever since, contributing to the downward spiral that had nearly destroyed his career before his encounter with the nexus entity had given him new purpose.

With his enhanced perception, he could now recognize the patterns in those old killings—victim selection based on energetic signatures rather than merely opportunity. The symbols carved into the bodies, the way they had been drained of blood—it matched Viktor's methodology. The murdered graduate student, Maria Estevez, had been researching the same folkloric patterns that Nadia Marsh had recently documented.

The pieces were falling into place, connections emerging between past and present. Viktor hadn't just arrived in Daybridge recently—his influence had been present for years, preparing the ground for his final ritual through careful cultivation of the city's metaphysical landscape.

"The patterns were there all along," came a voice from behind him. "We just didn't have the context to recognize them."

Ethan turned to find Detective Simmons standing in the doorway to the rooftop, his weathered face solemn beneath the brim of his rain-spattered hat. The older detective had been reviewing cold cases with similarities to the current disappearances, finding connections that ordinary investigation methods had missed.

"How long have you known?" Ethan asked, studying his colleague with new appreciation.

"Suspected, not known," Simmons corrected, joining Ethan at the rooftop's edge. "Started putting it together after the bridge incident last winter. When things that aren't supposed to exist start showing up in police reports, you either drink yourself into denial or start looking for patterns."

Ethan nodded, respecting the older detective's pragmatic approach to the supernatural. "The Estevez case—"

"Was the culmination of a preparatory ritual," Simmons confirmed. "Seven victims, specific configurations, energy harvesting. Creating anchor points throughout the city that Viktor could activate years later." He handed Ethan a waterproof folder containing case files and photographs. "Found these in the archives. Thought they might help with tomorrow night's operation."

Ethan examined the photographs, recognizing ritual configurations like those they had disrupted at the warehouse and foundry. "These will help Nadia Marsh refine the counter-ritual design. Thank you."

"Don't thank me yet," Simmons replied grimly. "Those missing people we rescued from the cemetery chapel. Most are recovering, but three remain catatonic. Doctor says there's nothing physically wrong with them—it's like their consciousness has been partially extracted."

"Soul harvesting," Ethan murmured, recalling information from the Liber Signorum. "Viktor's been collecting energy for his final ritual. Even with the disruptions we've caused, he still has resources to draw upon."

"Which means tomorrow night at Blackwood Cemetery, he'll make his final play," Simmons concluded. "Captain Donovan has authorized full tactical support. Your supernatural friends on board?"

Ethan nodded. "Alexei Volkov has confirmed participation from the vampire factions. The werewolf packs are coordinating through Aleksander. Even the fae representatives have agreed to a temporary alliance."

"Never thought I'd see the day," Simmons remarked, genuine wonder briefly displacing his usual stoicism. "Daybridge's supernatural communities working alongside the police department. Guess it takes the potential end of reality to bring folks together."

"How are you handling all this?" Ethan asked, genuinely curious about his colleague's apparent adaptation to supernatural realities that had shaken his own worldview significantly.

Simmons shrugged, a slight smile softening his weathered features. "Thirty years on the force, you see things that don't make sense. Most cops file them away in a mental drawer labeled 'unexplained' and move on. I just kept that drawer open a crack, figured the truth would slip in, eventually." His expression turned serious again. "What about you? Ready for tomorrow night?"

"As ready as we can be," Ethan replied honestly. "The counter-ritual design is solid. Our allies are prepared. And we have something Viktor doesn't expect."

"What's that?"

"Hope," Ethan said simply. "Not just for survival, but for something better. Viktor's vision is built on control and domination—bending reality to his will. Ours is about restoration and balance."

As they stood watching the storm over Daybridge, Ethan felt a curious calm settle over him despite the approaching confrontation. The connections between past and present, between conventional reality and supernatural dimensions, between individual lives and cosmic forces—all were becoming clearer, forming a pattern that transcended mere coincidence or chaos.

Tomorrow night at Blackwood Cemetery, that pattern would reach its culmination. And Ethan Reeves, once a broken man drowning in guilt and failure, would stand alongside allies both human and supernatural to determine the fate of reality itself.

The rain continued falling, washing away the past and clearing the way for whatever future awaited them all.

CHAPTER TWENTY-FOUR
CONVERGENCE POINT

Halloween night descended on Daybridge with unnatural swiftness, the sun seeming to plummet below the horizon rather than setting in its usual gradual descent. As darkness claimed the city, storm clouds gathered above Blackwood Cemetery in geometric formations that defied meteorological explanation, their swirling patterns visible from miles away.

Lightning pulsed within the clouds in precise rhythmic sequences, illuminating the cemetery grounds in brief, stark flashes that revealed the gathering forces. Along the perimeter, members of Daybridge's tactical response team established positions behind specially reinforced barriers, their standard equipment supplemented with modifications designed by Nadia Marsh to counter necromantic entities.

Detective Ethan Reeves stood at the cemetery's main entrance, his enhanced senses detecting both physical movement and metaphysical currents throughout the grounds. Beside him, Alice Chen coordinated communications between the various groups participating in their unprecedented alliance—police officers, academic specialists, and representatives from supernatural factions who had traditionally remained hidden from human affairs.

"Perimeter secure," she reported, her voice steady despite the tension evident in her precisely controlled movements. "Vampire contingent in position at the eastern approach. Werewolf pack covering the western woods. Nadia Marsh has completed the counter-ritual preparations at the nexus points."

Ethan nodded, his attention focused on the central chapel where Viktor would most likely emerge to complete his final ritual. Though they had disrupted his preparations at both the warehouse and the foundry, the necromancer had continued gathering power through secondary channels, adapting his approach rather than abandoning it entirely.

"And Lila?" he asked, aware that their most unpredictable ally had been unusually quiet during final preparations.

"In position at the southern nexus point," Alice confirmed. "She's maintaining the containment field that should prevent dimensional bleedthrough during the confrontation."

The air grew colder as midnight approached, frost forming on the gravestones despite the unseasonable warmth that had characterized the weeks leading up to Halloween. The dimensional thinning had reached a critical threshold, physical reality responding to metaphysical distortions with increasingly visible manifestations.

"He's coming," Ethan said suddenly, his enhanced perception detecting a distinctive energy signature emerging from the chapel. "Everyone to positions."

Throughout the cemetery, their allies moved with practiced coordination—tactical teams securing approach vectors, supernatural representatives channeling their unique abilities toward the containment framework Nadia Marsh had designed, academic specialists monitoring dimensional stability through specialized equipment.

Viktor Kalishnikov emerged from the chapel doors, his form simultaneously substantial and ethereal—partially materialized through necromantic energy rather than merely conventional physical presence. Around him, specialized entities maintained protective formation, their empty eyes scanning for threats as they established positions around the ritual site he had prepared.

"Detective Reeves," Viktor acknowledged, his voice carrying harmonic properties that caused physical discomfort in those without supernatural protection. "And the ever-resourceful Detective Chen. I must admit, your persistence has been... impressive."

"It's over, Viktor," Ethan replied, stepping forward while remaining within the protective boundary established through Nadia Marsh's counter-ritual preparations. "Your support network has been dismantled. Your captives freed. Your ritual sites neutralized."

"Over?" Viktor's laugh contained genuine amusement rather than merely theatrical effect. "You've caused inconvenience, certainly. Required adaptation. But over?" He gestured toward the sky, where the storm clouds had begun rotating in precise configuration above the chapel. "This was never about merely personal power, Detective. It's about fundamental transformation—the next evolutionary step in consciousness development beyond arbitrary limitations imposed by dimensional separation or existential categorization."

"You mean destroying the natural order," Alice responded, her analytical assessment cutting through his philosophical framing to the practical reality. "Collapsing the barriers between life and death, between separate realities that exist apart for very good reasons."

"Natural order is merely the status quo maintained by those benefiting from current limitations," Viktor countered, beginning to trace complex patterns in the air that left luminous trails hanging in the darkness. "Ask your partner about limitations, Detective Chen. About the freedom that comes from transcending conventional parameters."

As he spoke, the ritual site began to activate—concentric circles inscribed in the ground glowing with a sickly green light as the symbols carved into surrounding gravestones responded to his manipulation. The dimensional thinning accelerated, reality seeming to waver like heat haze around the chapel.

"Now!" Ethan commanded through the communication network connecting their allied forces.

Throughout the cemetery, their counter-ritual activated simultaneously —nexus points established at precise locations illuminating with pure white light that contrasted sharply with the sickly green of Viktor's working. Nadia Marsh's design, incorporating elements from multiple metaphysical traditions and enhanced through supernatural participation, created a containment framework specifically calibrated to counter the Khavisor Configuration.

Viktor's expression shifted from confidence to momentary surprise as he felt the counter-ritual engaging against his working. His hands moved faster, adjusting his approach in real time to compensate for the unexpected resistance.

"Clever," he acknowledged, genuine appreciation in his tone despite the opposition. "Triangulation effect utilizing complementary traditions rather than merely opposing force. Marsh has outdone herself."

But even as the counter-ritual established initial containment, Viktor's specialized entities began targeting the nexus points—attempting to disrupt the opposition framework before it could fully stabilize. The tactical teams engaged these entities with specialized weapons, while supernatural allies provided secondary defense layers utilizing their unique capabilities against necromantic constructs.

Ethan felt his transformation rising in response to the immediate threat, his connection to the nexus entity beneath Daybridge Bridge providing both enhanced physical capabilities and metaphysical anchoring against Viktor's attempts to distort local reality. With controlled intention, he allowed partial transformation—sufficient enhancement for combat effectiveness without compromising cognitive function or tactical coordination.

As the battle intensified across the cemetery grounds, Ethan, Alice, and Lila converged toward Viktor's position through coordinated approach vectors utilizing the protection provided by the counter-ritual framework. Their complementary capabilities—Ethan's transformation nature, Alice's tactical expertise with specialized weapons, and Lila's knowledge of Viktor's specific methodologies—created intervention potential exceeding what any individual opposition might achieve.

Viktor recognized the immediate threat as they approached critical intervention distance. With precise energy manipulation, he generated a dimensional vortex phenomenon combining both offensive capability and ritual enhancement functionality—creating localized reality distortion affecting physical movement and sensory perception within the defined operational zone.

Ethan felt momentary disorientation as conventional spatial parameters fluctuated, but his connection to fundamental reality structures through the nexus entity provided stability that allowed a continued advance despite the distortion. Alice and Lila experienced more substantial effects without similar protection, their coordination temporarily disrupted by the dimensional interference.

With deliberate focus, Ethan continued his approach toward Viktor while the necromancer accelerated his ritual implementation—attempting to complete critical components before effective opposition could be established. The air between them shimmered with conflicting energies as Viktor directed specialized attacks against the advancing threat.

Simultaneously, Alice recovered from the initial disorientation and implemented a specialized countermeasure developed through collaboration with Nadia Marsh—a technical approach specifically designed to neutralize dimensional distortion through harmonic interference patterns. Her precise application created a stability zone extending outward from her position, providing Lila opportunity to establish an energetic interface with the Liber Signorum she carried.

As Lila activated the ancient text's power, its pages began moving without physical manipulation—autonomous operation establishing a connection to dimensional forces that could counter Viktor's specific methodology. Her silver rings glowed with increasing intensity as she channeled energy through pathways established during their shared history but now directed toward opposition rather than collaboration.

The triangulation effect created by their coordinated positioning—Ethan's transformation nature providing reality anchoring from first position, Alice's specialized countermeasure establishing harmonic disruption from second position, and Lila's energetic interface with the Liber Signorum creating technical neutralization from third position—created specific configuration designed to neutralize the Khavisor methodology through targeted disruption.

Viktor recognized the immediate threat as the triangulation approached completion threshold. With desperate energy manipulation utilizing both remaining specialized entities and personal reserves beyond sustainable parameters, he attempted the final defensive operation—creating a localized reality distortion exceeding parameters previously manifested.

But despite significant power manifestation, Viktor's defensive operation encountered unexpected resistance through the triangulation effect. With coordinated implementation achieving critical threshold necessary for effective opposition, their countermeasure created visible effect through distinctive illumination pattern suggesting purification functionality.

Viktor attempted resistance against countermeasure implementation, his consciousness maintaining ritual activation sequence despite external interference through sheer determination. But as the triangulation effect continued enhancing countermeasure effectiveness, his opposition gradually weakened.

The final phase of countermeasure implementation created a distinctive manifestation as triangulation reached completion threshold—visible discharge expanding outward from central configuration with specific energetic signature indicating systematic disruption of the necromantic working.

Viktor experienced direct impact as countermeasure implementation achieved completion—distinctive effect targeting both physical manifestation and consciousness configuration. His resistance gradually weakened as implementation continued disrupting both physical structure and energetic patterns necessary for maintaining operational capability.

With final discharge expanding throughout the cemetery, countermeasure implementation achieved complete neutralization against Viktor's ritual—energetic patterns supporting both dimensional manipulation and necromantic manifestation experiencing systematic dissolution beyond recovery potential.

The necromantic entities supporting Viktor's operations experienced immediate dissolution as countermeasure disrupted energetic patterns necessary for maintaining artificial animation. Viktor himself experienced a significant transformation as implementation affected both physical manifestation and consciousness configuration—dimensional interface established through decades of partial transformation experiencing systematic disruption.

As the countermeasure completed its neutralization sequence, the dimensional distortion gradually stabilized throughout the cemetery—reality parameters returning toward normal configuration despite residual fluctuation requiring eventual equilibrium restoration.

Above Blackwood Cemetery, the unnatural storm clouds began dispersing, their geometric formations dissolving into more natural patterns as the dimensional thinning reversed. Throughout Daybridge, the metaphysical pressure that had been building for months gradually dissipated—reality's structural integrity restoring itself as Viktor's systematic manipulation lost cohesion.

The coordinated team maintained position until stabilization reached acceptable parameters—Ethan utilizing transformation nature for reality anchoring, Alice monitoring dimensional fluctuation through specialized equipment, and Lila assessing energetic patterns through connection with the Liber Signorum.

As their supernatural allies secured the perimeter and tactical teams began recovery operations throughout the cemetery, Ethan approached Alice and Lila, his physical condition reflecting both combat engagement effects and transformation energy expenditure.

"We did it," he acknowledged, voice reflecting both professional satisfaction and personal relief.

"Viktor's gone," Lila confirmed, her assessment balancing technical evaluation against personal knowledge. "Not destroyed completely—the countermeasure disrupted his physical manifestation and the necromantic energies maintaining his altered state, but consciousness fragments likely remain within the dimensional framework requiring eventual containment. But the immediate threat is neutralized. The ritual disrupted beyond recovery potential. Daybridge is safe for now."

"We should contact Captain Donovan," Alice suggested, professional responsibility immediately manifesting through practical focus addressing operational requirements.

As they initiated movement toward the cemetery entrance for extraction and subsequent debriefing, their collective focus remained on both immediate requirements and broader implications concerning future security protocols.

The battle for Daybridge had been won—not through individual heroics or isolated power but through collective wisdom and complementary capabilities working in harmony toward a shared purpose despite differing backgrounds or methodological approaches.

As dawn broke over the city, reality's structural integrity continued strengthening—dimensional boundaries restoring proper separation between worlds meant to remain distinct. The cosmic chess game had reached its conclusion, at least for now, with balance maintained through unprecedented cooperation between forces that had traditionally remained separate.

And in that cooperation lay hope for Daybridge's future—not merely survival against immediate threat but potential evolution toward a more integrated understanding of reality's complex nature and humanity's place within it.

~

CHAPTER TWENTY-FIVE

NECROPOLIS NO MORE

THE SUN ROSE over Daybridge with transformative brilliance, its golden light spilling across streets that had witnessed cosmic battle hours before. The dawn illuminated a city changed yet persevering, marked by the confrontation that had threatened reality's very foundation.

Unlike previous mornings when dimensional thinning had created unnatural atmospheric conditions, today's sunrise appeared remarkably ordinary—a return to normalcy that symbolized successful restoration of cosmic balance and reality integrity following Viktor's defeat.

The air still carried residual traces of energetic discharge from the countermeasure implementation, but these were already dissipating as natural equilibrium reasserted itself across the metropolitan area. Environmental sensors at the university registered a steady reduction in dimensional anomalies throughout the city.

In the abandoned industrial complex that had served as a battlefield for the final confrontation, Ethan, Alice, and Lila stood amid evidence of their hard-won victory. The specialized entities had disintegrated into fine dust that glittered with faint phosphorescence—the last remnants of necromantic energy gradually dispersing as dimensional barriers strengthened.

"The readings are approaching baseline," Alice confirmed, studying the specialized equipment Nadia Marsh had provided for post-operation monitoring. "Dimensional stability increasing across all quadrants. Whatever consciousness fragments remain from Viktor are insufficient to maintain coherent manifestation or systematic influence."

Her professional assessment reflected both scientific precision and personal relief. The data confirmed what they already sensed—their triangulation countermeasure had successfully neutralized Viktor's ritual and disrupted his physical manifestation beyond recovery potential.

Ethan nodded, his enhanced perception detecting subtle harmonization as reality parameters realigned toward natural configuration. The dimensional thinning that had progressed throughout preceding months was gradually reversing, stability returning to Daybridge's metaphysical framework.

"We should establish monitoring protocols," he suggested, balancing immediate relief against prudent caution. "Consciousness fragments might retain potential for limited manifestation during future dimensional fluctuations, particularly around seasonal thinning periods."

His transformation had fully receded, though residual heightened awareness remained—connection to fundamental reality structures providing insight regarding environmental conditions beyond ordinary human perception. The werewolf aspects of his nature had integrated more completely with his human consciousness through the confrontation's crucible.

Lila circled the ritual site, her silver rings occasionally catching morning light as she examined residual energy patterns. The Liber Signorum remained closed in her hands, its purpose fulfilled in the countermeasure implementation that had neutralized Viktor's working.

"You're right about monitoring," she agreed, professional expertise evident in her methodical assessment. "Viktor's consciousness was too deeply integrated with dimensional forces to be completely eradicated. Fragments will persist within the framework, though without sufficient coherence for independent manifestation under normal conditions."

Her voice carried both technical evaluation and personal knowledge— understanding derived from a shared history with Viktor and direct experience with similar phenomena throughout her career opposing necromantic manifestations worldwide. The confrontation had represented the culmination of a decades-long conflict between former partners whose paths had diverged dramatically following Prague incident.

"The Obsidian Chamber alliance should be maintained," Alice suggested, referencing the unprecedented cooperation between supernatural factions established through Alexei Volkov's diplomatic efforts. "Integrated monitoring protocols would provide more comprehensive coverage than any individual approach."

Her recommendation demonstrated strategic thinking beyond merely immediate victory celebration or post-operation relief. The collaborative methodology that had proven effective against Viktor's threat could evolve into sustained framework addressing future challenges through complementary capabilities and shared responsibility.

"Agreed," Ethan responded, professional focus immediately shifting toward implementation planning despite physical exhaustion following intensive confrontation. "Captain Donovan will coordinate with department resources, but supernatural faction involvement provides essential perspective beyond conventional parameters."

Their conversation represented a natural transition from crisis response toward systematic protection—evolution from reactionary intervention toward proactive maintenance ensuring Daybridge's continued safety against similar threats potentially emerging through dimensional weakness or cosmic imbalance.

As morning light strengthened across the industrial complex, they gathered their equipment and prepared for departure. The site would require specialized cleanup procedures developed through collaboration between conventional hazardous materials protocols and supernatural containment methodologies.

"Detective Simmons should be notified regarding historical case connections," Ethan noted, remembering his colleague's long investigation into patterns resembling Viktor's methodology. "The serial killings five years ago were clearly Viktor's preliminary work—victim selection based on specific energetic signatures rather than random targeting."

Alice nodded, already composing mental outline for comprehensive debriefing documentation. "Full disclosure to specialized division personnel will strengthen departmental response capacity for potential future manifestations. Institutional knowledge preservation ensures continued protection beyond individual involvement."

Their professional discussion reflected shared commitment to systematic improvement rather than merely personal accomplishment—focus on enhancing protective frameworks rather than claiming individual credit for successful intervention against cosmic threat.

Outside the industrial complex, Daybridge was awakening to unexpected ordinary morning. Citizens emerged for daily activities unaware of the dimensional battle that had transpired overnight, or cosmic threat neutralized through coordinated intervention combining conventional law enforcement, specialized magical knowledge, and supernatural alliance cooperation.

Emergency services had responded to isolated incidents throughout the metropolitan area—disturbances attributed to conventional causes rather than manifestations of Viktor's final desperate attempt to complete ritual activation sequence. The general population remained blissfully unaware of how close reality had come to fundamental disruption.

As they approached their vehicle, Ethan paused, enhanced perception detecting familiar energy signature approaching from northern perimeter. Alexei Volkov emerged from morning shadows, his human form betraying little of the vampire's true nature.

The vampire elder maintained a respectful distance, acknowledging territorial boundaries while simultaneously indicating a desire for brief communication. His posture conveyed neither aggression nor submission—balanced position appropriate for interaction between representatives of different factions following temporary alliance conclusion.

"Detective," he acknowledged with a formal nod, voice carrying subtle resonance reflecting his supernatural nature beneath the human appearance. "The Crimson Court acknowledges your intervention effectiveness. Territorial stability benefits all Daybridge inhabitants regardless of specific designation or particular classification."

The statement represented significant diplomatic evolution beyond traditional vampire isolation or territorial exclusivity. Alexei's acknowledgment suggested potential for continued communication channel beyond merely crisis cooperation or temporary alignment during extraordinary circumstances.

"Your assistance was crucial," Ethan responded, matching formal tone while maintaining genuine appreciation. "The confrontation outcome might have been significantly different without your coven's intervention against specialized entities protecting ritual configuration."

Their exchange established a foundation for potential future cooperation without requiring immediate commitment or formal alliance beyond current interaction. Both recognized mutual advantage in maintaining open communication channels while respecting established boundaries and operational independence.

Alexei nodded once more before withdrawing toward the northern sector—movement neither hurried retreat nor lingering presence, but deliberate departure following completed communication objective. The interaction represented promising development within Daybridge's complex supernatural ecosystem where traditional isolation had previously limited collective response potential against threats affecting multiple communities.

As they continued toward the vehicle, Alice's communication device signaled incoming transmission from department headquarters. Captain Donovan's voice emerged through the secure channel, professional tone carrying underlying relief despite maintaining formal communication protocol.

"Central has been monitoring specialized division frequency band," he informed them, referencing encrypted communication system established for supernatural operations following departmental reorganization. "Preliminary reports indicate significant anomaly reduction throughout the metropolitan area. Dimensional stability readings approaching normal parameters across all sectors."

The information confirmed their field assessment while providing a broader perspective regarding citywide conditions beyond immediate operational area. Captain Donovan's leadership had evolved to include both conventional law enforcement oversight and specialized division management addressing supernatural phenomena beyond ordinary parameters.

"Full debriefing scheduled for 1400 hours," he continued, establishing a clear timeline for comprehensive information exchange regarding successful neutralization operation. "Nadia Marsh will attend with preliminary analysis regarding dimensional stabilization progression and potential residual effect monitoring requirements."

The structured approach demonstrated institutional evolution beyond merely reactionary response toward a systematic methodology addressing complex phenomena extending beyond conventional parameters. The Daybridge Police Department had adapted to incorporate a supernatural division without compromising core mission protecting metropolitan population against threats regardless of specific origin or particular classification.

"Confirmed," Alice responded, professional acknowledgment indicating information receipt and schedule acceptance. "Team returning to headquarters for preliminary documentation and equipment processing before formal debriefing."

As they departed industrial complex toward central Daybridge, morning traffic flowed with remarkable normalcy—citizens proceeding through daily routines unaware of the cosmic battle that had transpired overnight, or reality disruption averted through coordinated intervention combining multiple methodologies beyond conventional response parameters.

"They have no idea," Ethan observed, watching ordinary morning unfold across metropolitan landscape transitioning from the industrial zone toward commercial district. "Everything they know, everything they are—it could have ended last night if the ritual had completed as designed."

The observation carried both professional assessment and personal reflection—recognition of both intervention significance and responsibility burden inherent in protecting population unaware of threats extending beyond ordinary parameters into territories where reality itself might be compromised through dimensional manipulation or cosmic imbalance.

"That's why we do this," Alice replied, her voice carrying quiet conviction beneath professional tone. "Not for recognition or gratitude, but because someone needs to stand between them and forces they can't comprehend or confront through conventional means."

Her statement captured essential purpose beyond merely professional responsibility or institutional obligation—commitment transcending official parameters toward fundamental protection regardless of personal cost or professional sacrifice potentially required through extraordinary service beyond ordinary expectations.

Lila remained silent during this exchange, her expression suggesting complex internal processing regarding personal history and professional evolution throughout decades opposing Viktor's activities worldwide. The confrontation had represented the culmination of a journey beginning with the Prague incident that had established a soul bond subsequently shattered through divergent ethical frameworks and opposing methodological approaches.

As they approached the departmental headquarters, morning light illuminated the city gradually returning to normal operations—dimensional stability strengthening throughout the metropolitan area as natural processes continued restoring equilibrium following artificial disruption neutralization through specialized countermeasure implementation.

The cosmic chess game had reached a conclusion; pieces returned to starting positions through successful intervention against Viktor's attempt to fundamentally alter reality's parameters through permanent dimensional breach. But all three recognized that vigilance remained essential—Daybridge's unique position as a dimensional nexus point ensuring continued vulnerability requiring sustained protection beyond merely temporary intervention or occasional response regardless of current stability or apparent normalization following successful confrontation resolution.

Their collective commitment transcended merely professional responsibility or institutional obligation toward an essential purpose protecting reality itself against forces extending beyond conventional understanding or ordinary parameters. The necropolis Viktor had envisioned would never materialize through their determined opposition combining complementary capabilities toward a shared purpose despite differing backgrounds or methodological approaches.

As departmental headquarters came into view, they shared a brief glance acknowledging both significant accomplishment and continuing responsibility. Daybridge would never become a necropolis. Their determined protection and integrated response methodology had proven effective against extraordinary threats. They had defended reality itself against forces seeking fundamental alteration or cosmic disruption. The specific motivations or methodologies of practitioners attempting dimensional manipulation had been countered successfully. Together, they had maintained the natural limitations governing reality's operation within their city. The battle for Daybridge's soul had been won, at least for now.

· · ·

The sun continued rising over Daybridge, illuminating a city preserved through their intervention—necropolis no more but a vibrant metropolitan area continuing existence through successful protection against a cosmic threat neutralized through a coordinated response combining conventional law enforcement, specialized magical knowledge, and supernatural alliance cooperation beyond what any individual approach might achieve independently regardless of personal power or specialized expertise.

They had succeeded where others might have failed, not through individual heroics or isolated capability but through an integrated methodology combining complementary approaches toward a shared objective despite differing backgrounds or specializations. Their coordinated implementation had protected reality itself against fundamental alteration through dimensional breach neutralization and ritual disruption beyond recovery potential despite advanced progression or sophisticated methodology employed by a practitioner whose capabilities extended beyond ordinary parameters through decades of research and preparation following transformative experience.

As they parked at departmental headquarters for preliminary documentation and equipment processing, morning light spilled across the windshield. A formal debriefing with Captain Donovan and Nadia Marsh awaited them inside. This dawn symbolized more than just the conclusion of their operation. It represented a new beginning, a restored balance to Daybridge. Their continuing protection extended against forces beyond conventional understanding. They had defended reality itself against dimensional manipulation and cosmic disruption. Daybridge remained uniquely vulnerable as a dimensional nexus point. Here, the boundaries between realities naturally thinned during certain temporal alignments and astronomical configurations. Yet for now, the city was safe again.

Daybridge would continue under their protection—necropolis no more but thriving city preserved through their determined intervention against cosmic threat neutralized through integrated response methodology combining multiple approaches toward a shared objective beyond what any individual capability might achieve independently regardless of personal power or specialized knowledge.

The sun rose higher over the metropolitan landscape. Daybridge was returning to normal operations. The necropolis had been averted through their successful intervention. They had protected the city against dimensional manipulation before it reached completion threshold. Reality remained within reversible parameters and recoverable configuration. The practitioner's sophisticated ritual implementation had failed. His attempt at cosmic disruption through advanced dimensional breach had been neutralized. What might have become a permanent reality alteration remained merely a temporary fluctuation. The localized phenomenon lacked both significant duration and substantial stability. Daybridge would live to see another day.

Their work would continue beyond merely current success or particular victory, vigilance maintained through integrated monitoring protocols and sustained cooperation between conventional law enforcement and supernatural factions following unprecedented alliance established through diplomatic efforts extending beyond traditional isolation or factional exclusivity toward collective responsibility protecting shared environment against threats potentially affecting multiple communities regardless of specific designation or particular classification within Daybridge's complex metaphysical ecosystem.

Necropolis no more. Daybridge had been preserved through their protection against cosmic threat. They had neutralized the danger before fundamental alteration occurred beyond recoverable parameters. The city remained in reversible configuration despite the sophisticated methodology employed against it. Their opponent had used advanced approaches developed through decades of research and preparation. His capabilities had extended beyond ordinary limitations following a transformative experience. That experience had established the foundation for this confrontation. Their successful intervention combined complementary capabilities toward a shared objective. They had triumphed despite their differing backgrounds and methodological approaches.

. . .

As they entered departmental headquarters for preliminary documentation and equipment processing before formal debriefing, morning light streamed through the windows. It symbolized both their significant accomplishment and continuing responsibility. Success had been achieved through an integrated methodology. Vigilance would be maintained through sustained cooperation. This would ensure Daybridge's continued protection against similar threats. Such dangers could potentially emerge through dimensional weakness or cosmic imbalance. Their origin or classification extended beyond conventional parameters. These threats operated outside ordinary limitations typically governing normal operations. They required an exceptional response and specialized methodology beyond standard protocols. Ordinary procedures would not suffice without enhanced capability. Expertise regarding intervention effectiveness remained essential. Their neutralization potential depended on maintaining this specialized knowledge and cooperation.

Daybridge continued under their protection—necropolis no more.

EPILOGUE: SHADOWS
LURKING

The city of Daybridge lay quiet beneath the pale light of a waning moon. Streets that had witnessed a cosmic battle just weeks earlier now appeared remarkably ordinary, a testament to both physical reconstruction efforts and dimensional rebalancing following Viktor's defeat.

Ethan Reeves stood on the precinct rooftop, enhanced senses monitoring the night with practiced vigilance. The autumn air carried crisp notes of fallen leaves and distant woodsmoke—normal seasonal scents that brought welcome familiarity after months of unnatural atmospheric conditions.

Yet beneath these ordinary aromas, his heightened perception detected subtle discrepancies—faint traces of dimensional thinning persisting in specific locations throughout the metropolitan area. Nothing approaching critical threshold, but present, nonetheless.

The official reports declared complete resolution: threat neutralized, dimensional stability restored, case closed. But Ethan knew better. Some shadows ran too deep for total elimination, some wounds in reality's fabric required extended healing beyond immediate intervention.

Footsteps approached from the rooftop access door—familiar rhythm he recognized without turning. Alice Chen joined him at the railing, her expression thoughtful as she surveyed the city below.

"Nadia Marsh's latest readings show continued improvement," she reported, practical assessment balanced with cautious optimism. "Dimensional stability at ninety-three percent across all sectors, up two points from last week."

Her voice carried professional precision without concealing the subtle undercurrent of fatigue that lingered weeks after their confrontation with Viktor. The physical injuries had healed, but the experience of facing cosmic disruption left deeper marks.

"The northwestern quadrant still shows elevated fluctuation patterns," Ethan noted, referencing anomalies his enhanced perception had detected during their patrol earlier that evening. "Nothing critical, but worth monitoring."

Their conversation reflected the new normal—professional assessment of metaphysical conditions alongside conventional crime statistics, enhanced perception working in tandem with scientific measurement to maintain comprehensive awareness of Daybridge's complex status.

The departmental reorganization had been formalized following their successful intervention. Captain Donovan now officially oversaw the specialized division addressing supernatural phenomena, with Ethan and Alice as senior investigators focusing on dimensional stability and paranormal threats beyond conventional parameters.

"Aleksander's pack reported unusual activity near the old cemetery last night," Alice mentioned, referencing the communication channel maintained with werewolf representatives following their temporary alliance during the confrontation with Viktor. "Probably just seasonal thinning with Halloween approaching, but they've increased patrols in that sector."

The cooperative framework established through the Obsidian Chamber alliance had evolved beyond the immediate crisis response toward sustained monitoring protocol. Various supernatural factions maintained regular communication regarding unusual phenomena, sharing information through channels established by Alexei Volkov's diplomatic efforts.

"Good," Ethan acknowledged. "The more eyes watching, the better our chances of early detection if any consciousness fragments attempt manifestation during natural thinning periods."

His statement reflected practical caution rather than paranoia. Viktor's physical form had been neutralized through their triangulation countermeasure, but complete eradication of consciousness fragments integrated with dimensional forces remained impossible. Vigilance would be necessary for the foreseeable future.

Alice nodded, her expression momentarily distant as she recalled Nadia Marsh's briefing regarding potential long-term implications. "The monitoring network at least gives us comprehensive coverage beyond what any individual approach could achieve."

The collaboration between conventional law enforcement, academic research, and supernatural factions represented unprecedented integration of complementary methodologies. Nadi Marsh's office served as a central coordination point, synthesizing data from multiple sources into a comprehensive assessment regarding Daybridge's dimensional stability.

"How's Jake doing?" Ethan asked, shifting focus from professional assessment toward personal concern for the bookstore owner who had provided crucial assistance during their investigation despite significant personal risk.

"Better," Alice replied. "Crossroads Books reopened last week. The protective wards Lila established before her departure seem to be functioning effectively. He's even talking about expanding the occult section."

Her small smile acknowledged the irony—traumatic experience with actual supernatural phenomena increasing rather than diminishing Jake's fascination with esoteric knowledge. His bookstore had become the unofficial information hub for civilian awareness regarding protective measures, though public framing emphasized historical folklore rather than practical application.

Ethan's expression grew more serious. "Any word from Lila?"

The question addressed the most significant loose end following their confrontation with Viktor. Lila had disappeared immediately after the debriefing with Captain Donovan, leaving only a cryptic note regarding "unfinished business" potentially connected to other manifestations beyond Daybridge's immediate vicinity.

"Nothing concrete," Alice responded. "Nadia Marsh received a package containing additional pages from the Liber Signorum last week. No return address, but the handwriting matched Lila's distinctive style."

The continued connection maintained through indirect communication suggested potential future collaboration if circumstances required, though Lila clearly preferred independent operation addressing broader implications beyond Daybridge's immediate situation.

As they contemplated the quiet city below, Ethan's enhanced perception detected a subtle shift in atmospheric conditions—nothing alarming, merely natural fluctuation as dimensional parameters continued gradual stabilization following the disruption.

"We should expand the training program for patrol officers," he suggested, professional focus returning to practical improvements enhancing departmental response capacity. "Basic recognition protocols at a minimum, ensuring proper escalation for unusual phenomena encountered during routine operations."

Alice nodded, already mentally outlining implementation framework. "Captain Donovan approved preliminary curriculum yesterday. Detective Simmons volunteered to assist with the historical pattern recognition module based on his research into previous manifestation cycles."

Their colleague had found valuable purpose applying his extensive historical knowledge toward practical protection methodologies. The case files he had meticulously preserved through decades provided crucial context regarding cyclical phenomena throughout Daybridge's development.

"Good," Ethan acknowledged. "Institutional knowledge preservation ensures continued protection beyond individual involvement. The more officers with basic awareness, the more comprehensive our coverage."

Their discussion represented a natural evolution beyond an immediate crisis response toward systematic protection framework— infrastructure development ensuring sustained vigilance regardless of specific personnel or circumstances.

As night deepened around them, stars visible through the unusually clear autumn sky, Ethan considered how profoundly their lives had changed through confrontation with forces extending beyond conventional understanding.

"Sometimes I still can't believe what we encountered," he admitted, rare moment of personal reflection beyond professional assessment. "Everything we thought we understood about reality..."

Alice placed her hand on his arm, gesture conveying both understanding and shared experience beyond merely verbal acknowledgment. "Yet here we are, still standing. Still protecting Daybridge."

The simple statement carried profound significance—affirmation of a continued purpose despite confronting forces that might have overwhelmed lesser individuals or shattered conventional worldview beyond recovery capacity.

"I've been reviewing case files from neighboring jurisdictions," Alice continued, professional focus returning to practical concerns. "Three unusual homicides in Riverdale last month share characteristics potentially connected to necromantic methodology, though significantly less sophisticated than Viktor's approach."

Her ongoing investigation demonstrated a commitment to proactive monitoring beyond merely reactive response—identification of potential emerging threats before manifestation reached a critical threshold requiring emergency intervention.

"Worth checking," Ethan agreed. "I'll contact Aleksander regarding potential patrol extension into the buffer zone between territories. Werewolf sensory capabilities provide detection advantages for specific energy signatures associated with necromantic activity."

Their operational planning reflected integrated methodology combining conventional investigation with supernatural resources— complementary capabilities enhancing collective effectiveness beyond what either approach might achieve independently.

As midnight approached, they prepared to resume patrol—systematic coverage of specific sectors identified through monitoring network as requiring enhanced vigilance due to residual fluctuation patterns or historical significance regarding previous manifestation cycles.

"Together?" Alice asked, question carrying meaning beyond merely operational coordination or patrol synchronization.

"Always," Ethan responded, the simple word carrying profound commitment beyond momentary acknowledgment.

As they descended from rooftop toward the patrol vehicle, the city appeared peaceful beneath autumn night—ordinary citizens unaware of both recent crisis averted through their intervention and continued vigilance maintaining a protective framework against potential future manifestations.

Yet beneath apparent normalcy, subtle indicators revealed Daybridge's transformation—iron fixtures incorporated into architectural renova- tions throughout downtown district, protective symbols integrated within decorative elements adorning public spaces, and specialized lighting installed through municipal improvement project officially designated for energy efficiency enhancement.

Their patrol route included specific monitoring points established through a comprehensive mapping program integrating Nadia Marsh's scientific measurements with historical data regarding previous manifestation cycles documented through Detective Simmons' research.

As they passed Crossroads Books, lights still illuminated the storefront despite late hour—Jake working late restocking shelves with specialized texts Nadia Marsh had requested following departmental funding approval for reference library enhancement.

"We should stop by tomorrow," Alice suggested, acknowledging both professional resource value and personal connection established through shared extraordinary experiences during the investigation into Viktor's activities.

Ethan nodded agreement, recognizing both practical utility and relational importance beyond merely functional interaction.

Their patrol continued through metropolitan sectors identified as requiring enhanced vigilance, Ethan's enhanced perception complementing Alice's specialized equipment for comprehensive monitoring beyond what either capability might achieve independently.

As they passed Blackwood Cemetery, the final confrontation site where Viktor's ritual had nearly achieved completion threshold necessary for permanent dimensional breach, Ethan detected subtle atmospheric shift—nothing approaching critical threshold requiring an immediate response, merely residual fluctuation natural to a location where significant energetic discharge had occurred.

"We should request updated monitoring equipment for patrol vehicles," Alice noted, professional assessment regarding operational enhancement.

"Agreed," Ethan responded, simple acknowledgment carrying professional support regarding improvement implementation.

Their patrol continued through metropolitan landscape appearing remarkably ordinary despite recent confrontation with forces extending beyond conventional understanding into territories where reality itself required defense against dimensional manipulation.

As midnight approached, their patrol returning toward central district following comprehensive coverage of prioritized sectors, Ethan sensed Alice's momentary hesitation.

"Sometimes I wonder if we'll ever truly understand what we encountered," she admitted, rare moment of philosophical reflection beyond merely professional assessment.

Ethan considered her question carefully; enhanced perception momentarily directed toward internal reflection rather than external monitoring. "I'm not sure complete understanding is possible," he acknowledged, perspective balancing professional assessment with personal insight. "But perhaps that's not the point. We protect Daybridge regardless of whether we fully comprehend what we're protecting it from."

Alice nodded, expression reflecting both professional agreement and personal connection.

"Together," she stated simply, the word carrying meaning beyond merely spatial proximity or temporal simultaneity.

"Always," Ethan responded, the simple word carrying profound commitment.

As they completed their patrol route returning toward departmental headquarters, night sky gradually lightening toward predawn illumination, they shared a comfortable silence reflecting partnership transcending verbal communication necessity.

The shadows might lurk throughout Daybridge's transformed landscape, consciousness fragments potentially retaining manifestation capacity during natural thinning periods, but vigilance remained constant through integrated monitoring protocol combining conventional law enforcement with supernatural faction cooperation.

Ethan and Alice would continue their protection—specialized division addressing supernatural phenomena beyond conventional parameters, enhanced perception working in tandem with scientific measurement to maintain comprehensive awareness of Daybridge's complex status.

One thing was clear—shadows might lurk throughout Daybridge's transformed landscape, but protection remained constant through their determined vigilance and integrated methodology.

A SNEAK PEEK AT WHAT'S NEXT!

Thank you for joining me on this journey through **Daybridge Necropolis: Where Shadows Keep Their Secrets.** I hope you enjoyed exploring the mysteries of Daybridge and getting to know its secrets.

The story doesn't end here—there's so much more waiting to be uncovered. I'm excited to give you an exclusive first look at, **Shadows of Vengeance: The Witch Queen's Return** the next book in the *Ethan Reeves Werewolf Detective Series*. Dive into the free chapter below and get a taste of what's to come!

Shadows of Vengeance: The Witch Queen's Return

Book Three in the Ethan Reeves Werewolf Detective Series

Prologue: Echoes of Vengeance

The town of Daybridge was a place where time seemed to have stopped, its cobblestone streets and ancient buildings whispering tales of a history steeped in both grandeur and sorrow. But beneath the quaint exterior, a darkness lingered -- a legacy of blood and fire that had never truly been extinguished. Like many New England towns,

Daybridge wore its colonial heritage as a tourist attraction, while carefully concealing the true horrors that had shaped its destiny.

On a night when the moon was hidden behind thick clouds, the air felt heavy with the weight of forgotten sins. In the heart of Daybridge, the old town square -- once the site of the infamous Witch Trials of 1692 -- stood eerily silent. At its center loomed a single, gnarled oak tree, its branches twisted like the fingers of the damned who had met their end there. Few tourists realized the oak wasn't merely decorative; it grew from soil soaked in the blood of the condemned, its roots intertwined with bones never properly laid to rest.

The iron benches surrounding the square bore subtle protective sigils disguised as decorative flourishes, their patterns unchanged since the Shadow Year of 1892. The streetlamps—modern fixtures designed to mimic gas lighting—contained blessed bulbs that illuminated more than just physical darkness. Every cobblestone had been laid according to ancient patterns, creating a ward that had weakened over centuries but never fully failed.

A figure moved silently through the square, its steps echoing the dread-filled marches of those long-past condemned souls. They paused at the oak, kneeling to brush gnarled fingers against bark that had seen countless horrors. Here, Mary Blackwood had screamed her innocence until the flames consumed her, clutching her infant daughter even as the smoke choked them both. There, Elizabeth Thorne, the midwife who had delivered half the town's children, had cursed her accusers with her dying breath, promising that their bloodlines would wither like autumn leaves.

The figure's hand trembled with both age and anticipation. For three centuries, this moment had been awaited—the perfect alignment of stars, the thinning of veils between worlds, the weakening of barriers established by founders who had built Daybridge not merely as a settlement but as a seal over something ancient and terrible.

The clock on the courthouse tower—a structure built and rebuilt three times, each iteration preserving the foundations that contained what slumbered beneath—struck midnight, its bell's resonance disrupting protective energies that had been reinforced by generations of Daybridge residents, many unknowingly participating in rituals disguised as historical preservation or civic pride.

From within the folds of their cloak, they produced the Bloodline Archive, its leather binding crafted from the skin of the executed, its pages stained with their blood. As it fell open, names blazed in crimson: Sarah Goodwin, hanged for healing the sick when the town's doctor had failed; Rebecca Clarke, drowned for speaking to her cats; Hannah Morton, burned for knowing too much of herbs and moonlore.

The book was no mere record of deaths but a living covenant between the witches and the land itself—a document that had been hidden, fragmented, and sought by the Septem Umbrae during the Shadow Year and the Dark Summer. Its pages contained not just spells but the true history of Daybridge's founding, the careful balance the coven had maintained between worlds, the protective measures they had established at key points throughout the town.

The figure began to chant, their voices carrying the weight of centuries. The ground trembled as spectral forms materialized -- women with proud, defiant faces and eyes burning with vengeance. Agnes Wheeler, whose prophecies had saved the town from plague, only to be rewarded with accusations of consorting with devils. Margaret Drake, whose only crime had been her beauty and her refusal to marry the magistrate's son.

One by one, the twenty-two spirits formed a circle around the oak tree, each bearing the marks of their execution. They hovered inches above the ground, their ethereal feet never quite touching the earth they had once walked. Their forms flickered between how they had appeared at the moment of death and idealized versions of themselves—proud, powerful, terrible in their spectral beauty.

The cloaked figure rose, revealing herself as Cassandra Blackthorn, the Witch Queen, last descendant of Salem's most powerful practitioner, who had fled to Daybridge only to be betrayed by those she trusted. Her eyes gleamed with power as she addressed the gathered spirits. "Sisters," she called, "too long have we watched our murderers' descendants prosper while our own bloodlines were cut short. Tonight, we reclaim what was taken."

Her form shifted between corporeal and spectral, neither fully alive nor truly dead—a being caught between worlds through powerful magic sustained by centuries of hatred. Her skeletal hands caressed the Bloodline Archive with terrible tenderness, like a mother stroking the face of a long-lost child.

The spirits swirled around her, each bearing the marks of its execution. Katherine Mills, her neck still bearing the rope's kiss. The Preston sisters, their flesh forever scorched. Little Alice Gray, barely thirteen, when they accused her of bewitching the minister's horse.

"For three centuries, Daybridge has forgotten its true purpose," Cassandra continued, her voice resonating with otherworldly power. "The founders built this town not as a home for the godly, but as a prison—a seal over the threshold where the barriers between worlds grow thin. We were its guardians, maintaining the balance, keeping watch over forces they could never comprehend."

The spirits murmured their agreement, their voices blending into a discordant chorus that made the protective iron benches vibrate with sympathetic resonance. Above them, the modern security cameras installed by the Daybridge Paranormal Defense Unit flickered and died, their blessed components overwhelmed by the concentrated spectral energy.

"We shall visit upon them the terror they showed us," Cassandra declared. "Let them feel the weight of chains, the bite of rope, the lick of flames. Let them know what it means to be hunted, to be blamed, to be condemned without mercy."

Her words echoed across the square and beyond, traveling through stone and soil to reach sensitive ears throughout Daybridge. In her apartment across town, Nadia Marsh woke with a start, Elizabeth's journal falling open beside her bed. At the PDU headquarters, monitoring equipment registered a massive spike in supernatural energy centered on the town square. In the Petersons' Victorian home, protective amulets began to glow with warning light.

"Tonight, we begin," Cassandra continued, "with the descendants of those who condemned us. One by one, they shall be taken—their lives feeding our resurrection, their blood renewing our covenant with this land. When all twenty-three have been claimed, the seal shall be broken, and what was imprisoned shall be free."

She turned to the spirit of Abigail Walker, who appeared more substantial than her sisters, a faint glow emanating from within her translucent form. "You have already claimed your descendant. Her essence strengthens you even now."

Indeed, Evelyn Walker's disappearance had been the first, triggering the investigation that now occupied Detective Ethan Reeves and his partner Alice Chen. Neither yet understood the full scope of what they faced—a vengeful ritual centuries in the making, designed not merely for retribution but for the complete undoing of Daybridge's protective purpose.

The spirits dispersed into the night, each seeking the bloodlines of their tormentors. They carried with them three centuries of pain, of rage, of waiting in the dark. Cassandra watched them go, a cruel smile playing across her lips. In her hand, the Bloodline Archive pulsed with dark energy, each page a record of debts to be paid in full.

"Let the werewolf detective and his partner chase their tails," she whispered to the darkness. "By the time they understand what truly happens here, it will be far too late. The boundaries between worlds grow thinner with each passing day, and when Halloween arrives, the final barrier shall fall."

She turned toward the courthouse, her spectral form drifting across the square without touching the protective cobblestones beneath. Her destination was the Necropolis—the ancient cemetery where the executed witches had been buried in unmarked graves, denied proper rites and remembrance. There, in chambers hidden beneath the oldest tombs, she had established her center of power, corrupting the protective wards into channels for vengeance.

The revenge of the witches of Daybridge had begun, and no power in heaven or earth could stop what was to come. The descendants of the accusers would learn that some sins echo through centuries, and some vengeance cannot be denied.

Yet unknown to Cassandra, forces were gathering against her. The Paranormal Defense Unit, led by Captain John Dixon, had already begun coordinating Daybridge's defenses—distributing protective implements disguised as historical artifacts, establishing watch rotations timed to lunar cycles, preparing specialized weapons effective against spectral entities. Ethan Reeves and Alice Chen were piecing together the connections between the disappearances and the witch trials, drawing closer to understanding the true nature of the threat.

And in her apartment surrounded by research materials, Nadia Marsh was translating her ancestor Elizabeth's journals, uncovering the truth about Daybridge's founding purpose and the protective measures that had stopped similar attempts during the Shadow Year of 1892 and the Dark Summer of 1963. The Chronicler's duty—to observe, record, and remember—provided the knowledge they would need if they hoped to save their town from what awakened beneath it.

Across Daybridge, protective measures activated as residents sensed the growing darkness—iron horseshoes over doorways, rowan wood stirrers in coffee shops, silver-threaded curtains in bedroom windows. The town, which had long disguised its supernatural defenses as historical preservation or architectural whimsy, was girding itself for battle, as it had done twice before in living memory and countless times before that.

In the darkness of the Necropolis, Cassandra opened the Bloodline Archive to a page marked with a ribbon woven from human hair. "The wheel turns again," she whispered to her absent sisters. "But this time, we shall not fail."

So begins our tale, in fire and shadow, in blood and justice long delayed. The witches of Daybridge had returned, and their rage would shake the foundations of the world.

ABOUT THE AUTHOR

Rae Stonehouse turned to fiction writing after establishing himself as a prolific author of self-development and professional growth books.

With over fifty published works helping readers navigate personal and professional challenges, he embarked on a new creative path with the Ethan Reeves Werewolf Detective Series.

When not weaving tales of supernatural sleuthing, Stonehouse continues to share his expertise in personal development through workshops and speaking engagements from his home in British Columbia.

The Ethan Reeves series marks his debut in fiction writing, blending his understanding of human nature with a newfound passion for urban fantasy.

Scan to continue to the next book in the Ethan Reeves Werewolf Detective Series:

https://my.linkpod.site/shadowsofvengeance or

Stay tuned for the expanding world of Daybridge in the Daybridge Chronicles and the Quantum Framework Series. There's a lot more info at https://my.linkpod.site/ethanreevesseries or

~

www.ingramcontent.com/pod-product-compliance
Lightning Source LLC
Chambersburg PA
CBHW020828260626
47169CB00003B/877